On the Corner of
Hope and Main

On the Corner of Hope and Main

A BLESSINGS NOVEL

Beverly Jenkins

wm

WILLIAM MORROW
An Imprint of HarperCollins*Publishers*

P.S.™ is a trademark of HarperCollins Publishers.

HarperCollins books may be purchased for educational, business, or sales promotional use. For information, please email the Special Markets Department at SPsales@harpercollins.com.

FIRST EDITION

Designed by Diahann Sturge

Map of Henry Adams © by Alexandria Sewell

Library of Congress Cataloging-in-Publication Data has been applied for.

ISBN 978-0-06-269928-2
ISBN 978-0-06-295220-2 (hardcover library edition)

20 21 22 23 24 LSC 10 9 8 7 6 5 4 3 2 1

To those finding the courage to let their light shine

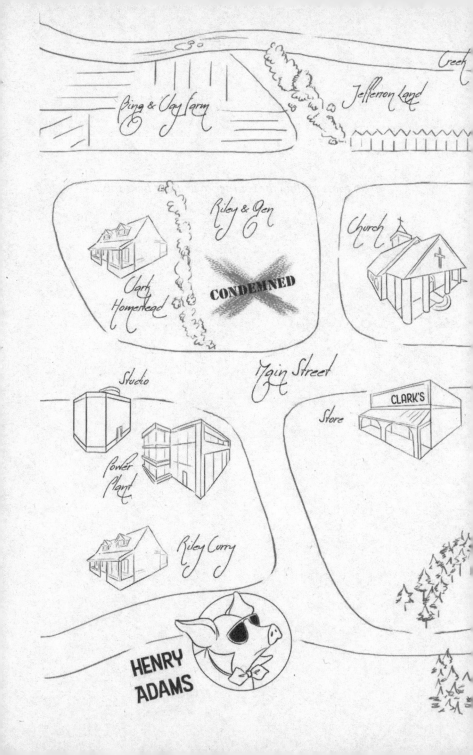

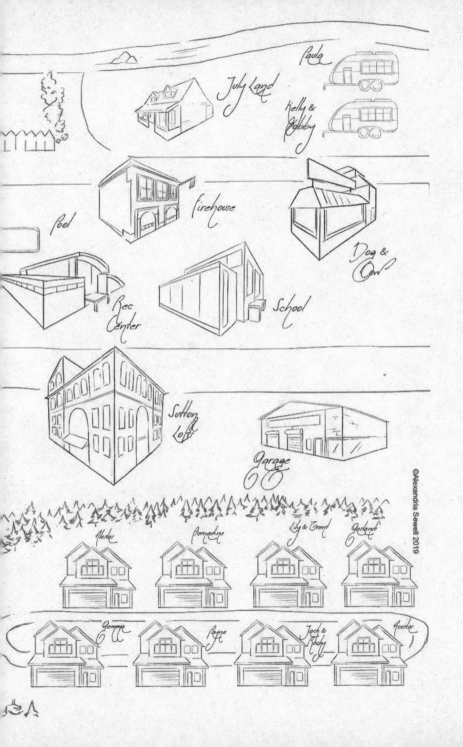

CHAPTER
1

Suffering through another boring workday, Leo Brown picked up the framed photo of himself and his ex-wife, Bernadine, from its place on his desk and studied it. Taken fifteen years ago during a Mediterranean cruise, the smiling faces reflected happy times. Or so he'd thought. He'd given her everything a woman could ask for—cars, jewelry, multiple homes complete with maids—but she'd wanted more: kids, love, and his presence in her life. She wasn't content with attending formal events tied to his job as a vice president of the world's largest oil conglomerate or posing with him during photo ops with foreign dignitaries. She'd wanted him. And as the years went by, they grew further and further apart. Cheating became his answer to the proverbial male midlife crisis, and when she caught him playing the two-backed beast with his secretary, she'd gotten revenge by taking him to divorce court and his bank account to the cleaners. He set the picture down.

In the years after, she made the news by using the settlement money to buy herself a town. Henry Adams, Kansas, a historic little place founded in the 1880s by freed slaves. Under her guidance, it rose from dirt poor and dying to a twenty-first-century jewel, and even he had to admit she'd done a great job. He'd also admitted to being still in love with her, so two years ago, with that in mind, he tried to win her back. At the same time, his company wanted to build a pipeline beneath her town's surrounding farmland and made him point man on the project. He figured it would be a win-win—woo his wife back, and secure approval for the venture. But she no more wanted the pipeline than him, and she convinced the farmers of the same by informing them of the health hazards it posed to their families and livestock, and the company's shoddy environmental record. Ninety percent of the farmers targeted declined. It was not only Leo's biggest failure as an executive, his employer, Salem Oil, found the dismal outcome so infuriating, he was downsized and out of a job before he could say, oil spill.

And now, he was in an entry-level position at Mega Seed, the nation's largest seed and tractor seller, making significantly less money. No longer rubbing shoulders with sheiks and European government officials, his time was spent with farmers, silo operators, and combine dealerships. He blamed Bernadine. Had she minded her own damn business, the pipeline would've gone through and he'd still be vacationing in the Maldives and Paris, and holding high-level meetings with Middle East princes and oil ministers that brought in billions. Instead, he was in a tiny office in Iowa, seated at a desk littered with seed catalogs and glossy brochures showcasing the latest in farm equipment. He no longer wielded power as a vice president, commanding multiple offices and people numbering in the thousands. Hell, he didn't even have a secretary. What he had was a cubicle in a space shared by three other company reps who hated him as much as he did them and the job. When he was first hired by Mega Seed, he hadn't minded starting at the bottom. It was a good way to acquaint himself with how the company operated and its products. However, after twelve months, he hadn't been put on the fast track as promised, and the people at the top were no longer taking his calls or replying to his emails. After bragging to his office mates about being destined for bigger and brighter, and leaving them behind to slog through fields of corn, sorghum, and soybeans, the lack of promotion was enraging, and embarrassing. Leo was almost sixty years old. At his age, he knew his prospects for climbing into the company's upper echelon were as bleak as the Iowa winter, but he didn't have to like it. He was accustomed to wielding power, and he wanted that again.

A beep from his laptop signaled an incoming email. He almost ignored it, but seeing it was from the CEO of his former employer, Salem Oil, he sat up, eyes wide and read it. Then read it again. Salem and Mega Seed were partnering on a joint project they wanted him to lead. His prayers had been answered. He quickly scrolled down to the email he'd gotten last night from Big Al Stillwell, a farmer in Henry Adams. Two years ago, Big Al had been one of the few supporters of the pipeline and had occasionally stayed in touch in hopes the project would be resurrected so he could be paid by Salem and buy back the land he'd lost to foreclosure after Leo left town. Leo hadn't been much interested in Al's updates on the town's goings-on. Now he was. Finding the email, he read that Henry Adams would be electing a new mayor and, according to Stillwell, there were no strong candidates. A kernel of a plan took shape. Leo owned various homes around the country and one was in Franklin, the town next to Henry Adams. How mad would Bernadine be if he returned and ran for the job? Damn mad, he figured, and his candidacy might even serve as a cover for the assignment he'd been handed. After taking a minute to respond to Big Al's email, Leo picked up his phone and called his old CEO.

CHAPTER
2

As the calendar welcomed October, the residents of Henry Adams basked in the fading warmth of fall. The kids broke out their fleeces and hoodies. Farmers stockpiled wood, cleaned up the now empty corn and soybean fields, put up hay for their animals in anticipation of winter, and stored their combines. Everyone knew by month's end, there'd be far colder temperatures, and maybe the first flakes of snow, so they enjoyed it while it lasted.

On this Saturday, the sun was shining, the temperature in the fifties, and Bernadine Brown, owner of Henry Adams, was behind the wheel of her new truck, Baby Four, on her way to a morning meeting at the Power Plant where she worked. Like the previous three versions, the truck was a cobalt blue Ford F-150, and the chrome was so bright you needed shades. Baby One had been destroyed in an arson fire set by Big Al Stillwell's vengeful mother, Odessa, angered by Bernadine's opposition to Salem Oil's proposed pipeline. Baby Two was totaled a short few weeks later when Odessa ran Bernadine off the road. This past summer, Baby Three was hauled to the junkyard after being shot up by members of the Russian Mafia who'd paid the town an uninvited visit. Bernadine thought the new truck might've needed to be a different color and given another name, but she'd chosen to stay with what she loved.

Five years ago, she purchased Henry Adams off eBay, and for a tiny town on the plains of Kansas, there'd been enough drama during her ownership for a Netflix series. Examples? Riley Curry's six-hundred-pound hog, Cletus, sat on a nasty old man named Morton Prell and squashed him to death. Crystal, Bernadine's adopted daughter, was kidnapped and held for ransom by her birth father, Ray Chambers, who was promptly given his comeuppance when a tornado killed him. Gold was discovered by a local farmer, and when a bunch of half-wits came to town looking for more, a riot ensued. Under Bernadine's guidance and limitless checkbook, Henry Adams had gone from barely breathing to a high-tech showcase with far-reaching Wi-Fi, solar streetlights, and a townwide security system that helped foil the plans of a revenge-seeking social worker who tried to burn down Gemma Dahl's home last year. A state-of-the-art school had been built, along with a new church and a rec center that served as the hub of the community. The town was thriving, but one never knew what kind of craziness a day in Henry Adams might bring, so Bernadine stayed on her toes.

She parked Baby Four in the parking lot of the Power Plant, the red, flat-topped building where she and the town's executives worked. Inside, she bypassed her office and went straight to the conference room to attend the first meeting of the newly formed Henry Adams Advisory Council.

Helping themselves to the breakfast buffet she'd ordered were town fire chief Luis Acosta; the town security VP, former colonel Barrett Payne; Mayor Trent July; and the town CFO, Lily Fontaine July, aka Trent's wife. Also on the council and seated at the table were Malachi July, Bernadine's former sweetheart—whom she chose to ignore—and Rocky Dancer James. Both were part owners of the town diner, the Dog and Cow aka the Dog. Next to Rocky was her husband, Jack James, the school's master teacher. To his right sat Marie Jefferson, superintendent of schools, and Dr. Reg Garland, town pediatrician. Also in the room were Reverend Paula Grant, and the Henry Adams matriarch, Tamar July, the ninety-plus-year-old mother of Malachi, grandmother of Trent, and ruler of everything and everyone—including Bernadine.

Once everyone had plates and were seated, Bernadine began the meeting. "I want to thank you for agreeing to be here this morning. We don't have a traditional town council anymore, but everyone here has contributed to Henry Adams's success and growth, so I'd like for us to act as a replacement and meet once a month."

"And the purpose?" Marie asked.

"Discuss items and issues that impact the town." And she gave examples. "Maybe Barrett wants to talk about new security systems, or you and Jack need updated school equipment, or Reg comes up with ways to ensure all the kids in our area of the county are vaccinated. I've been talking to each of you individually about the things you're handling, so I thought if we met once a month it would help eliminate some of the items on our calendars, and everyone would know what everyone else is doing. Does that make sense?"

Marie replied, "It does."

Jack added, "Sounds way more efficient."

Reverend Paula said, "I agree, because I may not know what's going on with Luis or Colonel Payne, for instance, if it isn't discussed at the regular town meeting."

Tamar said, "I think this is a great idea, Bernadine."

She was glad they were on board. She glanced at Mal. He met her gaze emotionlessly. She refocused. "So, first off. We have the election coming up. Anyone have thoughts on that—other than wanting Trent to stay in the job?"

He grinned. "No. I'm done. Someone else's turn."

"Do we have an Election Commission?" Barrett asked.

Bernadine had no idea. Lily shrugged and looked to Trent, who shook his head no.

Reverend Paula asked, "Is one needed?"

Barrett said, "I think so, yes. To have a commission setting parameters on what's allowed and not during the campaigning speaks to transparency."

"This is just a small town, though, Barrett," Trent said. "For mayoral elections, we don't even use printed ballots. People write down their choice on a piece of paper and put it in the box at the Dog. Has always worked. Why make it complicated?"

"Because this is no longer 1950, Trent."

Thin-lipped, he acquiesced with a tight nod.

Bernadine thought the system outdated as well but held off on saying so for the moment.

"Who's allowed to vote for mayor?" Luis asked.

"Anyone over eighteen with a Henry Adams mailing address," Mal answered.

"Which is how many?"

Trent shrugged. "Maybe eighty, eighty-five households. I'd have to check for an exact number, but I'm guessing a bit under two hundred people. Most don't bother voting for mayor. There's more focus on the state and national elections."

"Are there defined duties for the mayor?" Barrett asked.

Tamar replied, "Not anything written down that I'm aware of." As town historian, she'd know better than anyone.

"Don't you think there should be? Vague duties may have worked in the past, but this is a growing community now. Mayoral powers need to be codified."

"Why?"

"Suppose the mayor and Bernadine don't agree on something. Who prevails?" Barrett asked.

"I do," Bernadine replied to him frankly. "The person writing the checks carries the most weight. I'm not saying I'm right in every instance, but I'm always open to compromise or to being proven wrong, Barrett. You know that."

"So, what you're really saying is, the mayor has no power."

"No, I'm not. Trent advises, consults, and steers the ship in areas I know nothing about. We'd not be this successful were it not for his expertise. There's plenty of power in the hands of the right individual. Are you going to run?"

"Thinking about it."

"Then keep this in mind. Henry Adams needs a team who'll work together to get things done. If you want to waste time fighting over who holds the reins, the town loses." The colonel was a good man, but he was accustomed to being large and in charge, and that wasn't going to be helpful at the end of the day. This was not the Marine Corps, and she and the citizens of Henry Adams weren't recruits.

Barrett asked, "Who else is running?"

Lily replied, "Officially, only Riley Curry's expressed any interest so far."

Bernadine said, "For what it's worth, I think you'd make a great mayor, Barrett."

"As long as I don't step on your toes."

And sometimes he could be a jerk. "Yes."

Lily said, "I think what Bernadine just said about the ways Trent helps is a good mayoral job description: advise, consult, and offer expertise to the town owner."

Jack James said, "I agree."

Bernadine did too and asked Barrett, "Would you be willing to head up an Election Commission and report back as soon as possible so we can present the parameters at the town meeting next week? But if you decide to run, you'll have to step down."

"Of course."

She added, "And for the record, I agree that we need a better voting system than pieces of paper and a cardboard box." She gave Trent a smile.

Barrett responded, "Then the commission can come up with a plan. Anyone wanting to work with me on this is welcome."

Reg Garland spoke up for the first time, "I'll help."

Tamar weighed in. "So will I."

Bernadine was pleased by their responses. With Tamar on board, any of Barrett's over-the-top recommendations, such as all candidates had to be Marines, would be quashed.

Reg asked, "Trent, are you sure you don't want to run?"

"Positive. Only reason I was mayor to begin with was because people were tired of Riley's craziness and no one else wanted the job."

"I'm glad you stepped up, though," Bernadine told him.

"Without you, Henry Adams wouldn't be the success it is today."

"I'm not so sure you're right, but I appreciate you saying that, Bernadine."

She was right. Trent's engineering skills and calm, easygoing manner had been of unquestionable value on the quest to bring Henry Adams into the twenty-first century. None of the accomplishments would have been possible without him at the helm. The prospect of possibly having to work with Riley kept her awake at night, but she held fast to the hope that the voters had more sense than to elect someone with none.

With the election discussion settled to her satisfaction, Bernadine brought up the next item on her agenda. "Luis, are you and the family packed and ready to move in?"

"Yes, the kids are so excited, I don't think either of them slept last night. I didn't, either."

The Acostas' new home in the town's subdivision was finally ready. Since moving to Henry Adams, a bit over a year ago, they'd been living in one of the double-wides on Tamar's land. Luis and his two children and his mother-in-law, Anna Ruiz, were moving in later in the day. "Do you have enough help?"

"I've plenty. Between the Dads Inc. and some of my old fire crew members in Franklin, we should be done in no time." He glanced around the table and said sincerely, "I'm so thankful to be in this community. No one can ever accuse Henry Adams of not taking care of its people."

"Amen," Reggie replied.

That *care* was one of the things Bernadine took most pride in. No one was allowed to drift through life unloved and alone. If you stumbled and fell, there was someone to help you get back on your feet. In a way, she'd bought the town for that reason. Initially, it had been to give five, at-risk children a safe haven in which to grow. In the years since, Henry Adams had wrapped its arms around the Acosta family; Gary Clark and his daughters; Gemma Dahl and her grandson, Wyatt; and more recently, Gemma's two foster children, Lucas and Jasmine Herman. The residents had even extended a hand to Riley, ensuring he had a job and a decent place to stay, despite him being a one-of-a-kind pain in the behind. There was hope and caring on every corner, and no matter how large Henry Adams grew, Bernadine didn't want that to change.

As the small talk continued around the Acostas' move, her eyes strayed to Mal. She knew he wanted to reclaim his place in her heart, and she'd told herself she'd forgiven him for the embezzling he'd done, but beneath it all bits of anger lingered, along with doubt. As a result, the reconciliation was not going well. Even though she missed his balancing presence in her life, and the good times they'd had as a couple, a voice inside kept asking: *What if her wealth made him do something equally as dumb, or even dumber in the future?* He swore he'd learned his lesson, but male pride was a hell of a drug as her daughter, Crystal, often described problematic things. Truthfully, Bernadine had loved Mal July. She just wasn't sure a reboot of their relationship was possible.

With nothing else to discuss, the meeting adjourned, and everyone headed to their cars. In times past, had Bernadine been anywhere near her office on a Saturday, she would've sat down to work or grabbed some files to pore over at home. Instead, she did neither. She'd made a promise to herself to stop turning the world on weekends and relax like a normal person. It was difficult, though. Now that the owners of the new coffeehouse were no longer in town, the place would be run by the community college's culinary students. Late yesterday, the lease agreement had finally been sent back by the college's lawyers for her review. She also wanted to evaluate the architect's drawings for the new restaurant she and Rocky James were planning to open. Those things and more were waiting on her desk, but she ignored their siren call and stepped out into the October sunshine.

In the parking lot, Mal stood talking with Trent and Lily. Mal's eyes met Bernadine's, and the parts of herself that wanted to be with him warred with the parts that were still simmering. She'd never been so indecisive and was irritated at herself and at him for being the cause. To silence the inner debate, she got in her truck and drove toward home.

On the way, her phone buzzed. She activated the hands-free link. "Hey, Crys."

"Hey, Mom. Just reminding you about dinner at my place tonight."

"I haven't forgotten." Eighteen-year-old Crystal lived in one of the lofts in the newly renovated Sutton Hotel on Main Street.

"I have the food timed out, so I need you to be here at precisely six forty-five, okay?"

"Got it. What're you cooking?"

"It's a surprise."

Years earlier, that response would've scared her, but Crys was now an excellent cook, and Bernadine was looking forward to a good meal and to catching up.

"And Mom, this is an elegant dinner, so I need you to look nice."

Bernadine wasn't sure how to take that, but replied, "I'll throw on my gold."

"Good. See you later."

"Bye."

Bernadine entered her home in the small subdivision behind Main Street and stepped into silence. Crystal had moved out over the summer and Bernadine was still having difficulty adjusting to her absence. Crys was enrolled in the nearby community college and worked part-time as a waitress at the town's diner, so they rarely went more than a day or two without seeing each other, but she missed having her at home. In the five years they'd been family, she'd grown accustomed to the sounds of Crys's music flowing through the house, walking past her room and seeing her laughing with her friends on the phone, and being treated to whatever culinary magic she'd whipped up for dinner. She knew how much Crystal was enjoying having her own place, so kept the feelings of loss unspoken. A parent's job was to raise a child with as much love and understanding as possible, and when they became of age, to set them free to try their wings. She was saddened by her empty nest, but proud that the former teen runaway with the ugly blond weave had grown into a smart, stylish, and artistic young woman now living on her own.

Buoyed by that, Bernadine hung her jacket in the front closet. Her issues with Mal tried to rise, along with thoughts of the unattended work on her desk, but she pushed both aside. She was going to relax and to help her do that, she picked up the book written by the former First Lady of the United States and took it outside to read on the patio.

She'd been reading for half an hour when she was interrupted by her phone. BFF Tina Craig's name showed on the caller ID, so she set the book aside. "Hey, Ms. Tina. How are you?"

"I'm good. How are you?"

"Good. Are you on your way here?" Tina would be opening a bed-and-breakfast just as soon as it was built by Trent and the construction team.

"No. I'm stuck in Zurich. Malvina is being sued by the Prince of Whine for cutting off his support, so I'm here giving a deposition to her lawyers. How many times did we tell her not to marry him?"

"Maybe a hundred." Malvina Andreas was a member of the Bottom Women's Society, a group composed of divorcées of some of the world's wealthiest men. Bernadine and Tina were members as well. The Prince of Whine was Malvina's second ex-husband. His real name was Francisco but had been given the nickname because the former boy toy, ski instructor was a spoiled, whiny pain in the butt.

Tina added, "At least she listened to us about the prenup. He got to ride her gravy train for two years and now time's up."

"What's he suing for?"

"Five more years of gravy. He told the court he can't find a job."

She shook her head. "How long will you be there?"

"Two, maybe three more days. What's going on with you and Mal?"

Bernadine didn't respond.

Tina didn't let that stop her. "You need to either take the man back or cut him loose. This limbo is not fair to either of you."

Bernadine's continued silence didn't deter her friend, either. "We both know you love him, and yes, he screwed up royally, but he's owned it, apologized, groveled. That's way more than most men would do."

"He stole from me, Tina."

"Yes, but he also stole your heart, so, which means more at the end of the day? You can always get more money. With the investments I've set up, you're making money while you sleep. Can you find another man who's going to love you like he does?"

Bernadine sighed.

"And there's always the chance that he's going to get tired of waiting and decide to cut you loose, first. Then what?"

"I can do without a man, Tina."

"True, but can you do without that man?"

"I hate you right now," Bernadine told her.

"Yeah, yeah. Tell me something I don't know."

Bernadine smiled. "Get off my phone."

"I love you. Talk to you soon."

"I love you, too. Bye."

At the end of the call, Bernadine sat thinking about her problem with Mal and it came to her that her issues were rooted in how the reconciliation began. After his disastrous encounter with Ruth Smith's boxer brother that resulted in Mal being sucker punched and knocked out cold, he'd begged to be allowed to re-earn her trust. Instead of her taking that opportunity to come clean about the depths of her anger and disappointment, she'd done what most women were raised to do: she'd swallowed it and grudgingly agreed, putting his feelings first, thus sparing him the blasting he'd deserved. And because she'd let him off easy, and hadn't given voice to her feelings, her anger and resentment were roiling like lava, leaving her mad at him and more importantly, at herself.

MINDFUL OF CRYSTAL'S requested arrival time for dinner, Bernadine pulled into the parking lot of Sutton Hotel five minutes ahead of schedule. Getting out of her truck, she spotted Mal's truck parked a few spaces over. The salon and coffee shop were open, so she assumed he was either getting his hair cut or picking up a coffee. Because she had no solution to her relationship dilemma, she didn't want to run into him. So, entering the lobby, she headed straight to the elevator for the ride up to Crystal's floor.

Once there, she checked her watch. Seeing it was precisely 6:45, she knocked and was immediately welcomed in. "Hey Mom."

They shared a hug. Bernadine entered the apartment and saw standing in the middle of the room the man she'd hoped to avoid. Mal's surprise mirrored hers. They glared at Crystal. She gave them a guilty grin and picked up her purse and keys. "Everything's warming in the oven. Bon appétit."

Bernadine couldn't believe she'd been played by her own child. Before she could give her a piece of her mind, Crystal was out the door and gone.

Mal had the nerve to appear amused. "I guess she suckered you, too."

"You didn't plan this with her?"

He gave her a level look. "No."

Bernadine groused. "Wait until I see her again."

"I'm sure she meant well."

She rolled her eyes. "She needs to stay out of grown folks' business."

"You look nice."

"Thank you." She'd chosen a gray cashmere sweater with a cowl neck, black pants, and a pair of black suede short-heeled booties. "You look nice, too." In the time she'd known Mal, he'd never been one for suits. Instead he was wearing a nice blue shirt, bolo tie, pressed jeans, and a dark blue sport coat. His western-cut boots were black as was the Stetson in his hand. He looked like a dressed-up Wild West sheriff and was handsome as all get-out. She turned away.

"So," he said. "Since we've both been bamboozled, do you want to leave? Stay and eat with me? Your choice."

What she wanted was to read Crystal the riot act for playing matchmaker like she was Pearl Bailey in *Hello Dolly*. Tina's advice got the better of her, though. "I'll stay."

He offered a soft smile. "Good."

She didn't know what was more potent, his mustache-accented smile, or that fine dark chocolate face. Not even the remnants of his broken nose marred his visual appeal. "Let's see what she left us in the oven."

They found lemon pepper wings drizzled with honey, along with sliced and roasted little red potatoes, and seasoned green beans with shaved almonds. There was also a baguette of French bread. They filled their plates and took them over to Crystal's small, glass-topped dining table. In the center of it stood a vase of fresh flowers flanked by two candles Bernadine assumed were to be lit for atmosphere. Shaking her head at her child's romantic scheming, she removed the candles but left the vase.

They took their seats. Mal surveyed his plate then took a few bites. "Not bad."

"The girl can cook. No denying that," she replied.

They ate in a silence that felt both familiar and awkward.

Before the embezzlement, they'd shared countless meals filled with conversation and laughter. Now? The few meals they'd had recently lacked both. She glanced his way and he held her gaze for a long moment before turning attention back to his meal. When the reconciliation began, he'd sent daily hearts to her phone rather than call because easing slowly back into their interactions as a couple had been part of their agreement. But their talks had been as stiff and stifled as their dinners. Even though he'd done his best to draw her out, the barriers she'd erected remained in place. Apparently he sensed things weren't working because the calls and hearts had petered to a stop. This dinner was their first time alone together in weeks.

"I miss you," he said quietly and raised his eyes to hers as if to gauge her reaction.

"I miss you, too," she replied truthfully. And she did. What they had was special.

"So can we ease back into having dinner together again?"

Once again, she felt put on the spot. "Mal, look—"

He held up a hand. "It's okay. No need to explain. It's on me. I disrespected what we had big-time. I've begged forgiveness, and waited these past three months, hoping and praying we could start again. If you're not feeling it, cool. Let's just cut to the chase and end it. That way you can move on and I can, too. I'm sorry for the pain I caused you, baby. I truly am."

With that he stood, took his plate to the sink, picked up his Stetson, and left the apartment.

Stunned, Bernadine stared at the closed door, then snarled angrily at the man's nerve.

HOME FROM HIS barbering job at the Liberian Ladies and Gents Salon, Riley Curry surfed through the channels on his flat-screen TV hoping to find something worth watching. Now that Henry Adams had cable, there were hundreds of channels to choose from, but nothing looked interesting. In his perfect world, he'd still be at the salon closing up for the night instead of the sharp-tongued young woman in charge: Kelly Douglas. She was a friend of Bernadine Brown's daughter, Crystal, and lord help the world if the former foster kid didn't get her way, so Kelly was the boss and he just a lowly employee. Granted, Bernadine had thrown him a lifeline when he found himself homeless, by giving him a place to stay and a job, but he'd spent his entire seventy years determined to prove that he needed to be running things, even if it was just a barbershop.

Once upon a time, he'd been the Henry Adams mayor and thought he'd done a good job, though many disagreed. He remained convinced that his plan to merge the town with neighboring Franklin had been sound. That he would've received a substantial kickback once the agreement was signed was neither here nor there. Politicians were rewarded for such backroom deals all the time.

His musing was cut short upon seeing a familiar face on CNN. He quickly turned up the sound on the remote in time to hear the female reporter say: "In today's entertainment news, the hog known as Cletus has been nominated for the first ever Animal Oscar for his starring role in *Cletus Goes to Hollywood*. Trainer Ben Scarsdale says both he and the movie idol porker are delighted with the honor." The reporter moved on to the next news item, and Riley glanced over at the framed picture of Cletus in its spot on the fireplace mantel. He sighed. Cletus was the closest thing he had to a son and he missed him dearly. Riley told himself he'd gotten over the hog's betrayal of choosing to return to Los Angeles with Scarsdale. It was a lie, though. He'd not heard a word from either since that awful day Scarsdale showed up in Henry Adams to take possession of Cletus due to Riley's inability to pay the man's bill for his services, but Riley had been keeping up with his hog's rise to the top via the entertainment news shows and Cletus's Instagram account.

When Riley first got him as a piglet, he knew the hog was destined for stardom, and he told anyone who'd listen that one day Cletus would make him as rich as Howard Hughes. The prediction proved partly correct. Yes, Cletus was a star, but the only person getting rich was Scarsdale. There was nothing Riley could do but fume about it, however, so he spent his time cutting hair under Kelly's eagle eye, while plotting his own re-rise to power. He was going to run for mayor again. Trent July, who currently held the position, wasn't going to be on the ballot this time around, which in Riley's mind was a good thing. July had been responsible for hiring the hit woman who'd shot the owners of the coffee shop last summer. After which the Russian Mafia came calling on Henry Adams, resulting in a big shoot-out on the edge of town. Had Riley had any say in the matter, July would've been tarred, feathered, and run out of town for being the cause of the murderous debacle. Since he hadn't, he decided to be July's replacement. As far as Riley knew, no one else had thrown their hat in the ring, so he'd win by default. Once elected he guaranteed there'd be no assassins masquerading as school janitors on his watch. No siree!

In her office on Monday morning, Bernadine scrolled through the coffee shop lease agreement. With the shop's former owners once again leading anonymous lives in the government's Witness Protection Program, Henry Adams and the community college were partnering to run the place. The agreement spelled out who would pay for what in terms of salary for the student workers, supplies, maintenance, and how profits would be divided. She found the wording fair but wanted Lily to give the terms a look before signing on the dotted line. Bernadine had been in the office since 6:00 a.m. Still angry at Mal, she hadn't slept well the last two nights, so rather than spend another moment lying in bed tossing and turning she'd gotten up. Her hope was that work would give her something else to think about, but his action continued to gnaw at her. How dare he walk out as if he were the injured party instead of the one who put this whole mess into motion in the first place. There was her guilt, earned or not, that maybe she had strung him along too long and should have taken all his apologies in the spirit they'd been given and forgiven him. Also in play, as she noted before, was the common belief that women were supposed to assuage a man's hurt feelings rather than their own. She kept telling herself that she loved Mal and wanted to be with him, but was her decision to keep him at arm's length because she didn't want to be hurt again, or just a means to further punish him for choosing to let him off easy. She had no answers.

"Morning, Bernadine."

Bernadine swung her blue leather chair around to face the door. "Morning, Lil."

"You okay?" Lily asked.

"Of course. Why wouldn't I be?"

"You weren't in church yesterday, and rumors about you and Mal are flying around town like Ricochet Rabbit."

Bernadine leaned back in her blue leather chair and crossed her arms. "What're folks saying?"

"That you and Mal have called it quits."

"We have. His decision."

Lily paused. "Hate to be nosy but how are you feeling about it?"

Bernadine shrugged and said truthfully, "Honestly, I'm still trying to figure it out."

"Just so you'll know, Mal left town last night. He told Trent he was going to Oklahoma to hang out with Thad and the cousins."

"Hope he'll be safe on the road. Now, I need to get back to work. Would you look over your copy of the lease agreement for the coffee shop and let me know if anything needing tweaking jumps out at you?"

Appearing concerned, Lily nodded. "Okay, but if you want to talk. I'm here."

"I know. I'm good for now. Promise."

Lily didn't appear convinced. "I'll check out the contract."

"Thanks."

Lily made her exit and Bernadine returned to her computer screen. She didn't want to talk about Mal.

But folks in and around Graham County did. In homes, beauty shops, gas stations, and grocery stores Bernadine Brown and Mal July were the topic du jour. Rumors were rampant. One had it that Crystal had come back to her place to find them screaming at each other. Another version claimed Bernadine caught him embezzling again, and that he'd left town one step ahead of the law. Some folks agreed with her keeping him at arm's length, while others took Mal's side, proclaiming he'd done everything possible to make amends short of slaying a dragon.

As the days passed, Bernadine heard it all and ignored it all. She had work to do.

On Friday, even the kids at the Marie Jefferson Academy were discussing the situation. They loved Ms. Bernadine. Five years ago, she'd rescued Preston, Amari, Devon, and Zoey from the foster care system, arranged for them to move to Henry Adams and become adopted by awesome new parents. Seventeen-year-old Preston, aka Brain, was now the son of the Paynes. Sixteen-year-old Amari, and his thirteen-year-old little brother, Devon, were Julys. Zoey was now twelve, and her parents were town pediatrician Dr. Reg Garland and Grammy Award–winning singer Roni Garland. Although seventeen-year-old Leah Clark and her younger sister, Tiffany, weren't adoptees, Ms. Bernadine and Henry Adams provided them a safe harbor when their mom divorced their dad and left the family high and dry. The Henry Adams youngsters loved Mal, too. He was their OG, their town grandfather, and the dispenser of life lessons, even when the lesson was about what not to do—like embezzling.

At the picnic table during lunch, Zoey asked Amari, "Do you think Ms. Bernadine and the OG are going to get back together?"

Amari slipped his pastrami sandwich out of the Ziploc. "I don't know, Zo. Sounds like the split might be permanent this time. From what Crystal said, he left in the middle of the dinner she set up at her place. Now he's gone to hang out with the Oklahoma family."

Brain asked, "For how long?"

Amari shrugged. "Who knows, but I wish they'd get it together. They're good for each other—or at least they were. Ms. Bernadine cured him of running with the young girls, and he helped her slow her roll. Her working 24/7, 365, is going to give her a heart attack one of these days."

Leah, future astrophysicist and Brain's girlfriend, chimed in, "And we can't have that."

"No," Amari replied.

Robyn Grant, the newest teen in town, who usually never said anything at lunch, asked, "How long have they been together?"

"Just since we all moved here," Zoey said.

"Five years," Devon explained.

"Kind of a long time," Robyn said.

"Yeah, it is," Brain agreed, dipping a carrot stick into his small container of ranch dressing.

"It makes me sad," Zoey confessed.

Amari agreed. "Ditto."

After school let out, Robyn walked the short distance to the church to meet up with her cousin Paula, the town's minister. Robyn would be eighteen in a few weeks. By all accounts she should be preparing for college, if not already admitted, but she was behind academically for a number of reasons. One had to do with the inadequate school system where she'd lived before, and two having been raised by a grandmother who verbally and physically abused her for loving to read. Her grandmother Ardella was convinced a joy of reading would make Robyn believe herself to be better than everybody, keep her from focusing on her chores, and was useless because it didn't put money in her pocket or food on the table.

Last fall, Robyn learned that Ardella had played a hand in the death of Robyn's mom, Lisa. In truth, it hadn't been a shock because Robyn thought the old harpy capable of just about anything. Lisa's skull being found in the septic field behind their house in Oklahoma proved it. Lisa died when Robyn was two years old, so she'd never had the opportunity to know her mom or her love, something guaranteed to put a girl on a therapist's couch somewhere down the road. Good thing her cousin Paula had a degree in child psychology because Robyn was probably going to need help getting rid of all the anger and awfulness eating away at her insides, if she could ever work up the courage to talk about it.

Paula was also an Episcopal priest and Robyn now lived with her. Robyn didn't know her well but liked her mainly because during the few times Paula had visited Oklahoma when Robyn was young, she'd had always been concerned about Robyn's welfare and did her best to deflect some of

Ardella's ugly behavior. Paula never stayed more than a day, however. Robyn had always been saddened by her leaving and fervently wished she too was going to the airport to escape the ignorance and abuse that was Blackbird, Oklahoma, the place where both she and Paula were born.

Upon reaching the church, Robyn went inside, and in the blanketing silence took the stairs down to Paula's office. The door was closed, so she sat on one of the chairs to wait. A few minutes later, Paula walked out accompanied by Brain's mom, Mrs. Payne. Both women smiled upon seeing her, and Robyn smiled in return.

"How are you, Robyn?"

"I'm okay, Mrs. Payne." Robyn wondered what she and Paula had talked about.

"Are you going to the movies tonight?"

"Maybe."

She smiled. "I'm sure the other kids would love to have you hang out with them."

"I'll think about it."

After Mrs. Payne departed, Paula ushered Robyn into her office. "How was school?"

The book-lined space with its nice furniture and soothing, pale-yellow walls, seemed to mirror her cousin's personality and outlook on life. "School was good. Mr. James is the best teacher I've ever had, but he gives us way too much work."

"He's getting you ready to rule the world."

"I'm not sure how advanced geometry fits into that, but I'll take your word for it."

"Are you hungry?"

"Starved."

"I'm done here for the day. Do you want to grab dinner at the Dog?"

Robyn nodded.

"Let me get my jacket and we'll go."

The Dog, short for the Dog and Cow, was the town's diner. It was only a short distance away, so she and Paula walked. Like Blackbird, Henry Adams was a small town, but the two were very different. Henry Adams was modern and clean, and everyone in school had their own laptop. Blackbird was reeling from poverty, no jobs, and a school system so left behind, the civics books still listed Ronald Reagan as president. Blackbird had no grocery stores, no library, or entertainment, unless you counted the kids passing blunts in the field behind the dollar store. As soon as people were old enough to find a way out, they left. Paula had, and from what Robyn heard during her grandmother's trial, Robyn's mom, Lisa, had been trying to do the same. Her decision to leave set off a huge argument between Ardella, Lisa, and her grandfather, Tyree. The yelling morphed into shoving. Lisa fell over a table, broke her neck, and died. Thinking the police wouldn't believe the death accidental, Della and Tyree buried her behind the house and let Robyn grow up believing her mother had abandoned her. Swallowing the pain, she glanced Paula's way and met eyes filled with sadness. Robyn didn't know if it was for her, or a reflection of Paula's own pain. Having been raised by her aunt Ardella, Paula had suffered, too.

"Whenever you're ready to talk, I can find someone to help you work through the hurt."

Robyn replied softly, "I know." But she wasn't ready and didn't know if she'd ever be.

As always, the diner was busy but not as much as it would

be at dinnertime. The music on the jukebox was old school and competed with the laughter and conversations of the people seated at the tables and in the booths. Crystal Chambers Brown was at the hostess stand. Greeting them with a smile, she escorted them to a booth and left them to check out the menus. Watching her walk away, Robyn couldn't help but be envious. Crystal was always so confident and stylish, qualities Robyn lacked. Although they were close in age, Crystal seemed light-years more mature, and even had her own apartment. In fact, Robyn envied most of the Henry Adams kids. She knew many of them had grown up in foster care and had been through some difficult situations, but they were focused on their futures while she couldn't rid herself of her past. "I like Crystal."

"I do, too. She's come a long way, even in the short while I've known her. Everyone's real proud of who she's becoming."

The reply gave Robyn the impression that Crystal had gone through rough times too, but knowing Paula's profession kept her from divulging any details Robyn didn't ask for any. She was curious, though. She'd been in Henry Adams almost a year now, but all the trauma and drama tied to Lisa's death, Ardella's trial and subsequent incarceration, left her moving through life like a sleepwalker. She'd sort of made friends with Leah Clark but hadn't really invested the time or energy needed to form anything concrete. Leah and the other kids seemed to know she needed her space and didn't try to force her into their crew. Which Robyn appreciated. Now, however, she thought she might be ready to offer more of herself. They seemed to have a lot of fun, and she'd never had that in her life, either.

"A penny for your thoughts," Paula said.

"Just thinking maybe I need to hang out with the other kids more."

"Need to or want to? Sometimes those are two different things."

Robyn thought about that for a moment. "Both. I need to because I want friends. And I want to because I'd like to have some fun."

Paula seemed pleased. "Do you want to go to the movies tonight? They always sit together. I don't know what's showing but we can find out."

"I think I will go, and it doesn't matter what movie it is." Henry Adams had free movies at the recreation center on Friday nights and the entire community came out. Robyn had attended a couple of times but generally spent those evenings alone in her room savoring being able to read for as long as she wanted without being punished or yelled at.

"Good. So, now that that's settled, what are you having?"

"The OG burger and fries." The OG was a fancy cheeseburger topped with strips of bacon.

"I'll have the same."

A waitress arrived a second later and took their order.

Over at the Liberian Ladies and Gents Salon, Riley was finishing up Bing Shepard's haircut. After removing the cape with a flourish, he passed Bing a handheld mirror to check himself out.

"Good job, as always, Riley."

That pleased him. He'd been cutting hair in Henry Adams for nearly forty years, and even when everyone was mad at him, the men continued to sit in his chair because he knew his way around a pair of clippers.

Bing stood with the help of his cane and was reaching into his pocket for his wallet when he froze, eyes on the big-screen TV that dominated one of the salon's walls. "Is that Cletus?"

Riley glanced up just as Cletus waddled into view wearing shades, a garish Hawaiian shirt, and matching shorts. "Sure is!" Riley rushed over to Kelly's station to grab the TV remote to bring up the sound. It was one of the daytime entertainment shows, and the elfin host, a short blonde who liked to show off her dancing skills, wore a look of excitement as the hog and his trainer came over to the couch next to her desk.

Over in the ladies' section of the salon, Kelly stood up from her chair to watch. Marie Jefferson pushed up the dryer hood she was under, glanced up at the TV, and offered a head shake of disbelief. "Good lord."

Riley ignored her. The host spent a few minutes talking about Cletus's Oscar nomination, generating enthusiastic applause from the audience before asking about the hog's latest role.

"He's starring in *Cletus Goes to Hawaii*," trainer Ben Scarsdale explained.

"That's why he's all dressed up?" the lady host asked.

Scarsdale nodded.

"He could pass for Elvis," she pointed out. The audience laughed and applauded enthusiastically. Cletus threw his snout up and snorted as if in agreement and the place went wild.

A sour-faced Bing slapped a twenty-dollar bill into Riley's chest and hobbled out on his cane. Marie shook her head again, lowered the dryer hood, and returned her attention to the book she was reading.

But Riley was entranced, mad too, because he should've

been the one escorting Cletus around on the press and TV tour. Not Scarsdale.

The host thanked them for coming and told everyone to keep an eye out for *Cletus Goes to Hawaii*. Smiling at the applause, Scarsdale stood to leave. As he took a step away from the couch, his legs flew up in the air and he landed on his back. Everyone froze. Cletus snorted a laugh and waddled off.

Scarsdale, appearing both embarrassed and furious, was helped to his feet by the host's minions. She didn't look pleased, either. Riley guessed not many guests relieved themselves on her show's floor. Before they went to commercial, she made a sarcastic crack about Scarsdale needing to buy diapers for his pet.

Riley thought it served Scarsdale right and hoped Cletus didn't get in trouble for making his trainer a laughingstock before millions of Americans nationwide.

THANKS TO A heads-up from Lily, Bernadine had seen Cletus's appearance, too. As the show went to commercial after Scarsdale's fall, she was glad Cletus was now Hollywood's problem because he was hog non grata in Henry Adams.

She was reviewing Barrett's preliminary Election Commission guidelines when a light knock on her open door made her look up. Leo Brown. *Speaking of hog non grata.* Swallowing her surprise and feigning a politeness she didn't feel, she asked, "What brings you by, Leo?"

"Just thought I'd stop in and see how you're doing?"

As he entered, she sat back in her chair and folded her arms. "Why?"

He chuckled knowingly. "Still cold as ice, Bernadine."

She didn't respond.

"Mind if I sit?"

She did but gestured him to a chair anyway.

"I bought Big Al Stillwell's property from the bank. Having my house in Franklin moved there."

She tried not to show how appalled she was by that news, but apparently failed.

He smirked. "I knew that would get you."

"I'd say, welcome back to the community, but I'd be lying."

"And we can't have Mother Teresa lying, now can we?"

"Okay, because I want you out of my office, I'll bite. Why'd you buy the Stillwell place?"

"That property gives me a Henry Adams mailing address."

"And?"

"Maybe I want to run for mayor."

She couldn't suppress her snicker. "Like anyone's going to vote for you. I heard the oil company let you go."

He bristled. "True."

"And you're now working for Mega Seed."

"Honored that you've been interested enough to keep tabs."

"Only in case you slithered back into the county." She wondered if he'd been with the company long enough to be aware of the lawsuit filed against Mega Seed by the Black Farmers Association.

He continued, "As far as people not voting for me, you'd be surprised how many farmers still resent your meddling with the pipeline."

"Do tell. One pipeline break would've devastated their farms." *Arrogant asshat!* "And you think you'll get their votes? To what end? I still own the town. I may have no direct influence on the areas outside of it, but you can't move a pebble within the town's limits without my approval."

"True, but you having to see my face in yours every day? Priceless."

She shook her head. "Okay, Leo. You do you. Good luck with your plans for Henry Adams world domination. Anything else?"

He didn't appear pleased and she wondered why he thought the prospect of her having to work with him would cause her distress? It probably would if he had a Popsicle's chance in hell of winning, but since he didn't . . .

"I hear July got caught with his hand in the cookie jar."

"If you think bringing that up is going to push my buttons, try again. Better yet, just leave, Leo. I have better things to do than to sit here listening to your lame attempts to poke the bear."

"You think you got life by the balls, don't you?"

"No. Just yours, apparently, since you can't seem to stay away from me."

He stiffened. Anger hardened his eyes. He stood and stormed out.

Jerk. She went back to her screen.

The Election Commission's report was very straightforward. It included what they'd agreed on as the mayoral job description, in addition to an age and residency requirement. Candidates had to be at least eighteen years of age and have lived in Henry Adams at least thirty days. Personally, Bernadine wanted to raise the condition to ninety days in order to keep Leo off the ballot but knew that wouldn't be right. Besides, she'd get a bigger kick out of him losing fair and square, which she knew he would. The report aside, she wondered what Marie Jefferson would think of Leo's return? The last time he'd been in town, he'd treated her to a few weeks of Lifestyles of the Rich and Famous, but when she refused to sell him her land, he'd left her on the side of the road like a bag of discarded trash. She also wondered how Al Stillwell felt about Leo buying his land from the bank, not that he had any say in the sale. Her crusade against the pipeline cost Big Al's family the oil company money they'd needed to stay afloat, and she still felt guilty about that outcome. Last she'd heard, Big Al was living in Oklahoma and working in the oil fields. His mother, Odessa, convicted of arson and murder, was now serving time at the Topeka Correctional Facility and would undoubtedly die there. His daughter, Freda, had taken the reward money she'd earned from turning her grandmother in to law enforcement and moved to California to finish her college education. Dealing with the Stillwells taught Bernadine there were sometimes two sides to good deeds. One helpful. One not.

LEO WAS SIMMERING as he drove away from the Power Plant. He'd wanted to intimidate Bernadine but left verbally gelded instead. Gone was the wife who'd been deferential and accommodating, who'd never questioned or offered conflicting opinions. Back then, whenever he'd said, jump, she'd asked, how high. Now, in her place stood a confident, savvy, ballbreaker he barely recognized. He'd gotten a taste of her transformation during the last time he was in town, and she was even more formidable now. Didn't matter, though. He wasn't going to slink away like a whipped dog. He owed her for the hit he'd taken to his job status and lifestyle. If elected, he couldn't really affect her hand on the wheel, but being able to stir the pot meant more. He doubted current mayor Trent July ever challenged her vision on things and simply went along to get along. Leo wanted to throw roadblocks in her path and have enough backing from people other than her personal crew to make her miserable. It wasn't much of a plan, but he was okay with that because it would serve as a cover for what he'd really come back to do. Being the pebble in her shoe was enough for the moment.

But to make the election seem like his true goal, he needed allies. According to Stillwell, the only person running for mayor was Riley Curry. During Leo's first visit to Henry Adams, Curry had been caught up in the mess with his hog and was out of town. Leo knew the man was a bit squirrelly but wondered if they could join forces. From what Stillwell relayed, Bernadine and her crew were not among Curry's favorite people, so getting him on team Leo might be easy. He had a few other potential partners on his list, but Curry was first.

To that end, he swung by the barbershop. Entering, he glanced around the high-end place, taking in the expensive wall-size mirrors, fancy seating, and sleek dryers. A young woman with elaborate braids was seated at a desk on the far side of the room and glanced up at his entrance. Curry, wearing a blue barber smock, had Trent July in his chair. Thinking about July's father, Mal, having been caught embezzling restored Leo's good mood. July gave him a hard stare. Leo replied with a smirk.

The young woman walked over. "May I help you?"

"Wondering if I can get a haircut?"

"Now, or do you want to make an appointment?"

"Now, if possible."

She looked over at Riley, who called back, "I'm almost done here."

"Can I get you anything while you wait?" she asked Leo. "Coffee, tea, soda?"

He shook his head. "No thanks. I'm fine."

She walked back to her desk, and he sat to wait his turn.

It didn't take long. As July headed to the exit, Leo taunted, "Heard your dad got caught embezzling."

"Heard the oil company took your life."

Leo stiffened.

July departed.

Curry took a moment to sweep up the hair and wipe down his chair before beckoning Leo over. Leo removed his suit-coat and handed it to Curry who hung it on a nearby coat-tree. Once he had Leo draped with the protective cape, Curry picked up the clippers and began.

"What's your name?" Curry asked.

"Leo Brown."

Curry paused. "Have we met? Name sounds kind of familiar."

"Not sure if we have or not, but I used to be married to Bernadine Brown."

"Ah." Riley resumed his task.

"I hear you're running for mayor."

"I am." There was pride in his tone. "Got the field all to myself, so far."

"You're a shoo-in then."

"Should be. Going to bring some sense to the madness Ms. Brown's been causing." He paused again. "No offense, of course."

"None taken. She's an ex for a reason. Not one of my favorite people."

Curry didn't respond.

Leo took a chance. "You like what she's been doing here?"

"Some of it yes, but I still question where she got all her money. Me and a bunch of folks are still hopping mad about the hit woman."

"Hit woman?"

"Yeah, she shot a man at Movie Night at the rec auditorium this past summer. Should've never been hired in the first place."

"Who hired her?"

"Trent July," he said, sounding disgusted. "And he should've been brought up on charges for not doing the background check like he was supposed to do."

Leo had heard about the attempted murder from Stillwell but didn't let on. "He hired a hit woman?"

"Yeah. She was posing as a janitor at the school. Had something to do with the government's Witness Protection Program. The FBI was here and everything. Along with the Russian Mafia."

"The Russian Mafia! People here must have been pretty freaked out."

"They were, but nobody had the courage to call out Ms. Brown and her gang of fools, but me."

"I see."

"I used to be mayor here until she came along. Bought everyone off with her money and rebuilding the town. I do like that we have cable now, though."

"Can't live without cable."

"Nope. Only way I can keep up with my hog."

Leo played dumb. "Your hog?"

"Yeah. The famous hog in Hollywood. Cletus. I raised him from a piglet. Trained him and everything. Scarsdale, he's the trainer now, basically stole him from me."

"Bernadine didn't help you get a lawyer so you could take this Scarsdale to court?"

"Are you kidding? 'Course not."

"She's not one of your favorite people, is she?"

"No."

"All the money came from her divorce settlement. Don't tell anybody, but my lawyer and I hid millions offshore and overseas." What Leo didn't reveal was that he'd lost most of it to a bad overseas investment.

Curry moved the clippers carefully around Leo's ear and grinned. "Good for you." Then asked, "Are you here on business?"

"No, planning to move here. Was going to run for mayor but now that I know you'd be such a formidable candidate, I'd be willing to help with campaign expenses instead, or be your campaign manager if you need one." He lowered his voice and whispered, "If the two of us hooked up, she'd have a stroke, I'd bet."

"You'd be willing to do that? Fund my campaign?"

"Yes," Leo replied with as much sincerity as he could muster. "Together we'd probably have her shaking in her boots."

Curry was eyeing him speculatively.

"Just think about it," Leo said. "I'm sure you have plenty of money to work with, but just in case you need help, I got your back. No strings attached."

"I'll keep that in mind."

Curry finished the haircut. Leo thanked him and handed

over a personal business card—not the ones he used for Mega Seed. "You can contact me at that number. I'm out at the old Stillwell place."

Curry viewed the card. "Okay. Thanks."

"You're welcome. How much do I owe you for the haircut?"

He quoted Leo the price. "Pay Kelly over at the desk."

"Let me give you a tip, though." Leo pulled out his wallet and handed over a crisp fifty-dollar bill.

Curry's eyes widened. "Thanks!"

"Small price to pay for the conversation, and the potential partnership. Hope to see you soon."

"You got it."

Leo paid Kelly and walked back out into the brisk October sunshine.

CHAPTER
4

Did you finish the Election Commission report?" Sheila Payne asked her husband, Barrett, as she sat down to enjoy dinner with him and their sixteen-year-old son, Preston.

"I did. Gave it to Bernadine earlier today."

"Are you really going to run for mayor?" Preston asked.

"I think so. Since Bernadine makes most of the decisions around here, there's not a lot to the job, but no one wants Curry anywhere near the controls, even if they don't turn anything."

"I think Trent's had plenty of control," Sheila countered.

"If you mean doing what Bernadine tells him to do, then yes."

Thinking how blind her husband could be at times, she asked, "What kinds of things do you think the town should be doing?"

"Growing, for one. The areas outside of Bernadine's control should be developed so more people can move in and we can begin building a tax base."

"Don't people pay taxes now?" Preston asked.

"State and national, but nothing locally."

"What would local taxes pay for?"

"New roads so we can attract more businesses. A coffee shop and the fancy restaurant she wants to build can't survive without a larger population."

Sheila disagreed. "The coffee shop is doing great business and the restaurant will, too. People here need a sit-down place to eat besides the Dog."

"I agree, so why not bring in one of the national chains?"

"Because you can get that in Franklin. No one wants to celebrate engagements or wedding anniversaries at a fast-food place."

He shrugged as if that was debatable. Sheila saw Preston give a tiny shake of his head as if his pops was a couple fries short of a Happy Meal.

Sheila said, "I think a woman should run for mayor."

Barrett sighed. "You ladies already run everything now. Why can't the men have the mayor's position?"

"Because there are no gender-specific roles, Barrett. There are even lady Marines now."

He shook his head as if *she* was short a few fries, but Sheila simply smiled and forked up a bit more of her salad. "So, if you do win, who'll head up town security?"

"I'm thinking of asking Luis. He's not doing much as fire chief."

"That might be a good choice. You may want to consider a woman, too."

"Like who?"

Preston said, "Rocky?"

Barrett looked skeptical.

More shortsightedness, she thought. "Preston may be on to something, but then again, Rock's probably too busy at the Dog, and she'll be part owner of the new restaurant she and Bernadine plan to build."

Barrett asked, "Are they still looking at the spot near the Power Plant for it?"

"Far as I know. I can't wait for it to be up and running." She could already see the diners all dressed up and coming in for date night and the aforementioned celebrations. Everyone loved the Dog, but an elegant place would serve the town well, too.

Changing the subject, Sheila said to Preston, "I saw Robyn over at the church today. How's she doing? Is she adjusting to being in Henry Adams?"

He shrugged. "She's doing okay, I guess. She's real quiet. Leah's been trying to be her friend but other than staying overnight at the Clarks a couple of times, she's been keeping to herself."

Sheila understood that very well. "Barrett and I moved all over the world, so I know how difficult starting life over in a new place can be. I wish there was some way to make her transition easier. I asked her about attending the movie tonight at the rec."

"Leah thinks we should let her roll at her own pace. When she's ready to be a Henry Adams kid, she'll let us know."

Sheila liked that. "Leah is a very wise young lady."

The praise for his girlfriend made Preston beam. "I think she's pretty awesome."

The doorbell sounded. Wondering who it could be, Sheila stood. "I'll get it."

Opening the door, she wished she hadn't because the

woman standing on the other side was Martina Nelson, a military surgical nurse and Barrett's former lover.

"Hi, Sheila," she said brightly.

"Marti."

"Was in the neighborhood and thought I'd stop by. Is my favorite colonel around?"

Sheila wanted to strangle her and throw her body off the porch. Instead she slapped a fake smile on her face. "Yes. We're having dinner. Have you eaten?"

"I haven't."

"This way." When they reached the kitchen, Sheila said, "Barrett, look who's here."

He stared at Marti then back at Sheila. He appeared to be a breath short of a heart attack. "What are you doing here, Marti?"

"Had a recruiting presentation in Topeka. It ended yesterday, so I thought I'd drive over and hang with you all for a few days before heading home."

Barrett's attention swung to Sheila again, and she hoped he knew Marti's presence wasn't wanted. Seeing the woman fanned the embers of the hurt and pain Sheila had all but buried. Many wives with cheating husbands blamed the other woman. Sheila blamed Barrett because rather than remain true to his vows he'd chosen adultery over their marriage. "Have a seat, Marti, and I'll get you a plate."

Tight-lipped, Sheila went to the cupboard, then dished up some pasta and meat sauce and set the plate in front of Marti before retaking her own seat.

After the first forkful, Marti gushed, "This is very good. Barrett's always been a great cook."

Barrett cleared his throat. "Sheila did the meal."

"Oh. Sheila, I'm sorry. I didn't know you could cook."

"Probably a lot of things you don't know about my mom," Preston interjected coolly.

That got Marti's attention. She appeared embarrassed. "You're probably right." She shot Sheila a hesitant glance before addressing Barrett. "So, how's life in small-town America? This is the last place I figured you'd retire to."

Before he could reply, Sheila interrupted. "Preston, since we're both done eating, how about we let these two catch up in private."

Barrett froze. Sheila sent him a brittle smile. "That okay with you, Barrett?"

He appeared unsure of his response.

Marti had no such problem. "That's so nice of you. It seems like forever since we've been together."

Barrett's attention remained focused on Sheila who stood. "Marti, I'll see you later. Preston, we can clean up the kitchen after Marti leaves, so come on with me."

They left and climbed the stairs to the second floor.

In the hallway, Preston asked, "He still seeing her?"

Sheila studied him curiously. Barrett's Marine unit held a reunion in Orlando a few years back and the Paynes attended as a family. Marti had been there, too.

"You know about them?"

He nodded. "Pops and I talked about it when you went to chill at that convent."

After the reunion, Sheila had taken time away from Barrett because she needed to think about her marriage, life, and her role in both. "Honestly, I don't think they're still an item." Or at least she hoped not.

"Good. At least she got rid of the Jheri curl."

Sheila laughed softly. "I love you so much, and thanks for standing up for me the way you did."

"Sons are supposed to."

He'd been loyal since the beginning of their time together as mother and son, and she couldn't imagine life without him. She'd miss him dearly when he went away to college. "You go hang out at the movies. I'll hole up here until she leaves."

"I can stay if you want company. We could do some Netflix or something."

"No. You go on. I'll be fine."

"You sure?"

"Positive."

"Okay. Tomorrow's Pizza Saturday, so Leah and Tiff are having everybody over to spend the night after the movies. Is it okay if I go?"

"Will Gary be there?"

"Of course."

"Then sure. If you need a ride to the Clarks after the movies, send me a text. I'll come or send your pops for you."

"Sounds like a plan."

Once again feeling blessed to be Preston's mom, Sheila went into her bedroom.

Downstairs in the kitchen, while Marti chattered about the recruiting presentation, Barrett's thoughts were on his wife. Marti's presence had caused Sheila pain. Oh, she'd hidden it well, and the old Barrett, the one who'd been driven by hubris, and hadn't thought about what his affair would do to his elegant wife, wouldn't have seen it, but the new and improved Barrett had, and his shame rose. The old Barrett thought he'd needed a Marti in his life. The rush of being with her compensated for the unexciting woman he'd viewed Sheila to be back then. Never mind that Sheila had followed him from Korea, to Germany, to the Philippines, and back to the States, all without complaint while making sure he had a home to return to after a grueling day on base. During those years, she'd suffered two miscarriages. After the last one, the doctors told her she'd never be able to bear children. He'd comforted her as best he could, but was secretly relieved due to his fear that the physical abuse he suffered as a child at the hands of his father would somehow rise in him, too. Her beauty and class had made him the envy of the other officers he knew, but that hadn't been enough for the old Barrett. In retrospect, he should've been on his knees every day thanking his wife for consenting to be in his life, not cheating with the woman now seated at Sheila's table in Sheila's home. "You have to go, Marti."

She stopped. "Go where?"

"Home," he said quietly.

"I will in a couple of days."

He shook his head. "No. Now. What we had together isn't something I'm going to do ever again. I love my wife."

She sat back and studied him silently. "Is that why you haven't called since Orlando?"

"Yes."

"Does she know about us?"

"She does."

"I see. My apologies for coming, then. I hope she knows how lucky she is to have you."

"It's the other way around. I'm lucky to have her."

She pushed back from the table and stood. "Thanks for being truthful. Been great knowing you. Have a good life, Barrett."

"You, too, Marti. I'll walk you out."

"Not necessary. Thanks, though." And she left.

Barrett sat there in the silence. For the past two years he'd tried to prove himself worthy of the lovely lady who shared his life. His affair would always be a dark hole in their marriage, so he'd done his best to make it smaller. If Marti's visit had widened it again, he wasn't sure what he'd do.

Upstairs, he found Sheila seated outside on the deck attached to their bedroom. When he stepped out to join her, she turned his way and the brittle forced smile stung his heart. "Hey," he said softly.

"Hey."

"Marti's gone. I—I told her she had to leave."

"Thank you for that, Barrett. I really didn't want her here."

"I know, and if you're wondering if I've been in contact with her since the reunion in Orlando, the answer is no and there won't be any in the future."

She turned to the open field that stretched to the horizon and remained silent for a moment before admitting, "Honestly, I did wonder."

"You had every right to. I wasn't exactly trustworthy."

"Or truthful," she added. He flinched, then told himself she had the right to point that out, too.

"I'm sorry if her being here reopened old wounds."

"It did, but my sessions with Paula have helped me be better at healing myself."

He knew she'd been meeting with the reverend. Personally, he couldn't see himself ever revealing his inner self to a
therapist, not even one as good a person as Paula. He was a
warrior and warriors kept things like that under lock and key.

"And Barrett, so you'll know, I'm going to run for mayor."

For a moment, he thought he'd misheard her. "What?"

"I'm going to run for mayor."

"You're kidding, right? Is this your way of getting back at
me about Marti? Not trying to be mean, but you don't know
the first thing about running a town."

The combative flare in her eyes signaled it had been the
wrong thing to say, but his bruised ego spurred him on. "Is
this something Paula put you up to?"

"No one put me up to this. I know you think I'm not the
brightest bulb in the box, but that's because I've dimmed myself all these years so you could shine brighter. I graduated at
the top of my class, Barrett. My IQ is probably just a bit south
of our son's."

His eyes went wide.

"And I've never mentioned it before because I was raised
to be a good little military wife, content to be in the background and let her man lead. But doing so has wrecked my
self-esteem and made me so mousy and uninteresting, I don't
even know who I am anymore. So, I'm running for mayor,
for me," she declared, jabbing a red-tipped, manicured finger
forcefully in her chest for emphasis. "Not because Paula put
me up to it, not because you cheated on me with a woman
with a Jheri curl, but because I'd make a damn good mayor.
And if you don't like it, you can kiss my behind."

He almost fell off the deck. She strode past him and inside, leaving him to wonder who this woman was and what she'd done with his wife!

STANDING IN THE snack line for Movie Night at the rec, Robyn saw some of her schoolmates behind the counters and tables taking orders for popcorn, hot dogs, drinks, and everything else listed for purchase on the hand-lettered sign on the wall. When her turn came, she stepped to the table manned by Amari and Leah who smiled at seeing her. "Hey, Robyn. What can I get you?"

She ordered popcorn and a cola. "Can I sit with you all?"

Leah nodded. "Sure. We're behind Zoey and Devon's crew, so grab us a row and we'll be down when we're done working."

"Okay." After paying for her order, Robyn left the crowded area and headed to the seats. She'd never been given the job of holding down seats for friends before and was admittedly nervous that she'd somehow mess up and pick a row no one liked. She saw Zoey waving crazily and it took her a moment to realize, the signal was for her. Feeling better, she made her way down the aisle to where Zoey sat with her set of friends.

"You're going to sit with us?" Zoey asked.

"Leah said for me to pick out a row near you guys."

Devon said, "They usually sit two or three rows in back of us."

Wyatt cracked, "Can't have anybody thinking they actually know us."

Robyn eyed him, wondering if he was serious.

Lucas Herman came to her rescue. "That's a joke, Robyn."

"Oh."

"Ignore him," Zoey said, glaring Wyatt's way. "He thinks he's the king of sarcasm, but he's really just a pain in the butt."

"You're going to marry this pain in the butt one day."

"Only if you turn yourself into RM."

Alfonso Acosta snickered. "Burn."

Robyn wondered if every little girl in the world was in love with the members of BTS?

Devon boasted, "She's marrying me."

Zoey rolled her eyes. "Yeah, right."

Robyn noticed they threw shade at each other all the time, but never in a mean-spirited way. It was obvious they cared about one another. She'd only had a couple of friends in Blackbird, but her grandmother's reputation as a witch meant none of them wanted to hang out at her house, and she certainly wasn't allowed to hang out at theirs. Being around the Henry Adams crew made her wonder if her life would've been different had she grown up with a group of caring friends.

"You okay?" Lucas asked.

His question brought her back. "Yeah. I'm going to get the seats. I'll see you later."

"We're all spending the night at Leah and Tiff's," Zoey said before Robyn left them. "Are you going?"

Robyn had no idea what she was referring to. Her first instinct was to say no, but she reminded herself that she was supposed to be trying to build some friendships. "Let me talk to Leah, and I'll let you know."

Zoey smiled. "Okay."

Robyn picked seats two rows behind Zoey and the others. Settling in, she took a sip of her icy cola and glanced around the crowded noisy auditorium. Cousin Paula was seated up near the door. Beside her was Wyatt's grandmother, Ms. Gemma. Next to her was a tall dark-haired man Robyn didn't know. She wondered who he was, then heard her grandmother's voice rage in her head about staying out of folks' business. She sighed and wondered if she'd ever escape that voice? Paula planned to visit Ardella in prison sometime soon. She'd asked Robyn if she wanted to go, too. She didn't. Maybe she'd change her mind when she got older and the memories of being punched, slapped, and screamed at didn't hurt so much. For now, she didn't care if she ever saw her grandmother again.

Leah joined Robyn a short time later and by then every seat in the auditorium was filled with people of all ages, races, and sizes. They were attired in everything from jeans and T-shirts to nice suits and dresses. "Do people come here on dates?"

Leah nodded. "All the time. Not much else to do on a Friday night around here."

"It was the same way back home, but at least you have this. Zoey said you're having something at your house after the movies?"

"Yes. Tomorrow is Pizza Saturday with our uncle TC, so everybody's going to sleep over and hang out. You're welcome to come if you want."

"I'll have to ask cousin Paula."

"Okay; let her know the girls will be sleeping upstairs in our bedrooms, and the boys will be in the basement. My dad is real serious about being the chaperone."

"Do I need to bring anything?"

"Just your sleep stuff. Zoey and her girls will be in Tiff's room. You can sleep there or in my room like you did the last time you came over."

"Thanks, Leah." The last time, Robyn had just moved to town and was so overwhelmed by being in a new place, and all the drama tied to the trial, and being so unsure of herself, she hadn't had a good time.

"Hope Reverend Paula says yes. We always have big fun."

Robyn hoped she'd say yes, too.

And she did. After the movie, Paula drove her home and Robyn quickly threw her overnight gear into her backpack. When they reached the Clark residence, Robyn said, "Thanks for letting me come."

"You're welcome. Are you going to stay and make pizza tomorrow afternoon?"

"I think so. I'll text you when I need to get picked up."

"Sounds good. Have a good time."

Paula waited in her truck while Robyn rang the bell. When Mr. Clark answered the door, Robyn waved goodbye to Paula who then drove off.

"Good to see you, Robyn," Mr. Clark said. "Everybody's downstairs. You can put your backpack and jacket on the pile there and go on down."

"Thank you."

After adding her backpack and jacket to the mound of others, Robyn made her way down the stairs to the sounds of BTS and laughter.

Tiffany called out, "Robyn's here!"

Cheers followed, leaving her both embarrassed and happy.

The evening was the most fun Robyn ever remembered having. There was salsa and chips, pretzels, soda, and a big platter of grapes. Brain and Amari, Tiff and Leah, and Devon and Alfonso did battle with *Fortnite Save the World* on competing flat-screen TVs. Lucas and Wyatt declared war on each other on the Ping-Pong table, while Jasmine, Zoey, and Maria Acosta competed for the title of Queen of Jacks. It was loud and crazy, and Robyn spent her time going from competition to competition, laughing at the smack talk, watching victory dances, and commiserating with the agony of defeat.

At 1:00 a.m., Mr. Clark came down and announced it was time to close down the fun. There were a few groans, but no real complaints. They spent a few minutes cleaning up and putting things away. Once done, the boys began laying out their sleeping bags and the girls trooped upstairs.

Robyn and Leah had just changed into their sleep gear when a knock on the closed bedroom door sounded.

"Come in," Leah called.

It was Tiffany. She looked upset.

"What's wrong?"

"How often do you go through Brain's phone?"

Confusion lined Leah's face. "Never."

Tiffany seemed surprised. "Why not?"

"Duh, because it's his phone." Leah studied her sister. "Whose phone do you want to go through?"

When Tiffany didn't answer, Leah said, "I know this isn't about Amari."

Tiff came to her own defense, "Girls online talk about going through their boyfriends' phones all the time."

"Number one, you and Amari aren't really official, and two, people online set themselves on fire and eat detergent pods. Why would you take relationship advice from them?"

Tiff dropped her head.

Leah said, "I assume you asked him, so what did he say?"

"For me to leave him alone and come back when I grow up."

Robyn winced inwardly.

Leah said, "Dumb move, baby sis."

"But how am I supposed to know if he's calling other girls?"

"Five-letter word: trust."

Tiff blew out a breath. "You're no help at all." And she left.

Leah looked over at Robyn. "If she keeps acting like my mom, we may need to get an exorcist."

A short while later, they were lying in their respective beds talking quietly in the dark.

"Thanks for inviting me," Robyn said. "I had fun."

"Good. Do you like living here?" Leah asked.

Robyn thought over her response. "I didn't at first, but I don't think it had anything to do with being here specifically. I'd've probably been unhappy wherever I ended up. All the drama with finding my mom's skull in the yard behind the house, and my grandmother going to jail. It was a lot."

"The first time you slept over you didn't seem comfortable."

Robyn admitted, "I wasn't a very good guest."

"I thought you didn't like me."

"No. That wasn't it. I was just—let's say I was kind of intimidated."

"By what?"

"You."

Leah laughed. "Me?"

"Yeah. I came in this room, and you had a telescope, and your own flat screen, a ton of books—fiction—not schoolbooks. My grandmother never let me buy books." She chased off the sadness that bubbled up and continued, "You had a closet full of clothes and shoes—and I didn't have any of those things. I do now, but last year, no."

"I wanted you to come over because I hoped we could be friends. Everybody in the crew has a counterpart except me."

"You have Preston, though."

"I do and he's great, but I don't have any girl buds. Crystal and I are sorta tight but she's older and has her own college friends."

"You really want to be friends with me?"

"No, Robyn, I'm just lying, and I hate your guts."

Robyn laughed. "Okay." She thought about all she'd endured and said quietly, "I'd like a friend, somebody to talk to, hang with. My life's been a mess. Lots of pain."

"I have my share, too. My mom's crazy. It's good we have Reverend Paula. She's been great helping me deal with all my mama drama."

"She's helped me a lot, too. I got stuff inside I need to get out, but just thinking about having to talk about it hurts, you know?"

"I do. So if you want to talk I'm here."

"Same."

There was a silence for a moment before Leah asked, "Do you like waffles?"

"I do."

"I'm making them for breakfast. My friend gets the first one."

"Being your friend is a good thing, then. Thanks for having me over, Leah."

"No problem. Good night, Robyn."

"Night, Leah."

Robyn made herself comfortable and drifted off to sleep. She had a friend.

CHAPTER
5

When Bernadine arrived at the Dog for Meet the Candidates Night, she claimed a table in the middle of the room. The place was filling up. She was pleased to see the kids had already claimed booths. Jack James and new teacher Kyrie Abbott had mandated the students attend as part of their civics curriculum. Rocky and her staff were putting the last touches to the buffet and bringing in extra chairs. Everyone was expecting a large crowd.

Lily and Trent joined her a few minutes later. Discussing the agenda with them, she looked up and into the hostile eyes of the entering Big Al Stillwell. Fear raced up her spine. As if aware of her reaction he gave her an ugly little smile and walked to a table in the back. Watching him go, Bernadine exhaled a shaky breath.

Sounding and looking concerned, Lily asked, "What's he doing here? I thought he'd moved to Oklahoma?"

Trent eyed Stillwell grimly. "Heard he's renting the double-wide Leo was living in before he moved his McMansion from Franklin. Not sure if he's back permanently or what."

Seeing Stillwell brought back memories of the nasty temper he'd turned on her, the deadly arson fire set by his mother, and his mother's attempts to run Bernadine off the road. She hoped he wasn't back permanently. She didn't want to spend her days and nights looking over her shoulder wondering if he was lurking nearby.

As more and more people arrived, Bernadine's concerns about Big Al faded. Riley strutted in smiling, shaking hands and garnering eye rolls from folks all over the room. Anna Ruiz, mother-in-law of fire chief Luis Acosta, entered with her grandchildren and immediately came over to Bernadine and thanked her again for their new residence.

"We want to have everyone over for dinner soon to celebrate."

"Just let me know."

"Will do."

As she left to find a seat, Bobby and Kelly Douglas came in pushing the double stroller holding their twins. Kiara and Bobby Jr., the town's little darlings, were getting bigger every day. Dad, Bobby Sr., was doing well as a student at the community college, and as Trent's right-hand man. Kelly was managing the hair salon as if she'd been a successful businesswoman all her life. They were fine young people and great parents. Bernadine was glad they'd made the decision to move from Dallas to Henry Adams to seek a better life.

Genevieve Barbour, Riley's ex-wife, was godmother to the twins and as she went to greet them, Leo walked into the diner. Bernadine did her best to keep the snarl from her face. Decked out in one of his tailored European suits—silver—and wearing an equally costly pair of Italian handmade loafers—brown—the sight of him made her want to punch him in his nose. As if having peeped her thoughts, he flashed her a grin before taking a seat in the booth where Big Al Stillwell was seated with a few farmer friends. The mayoral race was already enough of a hot mess with Riley's candidacy. Add Leo to the mix, and the election was headed for Crazy Town.

Eyes on Leo, Lily asked, "Is he really running?"

"He says he is. Whether it's for the long haul, or just until he aggravates me enough to jump off a roof is anyone's guess."

"He's not wanted here."

"Another one of the reasons motivating him, I'm sure." Knowing Leo, he probably wanted to lay the blame for his no longer perfect life at her feet, but Bernadine refused to own even a gram of it.

Her musings were interrupted by Lily's surprised voice. "What's Thad doing here?"

Bernadine was brought up short by the sight of Thaddeus July, the patriarch of the Oklahoma July clan, entering the Dog via his fancy white-and-gold-trimmed, motorized wheelchair. He was smartly dressed in a fawn brown, western-cut suit and matching boots. Twin gray braids hung from beneath the beautiful snow white Stetson covering his head. With him was Mal. His gaze brushed hers so dispassionately, her anger flared, but she let it go. By his side were Thad's grandsons, Diego July, Crystal's former heartthrob, and Griffin July, Amari's bio dad. The smiling Thad threw Bernadine a wink before motoring over to the table where his sister, Tamar, sat with Marie, Genevieve, and Gen's husband, TC.

Bernadine prayed aloud, "Lord, please don't let Thad be here to run for mayor, too."

"Don't even speak that," Lily replied with amused alarm.

But with all the other craziness going on, Bernadine thought prayer might be needed.

With a bang of his gavel on a table at the front of the room Trent opened the meeting. "We're here tonight to introduce the candidates for mayor of Henry Adams. If you plan to run, please stand."

Riley stood first, beaming in his black suit. Barrett followed. Griffin got to his feet, "My grandfather's running, so I'm standing for him, Thaddeus July."

"Jesus," Bernadine whispered and saw Tamar hang her head.

Leo stood. "I was going to run, but instead, I'm throwing my support behind Riley Curry."

Bing Shepard yelled, "Birds of a feather, lose together!" Laughter and applause followed that and Leo appeared angered by the reaction. Bernadine wasn't sure why. Neither he nor Riley were well liked.

Trent used his gavel to restore order. Once folks quieted, he asked, "Anyone else?"

Sheila stood and Bernadine gasped. She and Lily exchanged looks of astonishment.

"Sheila Payne," she said loudly and clearly.

Jaws dropped all over the diner. There were smiles too, from people like Gen and Marie. Amari and Preston executed a quick high five. On the other hand, Barrett eyed his wife like a malevolent dragon. Bernadine wondered if this was affecting their marriage. Yes, prayer was on speed dial.

Trent continued, "Once the candidates are certified by the Election Commission, a debate will be scheduled. Election will take place the second Tuesday in November. There will be formal paper ballots this time, and absentee ballots mailed to any seniors wanting one. At the next town meeting we'll float a list the seniors can add their names to for those ballots."

Rocky put up her hand.

"Yeah, Rock?"

"Are we allowed to write in anyone not on the ballot?"

"Yes, as long as the name isn't Trent July." He scanned the gathering. "Other questions?"

Riley asked, "Who's on this Election Commission?"

Trent rattled off the names, adding, "The commission members will be counting the votes. Barrett will be stepping aside, of course, since he's a candidate. The official polling place will be inside the Power Plant."

Bernadine saw Leo lean over and whisper something to Riley. He nodded and stood. "Ms. Brown shouldn't be allowed to publicly endorse anyone. It would be undue influence."

Bing called out, "You're still going to lose, Curry."

Snickers were heard.

Bernadine answered, "I have no problem with that, Riley. I won't publicly endorse anyone."

He nodded as if satisfied and retook his seat. She wondered if Leo had expected her to argue.

Trent scanned the room again for more questions. Seeing none, he brought the gavel down and the meeting was adjourned.

Mixing, mingling, and eating from the buffet followed. Bernadine left her spot and joined the group gathered excitedly around Sheila, just in time to hear Marie Jefferson say, "Knock us over with a feather, why don't you. You're really running?"

"I am."

Sheila looked proud and confident. Bernadine wanted to ask about Barrett's reaction to her surprising candidacy but didn't. Her curiosity would be fed eventually though—there were no secrets in Henry Adams.

Genevieve exclaimed, "Sheila, I'm so proud of you. At the next Ladies Auxiliary meeting let us know how we can help with your campaign. Lord knows we're not voting for Riley."

"Or Leo," Marie declared firmly, lasering a stink eye in his direction.

Bernadine wondered if the two had spoken since his return. If he had any sense, he'd give the town's school superintendent a wide berth, but that not being Leo's strong suit, drama was a certainty. Leaving Sheila with her supporters, Bernadine made her way through the crowd to the buffet. Former head cook Siz Burke was now working in Miami, but the new person guiding the kitchen, Texan Randy Emerson, was equally as talented, and as devoted to food both tasty and healthy. She helped herself to the fish tacos dressed with a creamy coleslaw and added a nice-size portion of blueberry salsa. Adding a small stack of whole wheat taco chips, she left the buffet and searched the diner for an open seat. Across the room, Tamar waved her over. On the way Bernadine was stopped by Lyman Proctor, the newly elected mayor of Franklin, who asked, "Curry doesn't have a chance of winning, does he? Working with him will be a nightmare."

"Only if they start building snowmen in hell."

Pleased, he toasted her with a salsa-filled chip, and she went on her way.

Tamar July's booth was crowded with family: Trent, Lily, Amari, Devon, Griffin, Diego, and Mal. Thad was seated like a monarch on his gleaming gold-trimmed chair.

Tamar said to her, "Tell my brother Henry Adams doesn't need a casino."

Bernadine almost dropped her plate and gave Thad a questioning look.

He smiled, eyes filled with mischief. "A lot of tribes have casinos."

Tamar said, "On tribal land."

"Our plot is tribal land if owned by a member of the tribe."

Diego chuckled softly. Griffin rolled his eyes.

Bernadine said, "We don't need a casino on any of the town's land, Mr. July." She felt Mal's eyes on her but she didn't acknowledge him.

"But think how much money it will bring in," Thad claimed.

"Think how much money it'll cost to build it."

"There is that, but I was hoping you'd be open to a loan."

"To whom?"

"Me, of course."

Amused, she shook her heard. "I may not be Seminole, but I know not to lend money to a coyote."

Tamar drawled, "Your reputation proceeds you, Thaddeus."

He asked Bernadine, "You sure?"

"Positive, sir."

"Then maybe I need to be talking to old what's his name."

Her brow furrowed with confusion. "Who's that?"

"Your ex."

"Ah. Be my guest, but he's a snake, and last I heard, snakes and coyotes don't play well together."

Tamar added firmly, "And after the way he treated Marie, he'll be lucky I don't fill his worthless behind with buckshot." She looked at her brother. "No casino. No Leo. No. Period."

He wasn't deterred. "We'll see what the populace says once I begin my campaign."

Lily asked him, "But how can you even run? You live in Oklahoma."

"Was born here, and still pay property taxes on the July plot. Makes me a legal resident."

Bernadine guessed she agreed with his take. She didn't want to, but if he was correct, then by law he had every right to throw his Stetson into the ring. Now, the names on the Henry Adams mayoral dance card were Riley, Barrett, Sheila, and Thaddeus the Coyote July. The ballot was officially closed. Any other candidates would need to mount a write-in campaign if they wanted the job. Mal drifted over to talk with Bing Shepard and Clay Dobbs. She walked away to mingle.

The Dog emptied out a short while later. Out in the parking lot, Bernadine waved her goodbyes as she made her way to her truck. She was still floored by Sheila's candidacy and wondered if she could really win. She wasn't discounting her because anything was possible, but conventional wisdom said Barrett would be the next mayor. Although he was no longer the rigid hard-ass he'd been when he and Sheila first moved to town, Bernadine knew they'd butt heads more than a few times over things both big and small, but his intelligence and well-proven desire to do what's best for Henry Adams would balance out any disagreements they might have.

Reaching Baby, she opened the door. Hearing Mal call her name, she drew in a deep breath and turned to meet his approach. "What's up?" she asked.

"Just want to apologize for walking out on you the way I did."

"No problem," she lied.

He looked off into the distance for a few moments before saying, "If we can't be a couple, can we at least be friends?"

"I don't see why not, but how about you let me get over this breakup first?"

"You've been acting like you are over it."

Steam built up inside. "No, I'm not. And you know why?"

"Why?"

"Because I let you off easy, Mal. I agreed to starting over because you put me on the spot. Instead of blasting you the way I should have that day at Tamar's, I played the goody-two-shoes girlfriend and kept my mouth shut. I'm still mad about that, and madder at myself for not telling the truth."

"I've apologized enough for five men. What else do you want me to say?"

"Nothing. Not a word. You're not the victim here, Mal. I am." That said, she got in her truck and peeled out of the parking lot. Halfway down Main, she realized tears were wetting her cheeks; she dashed them away and kept driving.

THE NEXT MORNING, Leo spent an hour on conference calls with his handlers from Salem Oil and Mega Seed. They wanted to know what kind of progress he'd made, if any. He told them about using the mayor's race as his cover and that he expected the operation's pace to increase soon. After the call ended, he read the report he'd had their investigators compile on Franklin's former mayor Astrid Wiggins. He wasn't sure if she'd be an asset to his plans or not. Due to her role in the Henry Adams gold riot, the cockroach infestation at Gary Clark's grocery, and imprisoning the kid she'd directed to plant the insects, she'd been relieved of her duties, and Mabel Franklin, the matriarch of Astrid's wealthy family, had come down on her like Godzilla stomping Tokyo. Astrid lost her mansion and her privileged lifestyle. She was now employed at the family convenience store/gas station and going home to a single-wide in a seedy trailer park. By all accounts, she hated Bernadine though, and that was an asset. He was certain he could use the animosity, but no idea how. Maybe meeting her would him help decide. In the meantime he decided to pay a visit to an old friend.

The Jefferson homestead could trace its establishment back to the town's nineteenth-century founders and had been handed down through the generations for nearly one hundred and fifty years. The nearly mile-long picket fence fronting the land had been painted white the last time he'd been around. Now it was green. The town used painting it as a novel way to punish the youngsters for bad behavior, so he wondered who'd drawn the short straw this time and why. Not that it mattered. He didn't care about the fence. His interest lay with the land. Two years ago, he tried to sweet-talk his way into buying it from owner Marie Jefferson by feigning a romantic interest. In the days of the founders, she'd've been called a spinster: older, never married, and no prospects of that status ever changing. He'd gifted her with expensive jewelry, taken her to Europe and the Maldives, and showed her what it was like to be on the arm of a wealthy man. When he asked her about selling him the land, she'd given him a flat-out no. So he left her and moved on. Now, he was back to screw with her for turning down his offer.

When he stepped onto the porch, she was standing behind the screen door awaiting his approach. Her eyes, framed by the cat-eye glasses she always wore, were hard. "What do you want, Leo?"

"Don't I rate a hello?"

"What do you want?" she asked, enunciating each word.

"To see if we could have dinner. For old times' sake. Can I at least come in?"

"No to both. Anything else?"

"Yes. I checked with the State of Kansas and you're way behind on your taxes, Marie."

Fear flashed in her face.

He smiled smugly. "So far behind that if you don't come up with a large chunk of change for the next tax cycle, you're going to lose this place to the bank. Your sainted ancestors are probably spinning in their graves."

"And you're here to gloat?"

He smiled. "Yes, but also to extend a helping hand. I'll pay the taxes in exchange for ownership. I'll even let you stay here until the Good Lord takes you home."

"No," and she closed the door in his face.

It wasn't unexpected. Still made him mad, though. Leo walked back to his car and got in. He took solace in the fact that due to the multiple times she'd already refinanced, there wasn't a banker alive who'd help her out. Her only option lay with Bernadine. Marie Jefferson was a prideful woman and having to ask for aid would probably kill her. She'd not want to go to Bernadine on her knees. Knowing she'd have to swallow that pride or lose her land was enough payback for him.

Driving away, he decided he enjoyed playing the villain.

At the small convenience store/gas station where Astrid Wiggins worked, Leo pulled up to one of the four pumps out front to top off the tank of his German import. A few other men were filling up, mostly locals he assumed by their attire and trucks. He noted their silent scrutiny as he replaced the nozzle but didn't let it bother him, until one called out, "You know, America builds cars, too."

"But they don't build *this* car," Leo shot back. "How about you mind your own business and I'll mind mine."

That earned him some ugly looks but he walked to the door without a further word.

The report on Astrid Wiggins included a picture, so he knew the kid behind the counter whose face was more acne than skin wasn't her. "Looking for Astrid Wiggins."

The kid raised his attention from his phone and eyed him for a moment, then inclined his head. "Over there."

Leo turned to see a woman mopping the floor. Next to her was a big yellow bucket with a mounted wringer attached. "Thanks."

He walked past a counter holding a small glass-faced oven with dried-out hot dogs rotating in it, and over to the large standing cooler filled with bottled water and beer she was mopping in front of. "Astrid Wiggins?"

She paused the mop. "Maybe. Who's asking?"

"Name's Leo Brown."

She went back to her chore. "And?"

He debated how to play this. "Two things. First, I'm the campaign manager for Riley Curry. Hoping you can direct me to some people he can count on for support."

She chuckled bitterly. "Riley Curry couldn't win if he was running unopposed. What's the second thing?"

"Bernadine Brown."

She stopped and met his eyes. "What about her?"

"I'm her ex-husband. I hear our opinions on her may coincide."

Leo saw her glance toward the windows. She appeared to

smile as she turned back. "If that means I don't like her, you're correct."

"Anybody else feel the same way?"

She resumed mopping. "Why?"

"Thought maybe we could all get together and form a club."

"Dealing with her cost me my way of life. Whatever you're planning, keep me out of it."

"You're sure? I could make it worth your while."

"I'm living in a trailer. If I go anywhere near her, my next address will be the street. So, no. And you might want to go check on your car."

He stilled. "My car? Why?"

"One of the nozzles from a pump is inside your driver's-side window."

Eyes wide, he ran to the exit.

"Do you know why this happened?" the county deputy Davida Ransom asked.

The furious Leo watched the fire truck drive away and the tow truck driver attach his car to the winch. "I think it was racially motivated."

"Because?"

"You're black and can't figure that out? Look where we are."

"Did you have an altercation that makes you believe it was racial?"

He told her about the man's comment on his vehicle.

She shook her head. "More than likely you were targeted for your response. Whoever did this probably perceived you to be a jerk, Mr. Brown."

His jaw tightened. "I want them charged."

"Can you give me a description?"

"Doesn't this place have cameras?"

"Unfortunately, they aren't working. The clerk admitted to being on his phone when a guy came in and asked for twenty dollars on the pump where you're parked. Said he took the money and turned on the pump. Didn't look up. So a description would help."

He threw up his hands. "They were white—all of them."

"I'll need more than that. Do you remember glancing at a plate or the make of any of the trucks?"

He didn't know a Ford from a Dodge. "They were just trucks."

"Okay. I'll file my report." She gave him a card. "Call me in a few days with the fax number of your insurance company and I'll see that they receive it. Maybe the insurance company can go after the owners for the clerk's negligence."

"That's all you can do?"

"Lacking any concrete description of the men who may have been involved, yes. I'm sorry. Do you have a way home?"

"No."

"Give me a minute to check in with my dispatcher and I'll drop you off."

Angry and humiliated, Leo grumbled a terse thank you. A few minutes later, she drove him away.

BERNADINE CLOSED THE FaceTime app on her phone. The session had been with Luis Acosta, informing her about the run he and the department made out to the Wiggins gas station to deal with Leo's car. That someone had deliberately pumped gas into it meant her ex pissed someone off, and since it was Leo it wasn't difficult to imagine. She was just glad there hadn't been an explosion or a fire, and Luis expressed the same. But who'd done it and why? Astrid probably hadn't been pleased, either. Due to the incident, the station would be closed until the state sent inspectors to make sure all the gasoline had been cleaned up. She wondered if Astrid knew who Leo was. Since Astrid's grandmother Mabel cut her off from the family teat, Bernadine hadn't heard a peep from her former nemesis. Those who'd seen her said she appeared to have aged quite a bit, which happens when you can't afford your Botox shots. The gray had grown out in her hair, too. People described her as haggard and worn, which Bernadine found fitting considering all she'd put her and Henry Adams through.

"Knock, knock."

She glanced up to see Marie in the doorway. "Hey."

Marie asked, "Do you have a minute?"

"I do. Come on in."

That she closed the office door behind her gave Bernadine pause, but she waited to see if that held any significance.

Taking a seat, Marie said, "Leo came by my place earlier."

Unsure how to respond, she replied simply, "Okay."

Marie stared off into the distance for a few moments, then said quietly, "He wants to buy my land. I told him no of course."

"Of course."

"I'm in a bind though, and he's trying to take advantage of it."

"What kind of bind?"

"I'm behind on my taxes. I'll be going into foreclosure soon if I don't pay. He taunted me about it."

Bernadine was surprised. Marie's deep sense of pride was

well known. Bernadine couldn't imagine what it must be costing her to lay her cards on the table this way, so she asked gently, "How can I help?"

She took a deep breath. "If you'll pay the back taxes, I'll sign my land over to you."

Bernadine stared. "I can pay them, but it's not necessary to give me your land, Marie."

"Yes, it is. When I die, there's no one to pass it down to. You'll keep it safe."

"What about your son?"

"He doesn't want it. If I leave it to him, he'll just sell it— maybe to Leo."

"Why is he so hell-bent on your property?"

"I don't know."

"Have you ever had a geological evaluation?"

"No."

"It might be something to think about."

"I can't afford it."

Bernadine studied her silently. "Do you need your salary increased, Marie? I can raise it a bit if that will help."

She shook her head. "That isn't necessary."

Bernadine sensed there was something Marie wasn't sharing. She wanted to ask why she hadn't paid her taxes, but that was too personal a question. They'd had issues before, specifically when she'd tried to warn Marie off Leo, and she didn't want them on the outs with each other ever again. "Will you let me look into the evaluation? If Leo knows something about your land that we don't, we need to find out what it is. I'll use town money."

"Okay."

"If it's any consolation, Leo pissed off the wrong person

a little while ago." And she related what she knew about the gasoline incident.

"Couldn't have happened to a nicer person," Marie said bitterly.

"I agree." Silence settled between them for a moment while Bernadine again wondered how Marie had gotten into such financial straits. "How do you want me to handle the tax payment and when?"

Marie opened her purse and took out some papers. "Here's what's owed and the due date. If you could make the check out to the state, that would be fine." Unshed tears stood in her eyes and her voice was soft. "I can't believe I'm having to do this."

"We all need help sometimes, Marie."

"If it was for something unexpected, yes, but this isn't that. I caused this mess by being stupid."

She was silent for a moment, then confessed, "I have a gambling problem."

It was the last thing Bernadine expected to hear.

"I've lost a ton of money this year and like everyone else with the addiction, I figured if I kept playing, I'd hit the jackpot and make myself whole again."

"Oh, Marie."

"I know. I've gone through my pension, my savings. I've nothing left, Bernadine."

Her heart ached.

"I did have enough sense to join Gamblers Anonymous, and it's helping me get my mind right, but in the meantime, I'm broke, and I refuse to let Leo take advantage of it."

"Don't worry. I have your back. Good to know you're seeking help."

"Smartest thing I've done. You'll keep this between us? Gen's the only other person who knows. She's the one who convinced me to get help."

"Of course. No one needs to know. I'll take care of the taxes, so don't worry about that. You concentrate on getting well."

Marie pulled a tissue from her purse and dabbed at her eyes. "Thank you," she whispered.

"You're welcome."

After Marie's departure, Bernadine sat in the silence and realized you never knew what people had going on behind the curtains of their lives. She knew Marie enjoyed going to Vegas, but that she had a gambling problem never crossed her mind. Thank god for Genevieve. Bernadine also sent up a thank-you for being blessed with the money she'd gotten in her divorce settlement. It allowed her to help in ways that mattered, and Marie's issue definitely qualified. Using the information on Marie's paperwork as a guide, she wrote out the check for the taxes and stuck it in an envelope. She'd drop it off at the Franklin post office before going home at the end of the day. Even though Lily July was Marie's goddaughter, Bernadine didn't plan to share any of what was discussed. A promise was a promise. If Marie wanted Lily to know, Marie would tell her.

CHAPTER
6

Riley had a problem. To realize his dream of becoming Henry Adams's mayor, he needed money. There were billboards to erect, yard signs to order, flyers featuring his likeness to distribute, and coffee klatches to hold. Between his tips, small salary, and the occasional five-dollar bills discreetly stolen from the salon's cash drawer, he'd barely managed to scrape together enough to buy an old car. His bank account couldn't afford campaign costs. What little extra he had went to food and to the State of Kansas as restitution for having helped himself to Genevieve's trust fund before she walked out on him and their marriage. He still thought the settlement unfair, but it beat being thrown in jail. Life would be different were he still Cletus's owner. Scarsdale was probably rich as Midas, enjoying fancy cars, five-star hotels, and expensive vacations, while Riley was stuck in Henry Adams trying to make ends meet. The only viable option was to throw in with Leo Brown, who had both the cash and clout. Granted, in the scheme of things, Brown wasn't well liked and probably viewed Riley as just another dumb country hick easily manipulated, but he'd been underestimated before.

After ending his shift at the salon, he called the number on Brown's card and was pleased to be invited to his mansion to talk. On the drive over, his old car with its bald tires and dying carburetor sputtered and protested the entire way, but it got him there. He parked and stepped out, taking a moment to enviously survey the grand mansion that looked so out of place against the open Kansas countryside. It was all fancy brick and windows, and he couldn't imagine how much it must have cost to build, let alone have it moved from Franklin. A few yards away stood the old Stillwell place with its sagging roof and plywood-covered windows. Compared to the grandeur of the mansion, it looked even sadder. Deciding not to worry about the oil spots his car would leave in the driveway, he walked to the door.

He was ushered inside by a middle-aged, red-haired white woman in a blue uniform. "Good evening, Mr. Curry. Please, let me take your jacket."

Riley handed it over, all the while marveling at the grand foyer with its high ceilings and fancy staircase. It reminded him of Eustacia Pennymaker's place in Texas. Thinking of her, he wondered if she'd help finance his campaign. Like Genevieve, she'd walked out on him, too. The answer was probably no, but it wouldn't hurt to ask.

"Follow me, please."

He was led into a large sitting room dominated by a sparkling white marble fireplace. There was an expensive-looking brown leather love seat, chairs in blues and greens, and lamps with crystal bases. Painted landscapes of mountains and ocean that probably cost more than he'd make in five years graced the soft gray walls.

She gestured him to one of the chairs. "Have a seat. Mr. Brown will be right with you."

Left alone, he looked around and imagined what it would be like to have so much wealth that you never had to worry about things like aging cars or a place to live. You could have more than one good suit and lots of fancy shoes. It was a lifestyle he'd aspired to for as long as he could remember but it had always remained beyond his reach.

Brown came in a short time later, dressed in a black cashmere crew neck and pressed khakis. On his feet were the costly loafers he seemed to favor. "How are you, Mr. Curry?" He extended a welcoming hand that showed off the gold diamond-edged watch on his wrist.

Riley dragged his attention from the timepiece and stood to accept the handshake. "Doing okay. How about you?"

The quick clasp of hands ended, and Brown said, "I'm okay, too. I was just getting ready to have some dinner. Have you eaten?"

"No."

"Would you care to join me?"

Reining in his eagerness, Riley replied as casually as he could manage, "If I won't be imposing."

"Oh, course not. Come with me. It's not very chilly, so let's eat in the solarium."

Riley had no idea what a solarium was but stood and followed. As he was led through the sprawling house, there was more artwork and fine furniture. They passed a room filled with bookcases, one that was set up as a theater, and another with a large pool table in the center.

Brown asked, "Do you play pool?"

Riley told the truth for once. "No."

The journey continued past a life-size Samurai soldier decked out in red and black armor, then an all-white kitchen that was the biggest he'd ever seen, then down a hallway into a huge room with walls and ceiling made of glass. The enormous floor-to-ceiling panes, set between polished beams of reddish wood, were so clean they were rendered invisible. He could see for miles across the open plains. Riley had been impressed by Eustacia's spacious Texas home, but Brown lived on an even higher level.

Behind him, Brown said, "Spectacular view, isn't it?"

"Yes." It was something.

"If I decide to stick around, I may put in some tennis courts and a pool in the spring."

Riley didn't swim or play tennis either, but he approved of the man's vision. He wanted to ask what would make him stay or leave but held on to the question.

A few yards to the right was a double-wide trailer and to the left the Stillwell barns. They were in even worse condition than the tumbledown house.

Brown said, "I'll be having those eyesores removed as soon as possible. I won't be doing any farming. Not really my thing." He smiled, so Riley did, too.

"Mine either."

They were interrupted by the arrival of the uniformed red-haired woman pushing a four-wheeled metal cart. On it were polished silver domes covering what he assumed was their meal, along with silverware, glasses, and a pitcher of water.

"Our dinner," Brown confirmed, sounding pleased, and directed Riley to the marble table and leather chairs set against one of the glass walls. "Hope you like lobster."

Again, tamping down his excitement, Riley nodded. He'd only had lobster a few times in his life, and not even Eustacia served it at home. He wondered if Brown ate this extravagantly all the time. If the man was trying to impress him, he'd succeeded.

The lobster was served with little fingerling potatoes, tossed with what tasted like olive oil—which he didn't like—and a salad with tomatoes and cukes. He didn't care for salads either but planned to eat everything because tuna and crackers awaited him at home.

Once they began eating, Brown asked, "So, Mr. Curry. What did you want to talk to me about?"

"My campaign," Riley said, diving into the meal while trying not to talk with his mouth full. "I'm not as financially set as I'd hoped and was interested in maybe taking you up on your generous offer of assistance."

"Ah." For a few long moments, Brown said nothing more, and Riley did his best not to squirm under his silent scrutiny. "What do you see as the foundation of your campaign?"

"Security. Henry Adams will never have another assassin if I'm elected."

"I remember you saying that. A noble focus."

Riley beamed.

"And in exchange for my assistance?"

Riley stilled. Looking into Brown's watchful eyes made him feel like prey, but he did his best not to show it. "What would you like?"

"Being able to run the campaign the way I think it should

be run. Tapping people to be on the team I believe would be beneficial."

"Like who?"

"Maybe Al Stillwell and a few of the farmers. Bernadine holds sway in the town core. Targeting outside voters will be the way to go."

To Riley the plan made sense. He also didn't want to be bogged down with the day-to-day minutiae of running the less glamorous aspects of the campaign. Having someone else handling details like scheduling and paperwork freed him to spend his time making appearances, shaking hands, and kissing babies. "Do you think you can get me on TV?"

"Possibly. What will be some of your other platforms?"

"Do you think I'll need something besides security?"

"I do. Maybe something that speaks to the needs of those who live outside of the town's core. After all, there are more of them than there are those kissing up to Bernadine. And we can also play to those men who may not want to vote for a woman. Stoking the gender divide could work in our favor."

Riley agreed. "Can I think about all this for a couple of days and get back to you?"

"Sure, and in the meantime, I'll think about what kind of financial assistance I can offer and how much."

Riley liked the sound of that.

The end of the discussion coincided with the end of the meal and Brown stood.

Riley did, too.

"Time for my after-dinner cognac. I'll be in touch. The maid will show you out." Brown exited the room.

Riley was stunned by the abrupt departure but had no time to contemplate his dismissal because the maid appeared with his jacket and led him back through the mansion to the front door. A blink later he was outside in the rising dusk of the evening. Getting into his old car, he started it up and backed down the snowy white driveway. He felt good about the meeting but couldn't shake the feeling that he'd just made a deal with the devil.

Inside, Leo, seated in his den, sipped his evening cognac and thought about Riley Curry. He obviously didn't have a dime to his name, so saying he found himself not as financially set as he'd hoped was laughable. Leo had seen the envious eyes on his watch and the wonder on his face as they walked through the house. The man was a delusional boob, but for the time being, he'd be his boob.

The maid entered. "There's a Mr. Al Stillwell here to see you."

Leo didn't want to be bothered, but the man was another necessary component. "Put him in the solarium. I'll be there shortly."

Leo let him wait a full fifteen minutes before getting up to join him.

"Big Al. How are you?"

They shared a shake. Al was six feet three and his strong grip made Leo wince inwardly but he didn't show it. "How can I help you?"

"Want to talk to you about leasing my land back."

Leo scanned the determined dark eyes and the firmly set jaw with its sparse graying beard. Hoping to put him off, Leo said, "I'm not sure I can lease foreclosed property."

"You can. I asked the bank."

Caught off guard and needing a moment to regain his footing, Leo said, "How about we sit and talk for a minute."

Stillwell's attention was focused on the barns visible through the windows. "I'll stand. You had me wait fifteen minutes, so I figure you're busy and need to get back to whatever you were doing." He swung his attention to Leo, who was so thrown off by the icy regard, he instinctively shrank back. Stillwell showed a tight smug smile and turned back to the view.

Leo gathered himself. "If we're going to talk about a land lease, I'll need something from you first."

"Which is what?"

"I'm Curry's campaign manager. I'd like to set up a few meetings with him and some of the local farmers."

"Riley's got about as much chance of winning as a field rat outrunning a combine. Why are you really here, Brown?"

The intense eyes almost made Leo spill his guts then and there, but he reminded himself he'd made a living staring down Saudi princes and captains of industry far tougher and more powerful than this bedraggled Henry Adams farmer. "I'm here to throw a monkey wrench in Bernadine's well-run world, that's all, and I think you'd like to join me." Leo had been in Henry Adams during Odessa Stillwell's reign of terror and knew she'd be cooling her murderous heels in jail for the rest of her days.

He added, "Remember, Saint Bernadine is the one responsible for you losing your land to the bank. We can talk about a lease agreement down the road, but for now, I need you to set up a meet with the farmers." Truthfully, poor business practices were the reasons Stillwell lost his land, but pointing that out wouldn't bring him on board. Stillwell had been one of the staunchest supporters of the pipeline Bernadine helped kill, and he had direct access to the farmers Leo needed to further the plans of Mega Seed and Salem Oil's partnership. His cooperation was crucial, at least for now.

"Then draw up something in writing. My help, for the lease."

Leo stiffened.

"This isn't Riley you're dealing with," Stillwell reminded him. "You don't get something for nothing from me. My people farmed this land for seventy-five years. The soil is in my blood and I want it back."

Leo hadn't anticipated Stillwell being so formidable. No, he wasn't Curry. "Okay. Set up the meet, and after, we'll sign the agreement."

"Good, but if you try and screw me, you'll have more to deal with than gasoline in your fancy car." He paused as if letting that sink in. "I'll show myself out."

Watching the big man exit, Leo told himself he wasn't shaking, but he was.

BACK IN TOWN, Dads Incorporated, the support group made up of the fathers of Henry Adams, was holding its monthly meeting in Trent's basement. Because Barrett knew Sheila's run for mayor would likely be a topic of discussion, he'd tried to talk himself out of attending, but decided to go. Their collective advice about problems he'd had as both a husband and father had been helpful in the past, even though he'd balked at hearing it.

When he arrived, most of the others were there. Thinking he'd be roasted for having been upstaged by his wife, Barrett prepared for the potshots, but the men simply greeted him with friendly nods and that was that. Grateful, he helped himself to snacks and a beverage and sat down.

As the meeting began, the first item on the agenda was the trip to Fort Leavenworth to view the Buffalo Soldier Monument. The Dads did a getaway weekend with the sons once a quarter and had attended ball games, comic cons, and rodeos. At last month's meeting they'd set a tentative date for the monument trip, so Trent asked, "Is anyone unable to go?" Everyone seemed good with the date, so he continued, "I'll have Lily make our travel arrangements. Who's willing to bunk with Wyatt and Lucas?" Gemma Dahl was a single parent, so the Dads always made sure someone took her boys under their wing.

"They can hang with me," Bobby Douglas offered. "I like them both."

"Thanks." Trent looked over at Mal. "Are you coming with us?"

"Sure, if it's okay with the group."

Mal was slowly reestablishing his status in the community. Like everyone else in town, Barrett hadn't been happy with his embezzlement, particularly because of the terrible example it set for their sons. Luis spoke for them all when he got in Mal's face about the theft at a meeting over the summer. Mal, playing the victim, stormed out. He eventually came to his senses and did a townwide apology tour to beg forgiveness for his larcenous actions. Currently, he was on better terms with his friends, families, and the kids who'd looked up to him, but still wasn't trusted enough to handle the register or the books at the Dog.

The big Halloween party was the next item on the agenda.

A beaming Jack James said, "I have my costume."

Everyone smiled except Barrett. Because of the mess with Sheila, he was in no mood for costumed foolishness.

Luis asked, "So, Barrett. Do you have yours?"

The look he gave Luis spoke for itself.

"Get a costume, man, or find out from Gem if it's too late for her to make you one. We promised Tamar. Everyone's supposed to wear one. It'll be fun."

"And you can't come as a Marine," Reg Garland jokingly added.

When Barrett shot Reggie the same impatient look he'd given Luis, everyone turned his way.

Jack asked in a serious tone, "Something on your mind you want to talk about?"

Here we go. Barrett sighed with frustration. "Yes. I've got issues with my wife running for mayor. She knew I was going to run."

"Did you ask her why she wants to be on the ballot?"

"Yes. She said she thinks she'd be good at it, and then told me—" He stopped. "Never mind." He was still trying to wrap his brain around her startling last words.

"What did she say?" Trent asked.

Barrett's jaw tightened.

"Spill it, Barrett. You know there're no secrets here. We're going to find out sooner or later," Gary Clark told him.

"More sooner than later, probably," Jack pointed out.

They waited.

He surrendered and told them. "She said if I didn't like her running, I could kiss her behind."

Jaws dropped. Astonished looks were shared. Snickering and guffaws followed.

"Sheila said that?" an amused Mal asked. "The town's vice president of social affairs? The flower-planting Sheila?"

Barrett glared.

Reg asked, "Did Preston put human malware in her coffee?"

Barrett didn't care for the ribbing. "I know you all think this is hilarious, but I don't. She doesn't know the first thing about running a town." He thought back to the claims she'd made about her high IQ and wondered why she'd never revealed the information before. What else didn't he know about his wife?

Trent said, "Your wife's a pretty smart lady. She can learn, especially with Lily and Bernadine to help. I'll be around, too. I don't want the job but that doesn't mean I'll be moving to the Virgin Islands."

"You're supposed to be taking my side," Barrett tossed back.

Reg gave him a consoling pat on the back. "We're just playing with you. It's what we do. You know that."

Jack asked, "Are you going to withdraw?"

"No!"

Jack chuckled and raised his hands defensively. "Just asking, man. Sorry."

Barrett grumbled, "If you don't have any constructive advice, I'll just figure it out on my own." The idea that she might win was keeping him awake at night. "What if she wins?" he blurted out before he could stop himself.

Luis said, "You know, Barrett, as head of town security you already have the most important job in town. You don't need to be mayor."

Barrett eyed him coolly. "Meaning?"

"You keep us safe. All of us," Luis said, gesturing around the room with his can of beer. "Our kids, wives, everybody.

What you do for this town matters. Personally, I don't care if Sheila wins, as long as you're heading up security."

Trent added, "And if she does win, she's smart enough to keep you in that position. Riley, of course, would probably appoint Cletus's cousin, but since Curry has no chance of coming out on top, we won't have to worry."

Barrett admittedly hadn't thought about his role in those terms, but realized they were right. Keeping the citizens safe was of utmost importance. He hadn't been able to prevent the hit woman from nearly killing Sam Miller, but that screwup was on the FBI, not him.

Reg asked, "Better?"

He wasn't but nodded to move the conversation to something else.

Trent raised his beer. "To Dads Incorporated! Fixing dads is what we do!"

"Hear! Hear!"

But Barrett still wanted to be the mayor and wondered what might make Sheila drop out of the race.

WHEN BARRETT GOT home, Preston and Amari were lying on the living room's carpeted floor with a chessboard between them. Preston's face was lined with worry as he pondered his next move. Amari, looking quietly pleased, waited for Preston to decide.

Barrett studied the board and saw that his son had good reason to be worried. His BFF was three moves from declaring checkmate.

Without looking up from his impending defeat, Preston asked, "How'd the Dads meeting go?"

"It went okay."

"Are we all set to go to see the Buffalo Soldier Monument?"

"Yes. Is your mom here?"

Preston made a move and the smiling Amari quickly pounced.

"Aw, man!" Preston protested, now only two moves from being ended. "Why can't I ever beat you anymore?"

"Hey, you taught me; I wouldn't be this good if you hadn't."

Barrett always admired the way Amari supported Preston, even when he was kicking Preston's behind in chess.

Preston sighed. "Mom's over at Amari's talking to Ms. Lily about her campaign." Preston glanced up then, as if gauging Barrett's response.

Barrett kept his face neutral or at least tried.

Amari, eyes on the board, said, "I think we should ask Mr. Abbott if he'd like to go see the monument, too. I bet he's never seen it." Abbott was the new teacher.

Barrett was glad Amari pulled them away from talking about the election. "That's a great idea. You should run it by your dad."

"Will do. Checkmate, my friend."

Preston groaned.

Barrett smiled and left them to their game.

A short while later, he was in the bedroom using Google to read up on property taxation when Sheila came in. They'd been tiptoeing around each other since the declaration night at the Dog.

"How was your meeting with the Dads?" she asked.

He shrugged. "The usual. Preston said you and Lily were talking about your campaign?"

"Yes. She's going to be my campaign manager. Have you decided on yours yet?"

"No."

"Do you have someone in mind?"

He went back to the screen. "No."

"You really need to stop pouting, Barrett. This is a small-town election, not the presidency. Why can't you view the race as a friendly competition? It could be fun."

"I'm your husband. Do you have any idea how you running against me makes me look?"

"To whom?"

"To everyone. A woman is supposed to support her husband."

She replied calmly, "I've supported you for as long as we've been married. Every time you took on a new assignment, I packed up the household and moved. No pouting. No whining. No complaints. Me wanting to be mayor is about supporting myself for once. This has nothing to do with your ego and I'm sorry if you don't understand that."

Truthfully, his ego was bruised, and he didn't like having her point it out. It made him look small and petty. But he was the man. He was supposed to be wearing the pants. "If I ask you to drop out, would you?"

Her lips thinned and she shook her head as if he were truly pitiful. "I'll be sleeping in the guest room. See you in the morning." Calmly gathering her night things, she left.

He supposed he had his answer.

CHAPTER 7

In her office, Bernadine began her workday with a cup of coffee and her planner. The to-do list wasn't extensive but it was enough to keep her mind off Mal. First order of business was to start the wheels turning on the survey of Marie's land so they could see why Leo was so interested. According to the quick talk she'd had with Trent, the state of Kansas was at one time among the biggest producers of oil in the nation. Small independent companies had paid top dollar to lease land for drilling, and many farmers became millionaires overnight. In 2014, when the bottom fell out, companies pulled back on drilling and investments. The pipeline Leo's company wanted to construct two years ago hadn't been tied to drilling but to funneling oil from Canada to regions south of the state. The question as to why Leo was coveting Marie's land remained. Bernadine hoped the ground survey would offer an answer.

Another item on her list was the restaurant she, Rocky James, and Tina Craig were building. With the blueprints completed she needed to bring the parties together for a meeting.

Bernadine was excited to get started on the project. If all went well, folks in the area would be sitting down to some fine dining by spring. Rocky was looking over bios of chefs who might be enticed to run their kitchen, but they knew it wasn't going to be easy finding someone willing to relocate to basically the middle of nowhere. With the meetup with the architect in mind, Bernadine sent Rocky and Tina emails to see what their schedules looked like for the next couple of days. The sooner they could meet with the architect, the sooner they could get started. To her delight, both women replied immediately. Rocky indicated she was available any time. Tina sent back that she'd finally escaped the drama in Switzerland and would be in Henry Adams the following afternoon. Bernadine dashed off a quick email to the architect to propose they meet the morning after Tina's arrival and waited to see if that was agreeable.

While she waited for a response, she brought up on-screen the agreement her lawyers were putting together to facilitate the ownership transfer of Marie's land. Bernadine still wished Marie had a better solution, but like Marie didn't want the historic homestead sold to someone who might decide to build a fast-food place on the acreage. The land not only represented an important part of Henry Adams's history, but there were still kids to raise, and the parents needed the Jefferson fence. She was reading through the clauses when Trent and his assistant, Bobby Douglas, stopped by.

"I signed off on the coffee shop agreement with the college," Trent told her. "And the company I want to do the survey of Marie's land can't get here until next week."

"That's okay. What's on the mayor's agenda today?"

"We're on our way to meet with the crew that'll be lev-

eling the soil for Tina's B&B, so they can get started, then
Bobby and I will finish draining the outdoor pool and lock it
down for the winter."

"I wonder if Astrid is still mad that we named the pool
after her?"

"Probably."

Bernadine thought naming the community pool of a historic African-American town after a self-proclaimed bigot was
a treat on so many levels. "Let's hope she stays mad."

"And stays out of our hair," Bobby added.

Bernadine raised her coffee cup in agreement. "Amen."

After their exit, Lily entered and closed the door, which
confused Bernadine. "Why'd you close the door?"

"Super secret stuff."

Bernadine laughed. "Really? What kind of super secret
stuff?"

"Stuff on Leo."

Bernadine stilled.

Lily said, "No way he gets to come back to town and we
not know what he's up to."

Bernadine was even more confused.

"Last week, I ran into on old high school friend at the grocery store. Name's Jane Hubbard. Haven't seen her in a while,
so I asked what she'd been up to. Told me about her husband
and kids, and that she'd just taken a job that was supposed to
be a personal assistant. In reality it was more like chief cook
and bottle washer, but it pays well. Said the guy she works for
is a pompous ass. When she said Mr. Pompous Ass was named
Leo Brown, I almost fell over. I told her who he was, and his
history." Lily grinned. "She's now my spy."

Bernadine laughed. "What?"

"Yes, ma'am. I'm heading up the Henry Adams Counter-intelligence Unit."

She loved Lily Fontaine July so much. "I hope you're paying her?"

"I am. Do you want to hear my first report?"

"Yes."

"First, he's trying to sue Astrid for the mess with his car."

"Why?"

"Something to do with the clerk being on his phone instead of on his job when the pump was put in the window."

"Astrid won't be happy with that."

"Not a bit. He also had Riley over for dinner, and after Riley left, Big Al Stillwell stopped by. Jane said Leo looked shook when Big Al left."

Bernadine wondered if Leo knew Stillwell wasn't a person to mess with. Even though he hadn't been involved with the arson fire set by his mother or in running Bernadine off the road, she'd bet her condo in Spain that the apple didn't fall far from the tree. Mean and crazy was probably in Big Al's blood. "I wonder why Leo was shook?"

"She said she didn't know, but that Big Al didn't appear happy when he left."

"Doesn't give us much to go on, but it is interesting. Tell your friend not to take any chances playing Mata Hari, especially if she needs the job. I don't want Leo to find out she's tattling and fire her."

"We talked about that, but she said she'd keep her eyes open for me. Gives her something to do beside the cooking and cleaning."

Bernadine found this turn of events interesting, indeed. "Keep me posted."

"Will do."

They spent a few more minutes discussing the items on their respective to-do lists before Lily left to get her work done. Sitting alone, Bernadine wondered what secrets Leo might be hiding and if they would splash on the people she loved.

For the rest of the morning, Bernadine handled phone calls, emails, and texts. The architect confirmed the meeting for the proposed day. After sending the info on to Rocky and Tina, she scratched that off her list. At lunchtime, she called in a carry-out order to the Dog.

When Bernadine went to pick up her food, Toni Braxton was on the jukebox singing about seven long days and Mal was at the hostess stand.

"I called in a carryout," she said, wishing the memories of being with him would hurry up and fade away. Each time she saw him they rose like a whispering ghost.

"It's ready." Reaching behind him, he picked up the brown bag and handed it over.

"Thanks. You added the bill to my tab?"

He nodded.

For a moment time stood still. The ghost surfaced, reminding her what they'd lost. A tiny shard of hope struggled to gain life, and she wondered if he felt the pull of it, too. It didn't matter. A group of farmers entered, and their spirited laugh-filled conversation killed the moment and brought back reality. She gave him a terse nod of thanks and exited.

Bernadine returned to work to find Crystal seated in one of the office chairs, flipping through a magazine. "Hey, Crys." They'd had their talk about the failed dinner, so Bernadine was pleased to see her. Bernadine set her lunch on her desk. "What brings you by?"

"Ms. Sheila wants me to be the art director for her campaign, so I need to know if it's okay with you."

"Of course. Why wouldn't it be?"

"Me being your daughter doesn't make it illegal or anything?"

"Not that I know of, no. What kinds of things are you going to be doing?"

"Campaign posters, flyers, that sort of stuff. She said she'd pay me. And . . ."

The tone of that one word set off Bernadine's Mama Spidey sense, and she paused in removing her salad from the bag. "And what?"

"I had dinner with Diego last night."

Bernadine waited.

"It was just dinner, nothing else. I thought I'd tell you before you heard it in the streets. I know how it is around here. Folks know your business before you know it yourself."

"True."

"We were just catching up. He's getting his GED."

"That's great." And it was. "So no eloping to Zimbabwe?"

That brought a laugh. "No eloping to Zimbabwe, or anyplace else. Just a dinner between friends. He's still the finest guy on the planet, but I need more than fine from a guy."

"Listen to you being all mature."

"Just looking to have a relationship with somebody who has their stuff together. He's not there yet."

Bernadine was impressed. Two years ago, Diego, with his big motorcycle, bad boy persona, and multiple mug shots was all Crystal could see. When he finally and rightfully told her she was too young and too classy for someone like him, she'd been devastated.

Crystal stood. "I need to get to class. I'll text you this evening."

"Okay. Ladies Auxiliary meets this evening at Sheila's. I'll be home after we're done."

They shared words of goodbye. Crystal departed, leaving behind a very pleased mom.

THE MEN OF Henry Adams had Dads Inc., and the women had the Ladies Auxiliary. Like the men, the women used their gatherings to discuss town-related issues, their ongoing lives, and to support one another. In the past, most meetings were held at Tamar's place, but lately, they'd been rotating hosting and this evening they were convening at the Paynes' home. Anticipating their arrival, Sheila took in the beautifully appointed buffet table with its vase of fresh flowers, the extra seating, and the way the house sparkled. Everything was ready. The only thing not ready in other parts of her world was her husband. His continued unhappiness showed in his glum face, the lack of conversation at the dinner table, and his disinterest in her questions about how his campaign was going. The candidates' debate would be next week. She'd suggested they share their platforms to rehearse and refine their responses to any questions that might come up. He'd turned her down. She explained that her intent wasn't to steal his ideas, but he seemed not to believe that, so she gave up. He'd do his thing and she'd do hers. Separately. The refusal stung, however, and she supposed she'd been naïve to think they could compete in a friendly, mutually supportive way. As the doorbell sounded, Sheila sighed as she put aside her disappointment and went to greet her guests.

The meeting began the way they all did, with laughter,

food, and wine from Bernadine's cellar, and catching up on one another's lives. Roni Garland shared news of her latest music project. Tamar was questioned about Olivia's well-being with Thad July in town. Lily called Gemma out on something everyone noticed at the most recent Movie Night.

"So, how long have you been seeing Mike Freewater?"

Gemma's face pinkened and, over the laughter of the others, replied, "Not long."

"Details, Gem," Genevieve said. "Spill it, and don't leave anything out."

Gemma took a deep sip from her wine, as if needing bracing, then confessed, "I met him at the store about a month ago."

"And?" Bernadine prodded.

"God, he's so nice!" she gushed. "And considerate, and charming, and so unlike anybody I've ever had in my life before. He opens my car doors, likes jazz. Isn't bossy."

Lily asked, "How's he with the kids?"

"Jaz likes him as much as I do. I don't think the boys are convinced yet. They're watching him like he's going to carjack me."

"It's what sons are supposed to do," Tamar noted. "Glad Wyatt and Lucas are on their job. Mike and Trent grew up together. He's good people."

Bernadine asked, "Do we need to start planning another Henry Adams wedding?"

Rocky warned, "Don't answer her, Gem, otherwise she'll be booking the Taj Mahal."

Lily raised her glass. "Ain't that the truth."

"Both of you, hush!" Bernadine laughed.

Reverend Paula asked, "Is this serious, Gem?"

She shrugged. "I don't know. The last time I thought something was serious, he turned out to be married, remember?"

She was referencing an ill-fated hookup with one of her community college professors.

She added, "I'm going to take it slow."

"Keep us posted."

"As if I could do otherwise," she quipped with amusement.

More laughter.

Sheila thought this was the best group of women she'd ever had the pleasure to know.

"How's the colonel handling running against you?" Marie asked.

Sheila saw concern played out on faces around the room. "Honestly? Not very well. I was hoping we could make this fun, but as the kids say, not so much."

They looked sympathetic, which she appreciated.

Gen said, "How can we help?"

"Barrett's beyond any help at this point, but I'd like to run some of my platform ideas by you, and have you tell me what you think."

Everyone took seats and she began.

The discussion was lively. Some of the items she proposed drew enthusiasm. One in particular moved Bernadine to say, "That's a fabulous idea, Sheila. It should've been instituted when we first began construction."

Nods of approval followed that.

Tamar said, "Worked real well for the Dusters," referring to the African Americans who had first migrated to Kansas after the Civil War.

Sheila added, "I should have the basic research done in time for the debates next week."

Roni said, "I think you're going to blow people away with this."

"I hope so."

Sheila said, "Here's another idea. What do you think about making Henry Adams a Black History destination place? I'd like to explore getting the town put on the National Register of Historic Places and use some of the old photos and whatever other kinds of memorabilia people have in their attics and barns to start a museum. Not many people know about the Dusters but a museum might draw tourists."

Gen said, "And tourists bring revenue."

Tamar said, "We could resurrect the historical society to run things. I headed it up back in the day but once the town started dying, it fell by the wayside. Nobody was interested anymore."

Bernadine followed that by saying, "The big issue I see with it would be funding and overnight lodging. Visitors could stay in Franklin, of course, but I'd want that money to flow to us. We'll have Tina's B&B eventually, but I think making Henry Adams a historic destination place should be given serious consideration in the near future."

Lily said, "I think this is exciting, Sheila."

Nods of agreement followed.

Gemma said, "It's a much better idea than a casino. Was your brother serious about that, Tamar?"

"He says he is. But who really knows what he's up to? He left for home yesterday. Said he'll be back in time for the debates. Can you imagine a casino in Henry Adams?"

"We don't need a casino," Marie snapped.

Her tone drew everyone's attention.

Sheila agreed a casino wasn't needed. However, there was something in Marie's sternly set face that seemed to speak to more than the general consensus. Sheila didn't know what it was but rather than press for an explanation, she moved the agenda along.

They spent the rest of the meeting talking about how Gemma was coming along with all the costumes she was making for the upcoming Halloween party—she encouraged everyone to smack her if she ever volunteered to do something so time-consuming again. Discussion then moved to the Dads trip to the Buffalo Soldier Monument, and the update on how former town chef Siz was doing in Miami.

"He's homesick," Rocky said.

"Aww."

"Misses his family, Henry Adams, his dog—I never even knew he had a dog—but loves the weather, his new ride, and apartment. Said the head chef works him like he knows Tamar, though."

That drew smiles.

Rocky continued, "He says he's learning a lot."

Moving to a fast-paced city like Miami after being born and raised on the slow plains of Kansas had to be as adjustment for Siz, Sheila knew, so she was pleased to hear he was doing well.

The meeting ended shortly thereafter, and everyone pitched in for the cleanup. An hour later, alone again, Sheila gave thanks for the women of Henry Adams. From the day she and Barrett arrived, they'd inspired her to become more.

BERNADINE'S FRIEND TINA Craig hadn't wanted to endure the long ride from the Hays airport to Henry Adams, so she had her helicopter pilot touch down in the open field next to the fire station and Bernadine picked her up there. As the chopper flew off, the two friends rode to Bernadine's place.

"So, how are things?" Tina asked after placing her luggage in the upstairs guest room. "I'm excited to see the site for my B&B and the architect's final drawings."

Bernadine was, too. What didn't excite her was the prospect of discussing Mal, which she knew Tina would be bringing up at some point. "Things are good. So how long are you staying?"

"A week, maybe two. Depends on how soon I wear out my welcome and you give me the boot."

"No chance of that. Stay as long as you like."

"Good. I brought my laptop, so if anything pops up needing my attention, I can handle it."

"There's an empty office at the Power Plant if you'd prefer a dedicated place to spread out."

"No, I should be good here, but if I do, I'll let you know."

Bernadine was glad Tina had come for an extended visit and looked forward to her moving to town permanently.

"Can we grab some lunch? I had coffee and a bagel early this morning and I'm starving."

Lunch meant seeing Mal. "Sure, but how about we do lunch in Franklin, so we don't have to shout over the noise at the Dog to hear each other. Let me get my jacket and my purse."

As Bernadine turned onto Main Street and pulled up to the curb where the B&B would be, they viewed the flurry of noisy activity. Bobcats were leveling the ground and dumping the excess soil into the trailers of large semis. There were workers digging and men standing behind survey cameras. Trent and Henry Adams's construction boss, Warren Kelly, were in the center of the fray, while Bobby Douglas guided one dirt-filled semi off the site and beckoned in another. Seeing Bernadine and Tina, Trent walked over. "Hey there, Tina."

"Hey, Trent. I see you're busy getting my place ready."

"Trying to get as much done as we can before the snow falls."

"I appreciate it."

They spent a few more minutes talking before Trent said, "I need to get back." He bade them goodbye and returned to the site.

As Bernadine drove them away, Tina viewed the town center and said, "Whoever thought you and I would end up here?"

"I know." They'd both traveled and lived all over the world.

"There's a peace here that calls to the spirit," Tina said. "When the doctors told me to slow down after my heart attack—"

Bernadine's jaw dropped. "Heart attack! You didn't tell me you'd had a heart attack!"

"Did I leave that part out?"

"Tina, quit playing. You only said the doctors wanted you to dial back."

"I didn't want everybody worrying and fussing over me."

"But it's okay for me to worry and fuss now? Not good, girlfriend. When did this happen?"

"Last winter."

"So, telling me and the rest of our friends you were in Costa Rica with a new lover was a lie?"

"Nose-growing Pinocchio lie." She turned to Bernadine. "I'm sorry. I was scared—embarrassed."

"Embarrassed, why?"

"Because Captain Marvel Tina Craig leaps tall buildings with a single bound. She doesn't have heart attacks."

"You're mixing Marvel with DC, but I'll allow that."

Tina smiled before her tone grew serious again. "After the

surgery, I came face-to-face with my mortality, and it wasn't pretty."

"You should've reached out."

"I know, but I had enough sense to talk to my shrink and she was a big help."

Bernadine eyed the woman she considered a sister of her heart and didn't even want to think about how devastating losing her would've been.

"My heart issues made me realize life isn't about how many hours I work, my wealth, or any of that. It can end in a Thanos snap, so I'm planning to kick back and enjoy the time I have left—however long that may be—here in Henry Adams."

"Good." When her own mother passed away at an early age, Bernadine learned how short life could be, and the pain and grief remained buried deep inside. Knowing death is inevitable means nothing when you're a teen viewing your mama in a casket, it just hurts. Losing Tina would've hurt, as well.

Tina continued, "So, since life is short and we need to grab happiness by the balls, what's going on with you and Mal?"

Bernadine sighed and gave her the details of the disastrous dinner. When she finished, she warned, "If you say I told you so, I'm stopping this truck and putting you out."

Tina replied gently, "I'd never say that to you."

For a moment, she studied Bernadine silently, before asking, "How do you feel about it? Are you happy? Sad? Aren't sure?"

"Truthfully, getting the chance to tell him how mad I was has been freeing in a way."

"Was this during the dinner at Crystal's, too?"

"No, a few days later after the candidates' event at the Dog." Bernadine detailed what happened and added, "It took me all this time to figure out why I was still so pissed off even after all his many apologies. I never got to speak my mind because I was more focused on his feelings and playing the nice little girlfriend."

Tina nodded understandingly. "So after you called him out, what did he say?"

"I was too busy burning rubber out of the parking lot to care."

"A bit angry, were you?"

"A lot angry."

"And now?"

She shrugged. "I feel better knowing I told him the truth, and as for what happens next between us? No idea."

"Maybe now you two can find a way to go forward."

"Maybe. Either way, life's way too short to worry about it, though. Especially at our age."

"Amen."

LATER THAT EVENING, Leo Brown shook the hand of each of the twenty men who entered his expansive great room and directed them to the drinks and food prepared by his employee Jane Hubbard. They were simple farmers, underwater on their mortgages, and up to their necks in debt for equipment and seed. He wanted the room and food to show them what success looked like and make them as envious as Riley had been. Leo's mission was to seduce them with the prospect of accumulating their own wealth and have them eating out of his hand when the meeting ended.

Stillwell was one of the last to arrive. Dressed in gray denim overalls, he offered Leo a curt nod. The room was crowded so he took up a spot by the windows. The lease agreement he'd insisted upon hadn't been drawn up because Leo wanted to put it off for as long as possible. He'd tell Stillwell that the lawyers were still working on it. What he wouldn't tell him was that it would be worded in a way so as not to be legally binding.

"Is everyone comfortable?"

He saw a few nods. There was also skepticism on more than a few faces but he'd expected that. "I had Al invite you here this evening for a couple of reasons. First thing is why I think Riley Curry should get your vote for mayor of Henry Adams."

One of the men tossed back sarcastically, "Yes, please tell us."

Leo didn't care for that but kept going. "As it stands now, Ms. Brown is only concentrating her efforts on the town, but Riley and I believe she should be doing more for the families and farmers in the surrounding areas."

"You mean like hiring all the construction people she's employed who don't live in town? Or providing a new fire department, which we've never had before, or a new recreation center we all go to on Friday nights? Nope. She hasn't done a thing to help us outside the town limits."

A few snickers followed that.

"Mike Freewater, right?" Leo asked.

"Yes."

Leo remembered him as being one of the men adamantly opposed to the pipeline. "Pleased to see you again," he lied, hiding his contempt. "Thanks for coming tonight."

Another man spoke up. "Name's Lamar Ralston. Since Riley doesn't have two nickels to rub together, how's he plan on changing things?" By his graying blond hair and ruddy, sun-lined face, Leo estimated Ralston to be somewhere in his sixties.

"Corporations will pay good money for open land to build on. Riley will court these corporations."

"The same way he tried to sell out Henry Adams before Ms. Brown bought the place?" another man asked.

Ralston added, "Any man who'll steal from his wife is not someone I'll be voting for. Riley's as crooked as they come."

A tight-lipped Leo surveyed the room and realized this was not going the way he'd planned. He knew nothing about either of the mentioned incidents and mentally kicked himself for not vetting the old barber better, but that would be remedied soon. "I have business connections as well and will be putting out feelers on your behalf, too. In fact, I have letters of assurance from a few multinational corporations who've expressed interest given the right political climate."

"Like who?" Ralston challenged.

Lying, Leo rattled off a few companies he thought they'd be impressed by. The surprised looks many of the men exchanged in response proved he'd been correct.

Freewater asked, "Why would a big-tech company like the one you just named want to relocate here? There aren't enough potential employees with the kind of educational background they'd need."

"They're willing to train, and some will bring employees with them in order to hit the ground running. And when they come, they'll pay for the improvements in infrastructure because it will be in their best interests."

Freewater looked doubtful.

A heavyset man about Ralston's age spoke up for the first time. "Name's Elam Vine. So how does this benefit us farmers."

"You own the land they'll need. They'll pay top dollar. Some of you own hundreds of acres. Wouldn't you like to lease a portion, or sell outright to pay off your debts? Farming is difficult these days."

A buzz filled the room as men shared whispered conversations. Leo now had their attention. "To show the companies are operating in good faith, I've been instructed to give every man who wishes to be in on the ground floor of this a thousand dollars, with the hope that you'll consider giving Riley your vote, so this project can go forward."

More buzz.

"So this is a bribe," Freewater called out.

"No," Leo countered. "It's a down payment on the future of Henry Adams."

"No strings attached other than to consider voting for Riley?" Ralston asked.

"And think about attending his rallies if you care to and have the time."

"Why isn't he here?" Vine asked.

"He's home preparing for next week's debate. I need a show of hands of those interested." He glanced around the room.

Fifteen of the twenty eagerly complied.

Freewater stood up and walked out. Ralston, Vine, and two others followed his lead.

"Their loss," Leo said. He went over to the large silver chest positioned next to the fireplace. He'd purchased the antique in Bogotá over a decade ago. When he lifted the top and the stacks of money inside were revealed, their eyes widened. Leo calmly gave the men two stacks of twenties holding five hundred each. They viewed the cash wondrously.

"It's yours to spend however you wish," he declared, once the chest was closed again. "Does anyone have any questions?"

"How much do you think our land will be worth to the corporations?"

"That's yet to be determined, but I'll take a wild guess and say in the hundreds of thousands at the current market rate." He scanned the room. Some of the men were still staring in awe at the stacked money in their hand. "Anyone else?"

There were no other questions. "Then let's call it a night. Go home, and think about what we discussed. I'll let you know when we'll meet again. Thanks for your time."

The men left, Stillwell remained.

"Do you have the lease agreement?"

"My lawyers are working on it. They're busy people. They can't just drop everything for something as small as a property lease." He fought not to react to the menace Stillwell exuded.

"When do you expect them to find the time?"

"Probably a week. Maybe ten days."

"You have ten days. Not a day more."

"Don't threaten me, Stillwell."

"Or what? You going to call the police? We both know everything you said tonight was bullshit. Corporations aren't going to buy land here. You're as crooked as Riley, just better dressed."

Leo's jaw tightened. He wanted to plant a fist in Stillwell's face, but knew he'd get his butt kicked. The farmer was five inches taller and built like a silo. "Anything else?"

"Just this. You obviously think you're dealing with a bunch of ignorant farmers, but when the truth comes out, and it will, watch your back."

"More threats?"

"No. Just the truth." He strode out.

Later, the still angry Leo sat sipping his evening cognac and mentally reviewed the meeting. All in all it went well. They'd been mesmerized by the cash, but the thousands he'd doled out was a mere drop in the bucket in the scheme of things. Back at the height of his career he'd spent more on a suit and a pair of shoes. That the money had come out of the oil company's pocket and not his own made it even better. However, Stillwell was a problem.

"I'm heading home, Mr. Brown."

He looked up to see Jane Hubbard standing in the doorway. "Okay. Thanks for the help."

"You're welcome. I'll see you in the morning."

"Good night." He knew Jane was married but wondered if she played around? She wasn't bad-looking, but then again, any woman looked good to a man who'd been celibate for as long as he had. His celibacy aside, his thoughts drifted back to the meeting. Freewater was a problem, too. His huffy departure wouldn't have been such a big deal if the current plan didn't hinge so heavily on acquiring access to his land. Tomorrow he'd take a look at the county map and see if there was a way to bypass Freewater's place and still go forward. Until then, he'd keep putting things in place, get a full investigative workup on Riley Curry, and try not think about Stillwell looming like a thunderstorm on the horizon.

CHAPTER
8

The architect's name was Jody Pilgrim. She'd come highly recommended from another member of the Bottom Women's Society. Bernadine, looking up from the blueprints to the young woman from Nairobi, understood why. "This is spectacular, Ms. Pilgrim."

"Thank you. This is the first time I've designed a restaurant, but I took your suggestions, went online, checked out the layouts of some high-end, established places, and voilà."

"This is very nice," Rocky agreed, eyeing the drawing with its wide windows and sleek style.

Tina added, "And I love the cameo of the three women you have on the awning. Can we keep it as the trademark?"

"If you decide you want it, we can work out the legal issues. A graphic designer in my shop came up with it. I like it a lot, too."

Bernadine said, "I think the graphic is perfect." The head and shoulders silhouette of three women in period dress was encased in an oblong circle resembling a cameo. She liked other aspects and features as well: the spacious state-of-the-art kitchen, that the main room sat thirty people, and there was a separate space set aside for private gatherings. An outdoor dining area was another plus to the design, even if it would only be used during warmer weather.

"Ideally, if all goes well, construction should take about six months," Ms. Pilgrim offered.

"We'll see if that timeline jibes with our building crew."

"Not a problem. I'm told you should probably hire your chef as soon as possible just in case they want to tweak the kitchen layout."

Bernadine thought that made sense.

Tina turned to Rocky. "How's the search coming?"

"Have two chefs that may be candidates. A man and a woman. Keeping my fingers crossed."

A few more minutes were spent discussing logistics of the build and praising the design. When they were done, Ms. Pilgrim exited to meet TC Barbour for the ride back to the airport. After her departure, Rocky shared info on the two chefs she was considering. She passed Bernadine and Tina the bios she'd received from the first two applicants to respond.

The man wearing chef whites was named Thornton Webb. His round, dark-skinned face was seriously set. He looked to be maybe forty and owned a small, award-winning restaurant in San Francisco. Audra Perry, also in white, appeared much younger. She wore a smile that lit up her angular brown face. Bernadine found herself smiling back. "Which one would be your ideal pick, Rock?"

"Webb because he has more experience. Perry's an assistant sous chef in Kansas City. Not sure what we'd have to offer him in terms of big-city culture or amenities, but he seems genuinely interested."

Bernadine found her interest piqued. Why would a four-star chef want to trade San Francisco for the plains of Kansas?

"He's not in the Witness Protection Program, is he?" Tina asked.

Rocky laughed. "Lord, I hope not."

Bernadine agreed wholeheartedly. The drama tied to last summer's encounter had been enough to last a lifetime.

Rocky asked, "Do you two want to be in on the interviews?"

Bernadine and Tina nodded.

"Okay. They'll be here Monday evening. My plan is to hold the interviews Tuesday morning so they can head home that afternoon if they need to."

Bernadine thought that workable. There wasn't anything in the bios indicating the chefs' marital status. She wondered if they had family? "Would be nice if the B&B were up and running so we could offer them overnight housing."

"By the summer we'll be ready to house the pope if we need to," Tina pointed out.

Bernadine laughed. For now though, their guests would be staying in Franklin.

"Anything else you need from me?" Rocky asked.

Bernadine couldn't think of anything. Tina had no questions or concerns, either.

"Then I'll head back to the Dog and get on the lunch prep."

After her goodbye, Tina said, "Our restaurant is coming together."

"Yes, it is."

"Not sure which is more exciting, the restaurant or my

B&B. The B&B probably because it'll be all mine. Need to come up with a name for it."

Bernadine heard a knock and glanced over to see Trent July, Bing Shepard, Clay Dobbs, and Mike Freewater in her doorway. Concerned by their seriously set faces, she asked, "What's wrong?"

Trent said, "Can we bother you for a few minutes?"

"Sure."

As they entered, Tina stood. "I have some emails to catch up on. Is it okay if I use the conference room?"

Bernadine nodded.

She left and Trent closed the door.

"So, what's up?" she asked.

Bing said, "Leo."

She sighed. "Let me get a cup of coffee. Anyone want one?"

No one did, so after pouring the brew into her mug, she settled back into her chair.

After hearing Mike Freewater's tale of Leo's meeting with the farmers, Bernadine thought maybe she should've had a drink instead. "He gave them a thousand dollars? Each?"

"Yes."

Bing asked, "Have you heard anything about any corporations wanting to buy up farmland?"

"No, but I'll be asking around. Were you or Clay invited to the meeting?"

Clay shook his head. "Leo probably knew we wouldn't play along. I talked to a couple of the guys who were. They were pretty impressed by the cash. Some are already talking about how much they might get for their land."

Bernadine shook her head in disgust. "He's such a snake. I wonder what he's really up to, besides no good."

"Me, too," Trent replied.

Mike said, "He made a point of saying it wasn't a bribe. He called it a good faith payment from the corporations and asked that everyone think about voting for Riley and attending his rallies."

Bernadine sighed. "Okay. As I said, I've not heard anything about interests in land sales, but I'll see what I can dig up."

Mike said, "I probably should've stayed at the meeting so I could know what else is going on with this."

"Don't worry about that. I have it covered. I have another source of info on him."

Trent asked, "Really?"

"Yes, and I'm not telling you more than that." She asked Mike, "Was Big Al there?"

"Yes."

Bing asked, "Wonder if he took money, too?"

"Good question," Clay noted. "There're rumors that Leo's going to lease some of Al's land back to him."

"In exchange for what?" Bernadine asked.

"Another good question," Clay replied.

"It won't be out of the goodness of his heart, that's for sure," she added.

Trent said, "I'm wondering if Leo's in collusion with his old oil company buddies?"

They kicked that around for a few minutes, but with no concrete evidence, all theories remained just that—theories, so the men stood to leave.

Bernadine said to them, "Please keep me posted on anything else you hear, and I'll let you know what I find out about the supposed land sales interest."

They agreed and left.

Once she was alone again, Bernadine asked aloud, "What are you up to, Leo?" Turning to her laptop, she sent out a series of emails to try to find out.

Tina came back in a short while later and Bernadine filled her in.

"Interesting. Do you want me to get my network involved? Between the two of us we should be able to ferret out something."

"Would you?"

"Not a problem. This is going to be my new home. Can't have people shafting my neighbors. I'll head back to the conference room and see what I can find."

"Thanks, Tina."

"You're welcome."

Pleased with the added help, Bernadine resumed her search.

AFTER WORK, RILEY stood before the mirror in his bathroom trying out various facial expressions for his upcoming campaign flyer photo shoot. Leo Brown sent a text earlier saying he'd hired a photographer, so Riley wanted to be ready. He thought appearing serious might be a good look for the pictures, so he set his face, and viewed his solemn reflection. Deciding he appeared too aloof, he switched to a smile, then tried out one he deemed more thoughtful. He straightened his shoulders, raised his chin, and went for confident. Wondering if exuding intelligence might be better, he put on his reading glasses, eyed himself for a minute, then removed them. As the posing continued, he could already see the billboards and flashy newspaper ads sporting his face. He'd even come up with a tentative campaign slogan to brand himself: "Be Safe with Curry"—or something along those lines. He wanted the electorate to know that unlike Trent July, he'd not tolerate visits from hit men or hit women. One of his first duties as mayor would be to replace the Marine colonel guy as head of security with someone who knew what the heck they were doing. Had there been metal detectors in the rec center, the hit woman wouldn't have been able to enter with her gun. As mayor, he'd make sure metal detectors were everywhere, from the church, to the hair salon, to the Dog. No one would be shot on his watch due to shoddy security protocol, and he and the citizens would demand Bernadine Brown pay for the machines. He'd also demand the candidates get a look at the mayor's office to see what decor needed changing. After giving Colonel Payne the boot, the next person on the chopping block would be the current mayor's assistant. No way would he be keeping former thug Bobby Douglas as his right-hand man, not with all those scary tattoos. Pleased with his plans, he resumed posing.

An hour later, he drove out to Brown's mansion to meet the photographer. He'd showered, shaved, slicked down his thinning dyed hair with baby oil, and put on his new black suit with the new plastic red rose in the lapel.

Upon arrival, the housekeeper met him at the door and ushered him in. "Mr. Brown asked that I take you to the solarium. He'll join you momentarily."

She led him to the glass-walled room and left him there. A few minutes later, she returned with a shapely brown-skinned woman and a young man loaded down with bags and equipment.

The lady smiled at Riley. "Are you Mr. Curry?"

He puffed up. "I am."

She walked over and extended her hand. "I'm Madeline

Kroger. I'll be taking the photos. This is my assistant, Greg Bunt."

Riley shook her hand and nodded a greeting at the assistant. "Pleased to meet you." He looked on while they set up. Ms. Kroger walked around the room with a small light-measuring device. While she and her assistant discussed the best place to position the camera, Riley tried not to stare at how pretty she was. He saw no ring on her left hand and wondered if that meant she wasn't married; not that someone like her would be interested in a man his age, but once she got a load of his smarts and potential as mayor, it could happen. "Are you local, Ms. Kroger?"

She glanced over. "No. I'm from Kansas City."

"Ah. Long way from home."

"I am."

She moved behind the camera resting atop the tripod and looked through. Assuming she had the lens trained his way, he smiled and waggled his fingers in response.

Leo Brown entered wearing a cashmere sweater, nice black pants, and black loafers. He smiled at the lady photographer. "Thanks for coming, Ms. Kroger."

"You're welcome. My assistant, Greg."

He ignored the assistant and walked over to Riley. "Ready for your close-up?"

Putting on his confident face, he said, "I am."

Ms. Kroger said, "Let's get started then. Mr. Curry, give me a big smile."

"I'd like to start with something a bit more serious, if I may, and exude the confidence voters will be looking for."

She eyed him for a long moment before glancing at Brown,

who said, "How about we go with what Ms. Kroger wants for now, Curry. She's the professional."

Unhappy with the lack of support from Brown, Riley forced himself to smile.

She took a few shots then said, "Okay, now give me a variety of looks."

Happier, he went through the poses he'd practiced in the mirror. To mix things up, he did a couple with his hand beneath his chin like the author photos on some of the books in the library. He took his reading glasses out of his pocket and put them on and turned himself sideways, so she could get his strong profile.

"Okay, now. Let's get a few of you seated," Ms. Kroger said and directed him over to one of the big brown leather chairs near the glass walls. The camera clicked as she took more shots. "How about you stand behind the chair?"

"Should I look serious?"

"Sure."

So he gave her that. As she clicked, he placed his elbows on the top of the chair and rested his chin on his hands.

After a few more shots, she said, "That should be enough."

Riley agreed. "Can't wait to pick out the ones for the highway billboards."

She stared, looking confused.

He smiled proudly in response and watched as she and the assistant repacked their gear.

"I should have some copies for you to look at in a day or two," she told them.

"Sooner the better," Riley replied. "Mr. Brown and I need to get this campaign moving."

"I'll do my best. Finals won't be forwarded until I'm paid, of course."

"Mr. Brown handles things like that," Riley said importantly. "Send your invoice to him. Right, Mr. Brown?"

Brown studied him for a moment before saying, "We'll discuss payment once I decide how many we need."

Riley stiffened. He hoped Brown wasn't going to try and wiggle out of paying, or go with a lower number than Riley thought he needed. His supporters would want autographed glossies at all the rallies and coffee klatches he planned to have.

Gear packed, Ms. Kroger said, "Mr. Brown, I'll be in touch. Good luck with your campaign, Mr. Curry."

"Thanks."

"Let me walk you out," Brown said to her.

While he was gone, Riley debated whether to ask how many pictures Leo planned to order but decided not to. Brown hadn't looked happy talking about the payment and Riley didn't want his moneyman upset. Once the pictures were paid for and turned over, if there weren't enough, he'd figure out how to handle it then.

When Brown returned a few minutes later, Riley asked, "How do you think the photo shoot went?"

"It went well."

"Did you like my poses? I practiced them in the mirror before coming over."

"Are you ready for the debates?"

Miffed at not receiving the praise he'd sought, Riley replied, "I am. Been practicing that, too." He went on to tell Leo about the campaign slogan he'd come up with. "What do you think? Is it strong enough?"

"Sure. I want you to add something to your campaign promises for the farmers."

"Like what?"

"Mega Seed has a new seed strain they want to give out after you get elected, but I think we might want to do it during the campaign so the farmers will offer you more support."

"What kind of seed?"

"Corn and wheat. It's experimental, but guaranteed to increase yields by 20 percent. The company wants to have testimonials when they do the formal release so potential buyers know that the seed does what the company claims."

Riley thought it over. "Sure. I don't see why not. If it works, they'll be grateful to me and to Mega Seed."

"Exactly. We won't have the results until next fall's harvest, but I guarantee they'll be pleased with the way the seed performs."

"When do you want to give it out?"

"After the debate. We don't want voters to know you have a corporate backer, just yet. Mega Seed is making this offer exclusive to you."

Riley felt real important. "I like that."

"I knew you would." Brown pulled a thin sheet of paper out of his pants pocket. "This is from their research office. It lays out the talking points they want emphasized when the time comes."

Riley took the brightly colored brochure and gave it a cursory once-over.

"Study up on it, so you'll be prepared to answer questions at the big giveaway."

He nodded. "Will do."

"I'll talk to you in a few days. Jane will show you out."

As he departed, Riley was again bothered by Brown's abrupt dismissal, but decided not to get upset. After all, he was now being backed by Mega Seed.

Driving home, he wondered how much exclusive spokesmen were paid.

SHEILA, LILY, AND Crystal were in Lily's Lady Cave brainstorming the campaign.

"How's this for a slogan? 'Sheila Payne. A Vote for Henry Adams's Future.'" Sheila turned to gauge their reactions.

"I like that," Lily said. "Has a nice ring to it, as folks used to say."

Crystal nodded. "I like it, too. I took a marketing class last year and one of the things we learned was: simple is better. I think it's a nice slogan."

Sheila was pleased. The slogan was specific without being over the top and paired well with her vision as the new mayor.

Crystal said, "I'll do some sketches of flyers and posters and have them ready for you to look at by the next meeting."

"That would be wonderful."

Lily said, "Then I'll find a local printing company that won't break your budget."

"Please. Getting elected and having to live in the poorhouse won't be a good look."

They smiled in agreement.

Lily asked, "Anything else we need to tackle today?"

They'd discussed the budget, the artwork, finding a photographer to take Sheila's picture and worked on refining her message. "I think we're done for now."

"Okay."

Sheila and Crystal gathered their things. As they exited, they passed through the kitchen where Trent was at the stove frying shrimp.

"Smells good out here, Trent," Sheila said.

"Thanks. How'd the meeting go?"

"Went well," she replied. And it had.

"Okay. Pulling for you and Barrett."

"You only get to vote once, Mr. July," Lily pointed out. "You know that, right?"

"Yes, Mrs. July, but I can still support the only sane people on the ballot. I love my great-uncle Thad, but no way am I giving him or Riley my vote."

Sheila was glad to hear that, although she was sure Trent planned to choose Barrett on election day. She told herself that was okay. The men were good friends.

Lily walked them to the front door, and they said their goodbyes. Crystal got into her little car and drove away. Sheila crossed the street to her home and went inside.

Preston was at the dining table with his trigonometry book. He looked up. "How was your meeting?"

"It was good. How are you?"

"Be better if I understood this formula."

She laid her jacket on the chair and peered down at the page. "Which one?"

He pointed to it.

"Try this."

She picked up his pencil and worked the problem, explaining as she went. He stared at her as if she'd suddenly turned into Beyoncé. "You can do trig?"

Sheila chuckled softly. "I was president of the math club in college."

His eyes widened more. "How come you never said anything?"

"I was raised not to brag about my intellect. My parents were convinced I'd never find a husband if men knew how smart I was."

"That's dumb."

"True but I was encouraged to play dumb."

"Leah is smarter than me in a lot of ways, but I like that she's a brainiac."

"Many men don't, though."

"Does Pops know you can do an advance trig problem in under a minute?"

She sighed and thought about her issues with Barrett.

He answered for her. "He doesn't like it, does he?"

"I don't really know, Preston. I didn't tell him about my smarts until the day I decided to run for mayor. He was more upset by my candidacy than anything else."

"That's dumb, too."

She gave his shoulders a squeeze. "You're an awesome young man, Preston Mays Payne. Stay that way, okay?"

"Okay."

"Your pops won't be home until late."

"I know. He sent me a text about him staying after work to install the new cameras."

Barrett was upgrading the grocery store's surveillance equipment. "How about we do something simple for dinner like pancakes?"

His eyes lit up. "Awesome."

Because he'd had such an awful life before coming to Henry Adams, every time Sheila pleased Preston her heart swelled with love. "Need any more help with your trig?"

He shook his head. "That was the only problem I couldn't figure out. Thanks, Mom."

"You're welcome. Would you fry the bacon while I make the pancake batter?"

"Sure. Let me take my books to my room and wash my hands. Be right back."

As he ran up the stairs she headed to the kitchen to start the batter.

While they shared the cooking duties, they talked about school and other teen things.

"I don't think you'll have to worry about Robyn anymore. She and Leah are good friends now."

"That's good to hear." Sheila flipped the three pancakes in the skillet and waited for them to brown.

"She and Reverend Paula are going to Oklahoma this weekend to see Robyn's grandmother in jail. Robyn doesn't really want to go but said she felt bad about the rev going alone."

"I'm sure Paula could handle the trip without her."

"Leah tried to tell her that, but Robyn said she wanted to go and get it over with because she'd probably never go again."

"That's sad."

"Yeah." He used a pair of tongs to take the bacon strips out of the skillet and let them drain on a paper towel–covered plate. "I think they're going to see about selling her great-grandfather's house, too. He left it to the rev, Robyn said."

"I didn't know about them going to Oklahoma. I've been spending my time on the internet and at the Franklin library doing research for my campaign platform, so I've missed some things."

They moved their now done dinner to the table. Preston said grace and they dug in. Pouring syrup on her pancakes,

Sheila asked, "Anything I've missed in the Henry Adams world of teens?"

"Yeah. Amari decided he and Tiff aren't going to be official."

She paused. "Why not?"

"Because he won't let her walk him like a dog on a leash."

"And that means?"

"She's kind of controlling. Change that. She's big-time controlling. Leah said Tiff gets that from their mom."

"I see."

"He got mad at her after she wanted to look through his phone to make sure he wasn't talking to other girls."

"Doesn't trust him?"

He shook his head.

"Good relationships are built on trust." Barrett's affair with Marti taught her all about misplaced trust.

"Is there a way I can help with your campaign? I'm going to ask Pops too, so he won't think I'm playing favorites."

"If you could put up signs and pass out flyers at Movie Night when the time comes, that would be helpful."

"That sounds easy. Do you think you can win?"

"Some men, and women too, have issues with a woman running for office, but if I can overcome that I think I have a good chance. Your pops is the only other candidate I'm worried about. He'd make a good mayor. I'd make a better one, though."

Preston smiled. "I like that you're all about you, Mom."

"Do you?"

"Yeah. Shows you're confident."

"It's how I feel. I just wish I'd felt this way earlier in life."

"Reverend Paula tells us kids that we can't do anything about our past so look forward, not back."

"Wise words."

"Hard words, though. Sometimes I wish I could go back and stop stuff—like my bio dad dying in the car accident, or some kind of way of making the foster mother who wouldn't buy me an inhaler a better person so I wouldn't have to set her house on fire."

"I think we all wish we could go back and change things, but that might alter where we are today. Who knows if you and I would be family then. I like having you as my son."

"And I like being your son. Not many kids get to have two awesome moms."

"You are blessed." Preston had a good relationship with his bio mom, NASA scientist Dr. Margaret Winthrop. She became pregnant with him while in college. The wealthy Winthrops were descendants of a free black Revolutionary War soldier and her parents were appalled that Preston's father, the brilliant Lawrence Mays, grew up poor in Philly's inner city. They pressured Margaret to put the baby up for adoption. Before the two students could marry, Lawrence died in a car accident. A grieving Margaret, tired of fighting her parents, surrendered her son to the state's adoption agency and walked out of their lives. Margaret was currently searching for Lawrence's family. She wanted Preston to have closure and Sheila did, too. They both loved their son enough to not be threatened by connecting him with the Mayses, who would undoubtedly love him just as much.

After dinner, they cleaned up the kitchen. Preston went up to his room to finish his homework and hang out online with his telescope crew. Sheila settled in with a book she'd been reading to wait for Barrett to arrive. He'd been coming home later and later the past few days. He attributed it to the preliminary work tied to the store's upgraded security system. Sheila didn't believe him. She thought it had more to do with his moping over the election, but she kept her opinion to herself. His fragile ego made her as unhappy as his cheating had done.

OVER AT CLARK'S Grocery, Barrett put the schematics for the new security system into a drawer of his filing cabinet, took a seat at his desk, and opened the containers holding his dinner from the Dog. By all rights, he should be eating at home, but he didn't want to argue with Sheila and he could feel himself on the cusp.

A light knock on his opened door caused him to glance over and into the face of Gary Clark who said, "I thought you'd gone home. What are you doing still here?"

"We got done so late, I figured Sheila and Preston have already eaten, so I had a delivery sent over." In response to the skepticism on Gary's face, Barrett asked, "What?"

"It's the second time this week."

"Are you counting?"

"I am. Is something going on at home?"

Barrett looked away.

"Are you still upset about Sheila running for mayor?"

"And if I am?"

"You need to talk to Paula."

"Warriors don't talk to people about their problems."

"So, you do admit to having a problem."

Barrett bristled. He'd been tripped up by his own words. He didn't like it.

"Man, you're too good a person to be drowning in your own misogyny."

"Misogyny?"

"Yeah. Chauvinism, antifemale."

"I know what the word means, Gary, and I'm not that."

"You sure?"

"Positive."

"Then what's the issue?"

"She refuses to drop out."

"Why should she?"

"Because her husband is running."

"So, it's not so much misogyny as it is patriarchy?"

Barrett stared. "What is it with you and these feminist buzzwords?"

"I live with two bright, independent daughters, and I'm in love with an equally independent woman. I try and see the world through their eyes."

Barrett shook his head. This was not a conversation he wanted to have. "Men are supposed to lead."

"Lead, where?"

"In things that matter, and this election matters."

"In other words, what you want overrides what Sheila wants because you're the man? Am I hearing you right?"

Tripped up again, Barrett glared. "How about you go home and let me eat in peace."

"You got it. I'll see you tomorrow."

After Gary's departure, Barrett started in on his food. He'd never considered himself a chauvinist, at least not overtly, but admittedly the man being the head was how he'd been raised. He was a third-generation member of the Armed Forces and grew up watching his grandfather and then his father be the family decision makers. For the most part those decisions had been sound. Both his grandmother and mother worked outside the home: the former as a teacher, the latter as a nurse, so he had no problems with women and employment. Yet they'd deferred to their husbands in just about every way. If they disagreed, it was never expressed, at least not within his hearing. He thought back on the abuse his mother suffered at his father's hands but turned his mind away from those painful memories. What mattered now was that throughout his marriage to Sheila, she'd been deferential as well. Was this change in her really just her way of asserting herself, or tied to something more? Her claim of hiding her true self so he could shine brighter also gave him pause. All this time, he assumed she was content being in the background because she saw that as her role, and frankly, because he felt it his due, being the man and all. In his world, few military wives called themselves feminists, at least not on base. Now he had to wonder how they truly viewed themselves. He didn't want to be thinking about this; he simply wanted to run for mayor, not flounder in a marital version of the Corps Crucible that had him lost and in the dark.

After finishing his dinner, Barrett left the store to the cleaners and stockers of the night crew and drove home. Sheila was on the couch. Beyoncé was on the flat screen strutting and singing. At his entrance, Sheila paused the program. "Hey there." He saw her studying his face as if gauging his mood.

"Hey."

"The new system up and running?"

"It's installed. Testing starts in the morning. How are you?"

"I'm fine. How was your day?"

"Okay."

"Have you eaten?"

He nodded. "Had a delivery from the Dog."

"Oh."

He heard the disappointment in her voice. "I didn't know how long the work on the system would take."

"I see. Preston and I had breakfast for dinner. Pancakes."

They were trying not to acknowledge the elephant in the room and he certainly had no plans to do so. He turned his attention to the flat screen. "Is this the one with her and the bat?"

She chuckled, "No, this is the documentary she made during the run up to Coachella. It's amazing. These independent young women are in charge of their lives in ways that are so impressive."

He'd had enough about independent impressive women. "I'll let you get back to it. Going to check in with Preston, and then I have some reading to do."

She nodded.

He headed to the steps.

"Barrett?" she called softly.

He paused.

"I'm sorry this election is difficult for you."

He didn't know how to respond to her sincerity, so he offered a tense nod and climbed the stairs.

Preston was at his desk with his laptop open. "Hey, Pops. How's the new system?"

"Testing starts in the morning. How are you?" It had taken Barrett and Preston quite some time to bond as father and son, but now their connection was stronger than Barrett ever dreamed it would be.

"I'm good. Learned something amazing today."

Barrett smiled. "And that is?"

"Mom's a trig master."

Barrett was confused. "Trig, as in trigonometry?"

"Yeah, I was having issues with a problem, and she showed me how to work it in like less than a minute. Said she was president of the math club in college. Did you know that?"

Barrett shook his head. "No." One more thing to add to the list of things Sheila had never divulged.

"I think that's dope," Preston pointed out, sounding impressed. He scanned Barrett's face for a moment. Always perceptive, Preston asked, "You're not happy she's running against you, are you?"

Barrett didn't lie. "No. Suppose you were going to run for say, president of the Physics Club and Leah decided she was going to run, too. How would you feel?"

"Honestly? I be psyched. We like competing against each other. We do it with homework to see who finishes first. Sometimes I win, sometimes she does. If we were up against each other, we'd probably make a crazy bet and then go at it." He went silent for a moment, taking in Barrett again. "I guess you don't see it that way?"

"No."

"This isn't going to make you want a divorce, is it?"

Barrett knew issues between him and Sheila had worried their son in the past, and he didn't want this current disagreement to be of concern. "No. I'm just disappointed that she wants to be mayor, too."

"Why?"

"Hard to explain."

"Maybe talk to Reverend Paula. She's really good at helping figure stuff out. Nobody listens better than the rev."

He shook his head. "I'll deal with it on my own."

Preston shrugged. "Okay, but I'm proud of Mom and you, too. I think you'd both be great as the next mayor."

"Thanks."

"I can pass out flyers or put up signs if you need me to. I told Mom the same thing. I don't want anybody to think I'm playing favorites."

"Appreciate the offer. I'll let you know."

"And Pops. I still think you ought to turn this into something fun between you and Mom. Probably make you feel better than you do now."

Out of the mouths of babes.

Preston added, "At least think about it, okay?"

"Will do. I'll see you in the morning. Don't stay up too late."

Preston gave him a thumbs-up.

Leaving the room, Barrett wondered when had his son become the Wise One and he the Grasshopper?

CHAPTER
9

Friday after school, while her friends got ready for Movie Night at the rec, Robyn was in her bedroom zipping up the sides of her packed suitcase for the ride to the airport. She and cousin Paula were taking an evening flight to Blackbird, Oklahoma. Her stomach had been in knots all day at the thought of returning to a place filled with so many bad memories. More than once she wished she hadn't agreed to the trip, but she didn't want Paula to go alone—not that Paula needed help. In Robyn's mind accompanying her was the right and mature thing to do. And it wasn't as if she'd have to stay. As soon as Paula handled the paperwork for selling their grandfather Tyree's house and taking care of whatever else needed to be done, they'd be flying back to Henry Adams.

Paula stuck her head into the room. "TC's here to take us to the airport. Are you ready?"

"Yes." Picking up her fleece and her new, sky blue crossbody, Robyn raised the suitcase's handle and rolled it out of the room.

At 8:00 p.m., the small plane landed in Tulsa. They were met there by their uncle Calvin Spivey, who was just a few years older than Paula. He greeted them with strong hugs. "So good to see you both."

It was good to see him as well. He'd always been as kind to Robyn as her grandmother Ardella would allow, which hadn't been much since she hated Calvin as much as she hated his mother, Anna Lee. The story went that in high school, Ardella stole Anna Lee's boyfriend. After graduation, Anna Lee paid her back by stealing the affections of Della's widower daddy, Tyree. Calvin Tyree Spivey was born from that union.

"I'll take care of the bags," he said, as they reached his shiny black truck in the night-dark parking lot. "You two go on and get in."

Robyn climbed into the back and Paula took the shotgun seat. Calvin entered and started the engine. The drive to Blackbird would be two hours. "Where do you want to stay while you're here?" he asked. "Mama says you're welcome at her place. She has plenty of room."

Paula turned and asked Robyn, "What do you think? Should we accept?"

"I vote yes."

"I'm with you," Paula said. "Too many bad memories at Tyree's and Della's."

Robyn agreed. Exhaling a quiet sigh of relief, Robyn settled in for the long ride.

The porch light was on when they reached Anna Lee's. Calvin pulled up into the driveway and they got out just as his mother stepped onto the porch. In her copper bob wig, gold caftan, and matching low-heeled slides, her long gold nails and perfect makeup made her resemble a fading, brown-skinned movie star.

After welcoming them with hugs and kisses on their cheeks, she led them inside. From her last visit, Robyn remembered the big piano on the far side of the small living room. The top served as a bar that held liquor bottles in a variety of colors and sizes.

"How was the flight?" she asked.

"Not too bad," Paula replied.

Anna Lee gestured for them to sit, so Robyn and Paula sat down on the plastic-covered gold couch. Their hostess sat in one of the matching gold chairs, also encased in heavy, clear plastic.

"Cal, take their suitcases to the back and we'll figure out who gets what room later."

As he left, his mother said, "So glad to see you two. There's food in the kitchen if you're hungry."

They were.

"Ribs and baked beans in the oven, potato salad in the fridge. Go ahead and get you a plate. I'll be in in a minute."

While she moved to the piano to pour herself a drink, they walked to the kitchen. Washing their hands at the sink, they searched out plates and silver and pulled the food from the oven and the fridge. Cal joined them and made himself a plate too, and the three of them sat at the small dining table. Paula said grace and they dug in.

The food was delicious. Robyn thought back on all the boring white beans and chicken she'd eaten while living with her grandmother and wished she'd been living with Anna Lee instead. The meat on the ribs slid off the bones like melted butter, the beans were sweet and smoky, and the potato salad was to die for. She looked over at Paula, met her smile, and went back to her meal.

Anna Lee floated in. "Everything okay?"

"Very," Paula said.

"If I feed you good, you might want to come back," she said with a smile. "Having you here is a real treat. I don't get many visitors. There's only so much joy in drinking and Netflix." She looked to Robyn. "Are you happier?"

Robyn read the concern in her eyes. "Yes, ma'am."

"Good. Anyone who has a chance to escape this place should. College?"

"Next year. Need to catch up on some things."

"You always were a smart little thing, so that shouldn't take long."

A warmth spread through Robyn in response to the praise. She wished she'd had the opportunity to have known Anna Lee while growing up, but it was never allowed.

As the visiting continued, the adults talked about the sale of her grandfather's house. Calvin doubted it would bring in much. He wanted Paula to consider investing a small amount of money in it, and then renting it out instead.

"I'd try and get you some good tenants and keep an eye on the place," he said to her. "Maybe function as your landlord representative and see to repairs and such. This way you'd have a small stream of additional income."

"That's not a bad plan. I'll think about it."

Robyn asked, "What's going to happen to Gran's place?"

Anna Lee cracked, "I want to burn it to the ground, but Cal won't let me."

Robyn smiled even though she knew she shouldn't.

"Behave, Mama," Cal said grinning.

Paula said wistfully, "God forgive me but growing up, there were days I wished for a book of matches for both houses."

Robyn paused and looked her way.

As if thinking back, Paula was silent for a few moments, then waved it away, "Never mind. Let's talk about Della's house."

Robyn always sensed Paula's time growing up in Blackbird had been awful too, and this conversation seemed to confirm that. She wondered if talking about their experiences would help free them both? Returning to Blackbird reminded her of all the hurt, and she was tired of the memories chasing her like monsters in a nightmare. Maybe the time had come to stop running and face it down so she could find some peace.

Paula asked, "Has Della told anybody what she plans to do with her house?"

Calvin shook his head. "A storm took down a couple of trees on her property and damaged her roof. I went to the prison to ask her what she wanted me to do about it, but she refused to see me."

Anna Lee added, "Her neighbor's pretty sure the roof's leaking, so who knows what it looks like inside."

Robyn wasn't surprised that her grandmother refused to speak with Calvin, not even about her house. She'd always been as stubborn as she was mean.

Paula said, "When I visit her tomorrow, maybe we can talk about it."

"She won't see you, Paula," Anna Lee told her. "Robyn, either. I know you're a preacher and all, but you can't save a soul that doesn't want saving."

"I have to try. If she turns me away, that's on her."

Robyn thought Paula a better niece than her grandmother deserved, and a better person than Robyn herself would ever be. The true circumstances surrounding Robyn's mother Lisa's death were still a mystery, and it appeared Ardella would take the truth to her grave. If that happened, Robyn would hate her for the rest of her life.

Once the meal was finished, they all helped with the cleanup. Calvin went home after promising to stop by the next day after work, and Anna Lee escorted them down the narrow hallway to the two spare rooms at the back of the house. Both were small and clean and the beds in each were covered with matching floral comforters. "I used to put my grandkids in here when they visited, but after they moved away, they're apparently too busy to come see me so I can know my great-grands."

The sadness in her eyes matched her tone before it was masked. "Decide which room you want, and I'll see you at breakfast in the morning."

They wished her good night and she left them alone.

Paula asked Robyn, "Do you have a preference?"

"Not really. I can take this one and you can have the other room, if that's okay."

"It is." Paula spoke to the anxiety she knew Robyn was feeling, brought on from being in Blackbird. "We fly home tomorrow after the visit."

Robyn replied softly, "Good. I'm glad we didn't stay at Della's or Papa's."

"Me, too."

"Were they mean to you when you grew up here?"

"Yes. Very."

Robyn hesitated before asking her next question because

she wasn't sure if it would be too personal. "How long did it take for you to be okay?"

Paula sat on the bed and patted the spot beside her. Robyn took the invitation and Paula draped a comforting arm lightly across her shoulders. "Took me a while. Even though I didn't live here my entire life like you, the three years felt like an eternity."

"Gran slapped me a lot," Robyn whispered.

"Did the same to me. I tell myself I've forgiven her, but in my heart, I know I haven't. Not totally."

"I dream about her sometimes, and she's always screaming at me, or punching me or whipping me with that old extension cord she used to use, and no matter how fast I run away, she always catches me."

"I'm so sorry."

Robyn wiped at the tears on her cheeks. "Why's she so mean, Paula?"

"I wish I knew, baby. Maybe she doesn't like herself, or her life, or—I don't know. Whatever the reason, she had no right to take it out on you—or me." Paula met Robyn's eyes and said in a serious tone, "When I go see her tomorrow, you don't have to come."

"I know, but I want to. Maybe seeing her in jail and knowing she'll never hurt me anymore will help the nightmares stop."

Paula eased her closer. "You sure?"

Robyn nodded.

Paula picked up her purse and fished inside for a small pack of tissues that she handed over. Robyn pulled a few free and blew her nose. "Did you ever talk to a therapist or somebody like that about what happened to you here?"

"I did, but it took me years to admit I needed help. African Americans don't do therapy, at least that's what I was raised to believe. We're told those things aren't for us. We're supposed to handle our problems and move on, so I thought my hurt would fade away and fix itself. Like you, I had nightmares though, and I was so quietly angry, I developed ulcers my sophomore year in college. On the outside I was a had-it-all-together high achiever, but on the inside a boiling hot mess. Finally, one of my Spelman friends suggested I see her mom who had her own practice in Atlanta. Initially, I blew it off, of course, but she kept after me to the point I made the appointment just to shut her up." Paula smiled and Robyn mirrored it in return.

"So did it help you?"

"Oh yes. Thank the Lord for girlfriends. Her mom was a godsend. I worked through a lot of my issues while under her care. It wasn't easy though, because sometimes it's hard laying your problems on the table, especially to a stranger, but she was so compassionate and patient, that I changed my major from prelaw to psychology so I could do for other people what she did for me."

"That's a great story." Robyn quieted for a moment as she thought over what Paula had shared. "Do you think you could help me talk through some things?"

"Sometimes it isn't wise to counsel a family member."

"But I want it to be you, Paula. I think I'd be more willing to, like you said, put it all on the table."

She could see Paula thinking it over.

"Okay, but instead of making it formal and have you come to the office for appointments and all that, let's do our talking cousin to cousin over dinner, or when we're riding to the mall, or sitting out on the porch in the evenings. You talk, I'll listen, and if I have some advice that I think might be beneficial, I'll share it."

"I'd like that."

"Then in the words of Jean-Luc Picard, 'make it so.'"

Robyn threw her arms around Paula's waist and hugged tight. "Thank you."

"You're welcome. I'll always be here for you, Robyn. Always."

THE NEXT MORNING, the idea of seeing her grandmother again made Robyn's stomach roil so much she apologized to Anna Lee for passing on the big breakfast she'd prepared and settled on a piece of toast and juice.

Paula asked, "Are you not feeling well?"

"I think it's from going to see Gran. I'm nervous."

Anna Lee, sporting a red bob wig and dressed in skinny jeans and a snug green top that showed off her still trim frame, said sympathetically, "It's okay, baby. Going to see that old bat would make me not want to eat, either. I'll fix you a good lunch when we get back."

"Thank you."

The women's facility where Ardella was incarcerated was over an hour away. Anna Lee would be driving them, so after breakfast she backed her new, midnight-blue Mustang out of the garage and Paula and Robyn got in.

"Nice car," Paula said admiring the nice leather interior.

Anna Lee beamed. "Cal bought it for me out of his share from Tyree's will. It's the first brand-new car I've ever owned."

Robyn thought the car was sweet, too. Paula had also received money from their grandfather's will. She used some of it to set Robyn up in Henry Adams with new clothes, furnishings for her bedroom, electronics, and every book Robyn wanted to read. The rest went into an investment fund for Robyn's future, which made her cry. No one had ever done so much for her before.

As Anna Lee headed to the highway, Robyn watched the scenery. Growing up in Blackbird, she hadn't done much traveling because her grandmother never went anywhere, so she was seeing some of the areas for the first time. The towns they drove past with their big box stores, fast-food places, and malls all looked to be doing better than Blackbird, and she wondered what kind of lives the people led. Only after moving to Henry Adams did she realize how impoverished she'd been not just economically, but in experiences as well. Recently, Leah told her about the time she'd spent with Preston and his NASA scientist mom in Florida last summer, and all the cool things they'd seen and done. Zoey occasionally toured with her mom, Ms. Roni, and had been to cities like Paris and Rio. Most of the Henry Adams kids had flown on Ms. Bernadine's white jet. It was all astonishing to someone like Robyn, who two years ago didn't even know black people worked at NASA or owned their own planes. That she now had access to that same world made her want to scoop up all the kids in Blackbird and move them to Henry Adams so they could see a better life, too.

"Is this the prison?" Paula asked.

Anna Lee said, "Yes."

Robyn peered out the window at the beige-brick buildings surrounded by tall barbed wire. Unlike in the movies there were no guard towers. The complex, set back from the road, had few windows, all with bars. As they drove past, Robyn spied a lone tree in the large open field that surrounded the building. She wondered how many of the inmates could see it.

Anna Lee steered the Mustang into a car-filled parking lot adjacent to a flat-roofed, one-story building painted blue and white. It could've passed for a school or a doctor's office had it not been for the sign out front bearing the facility's name. Looking out at the building, Robyn swallowed hard as Anna Lee found an open parking space and braked.

Paula asked Anna Lee, "Are you coming in?"

"No. I'll wait for you here," she said, cutting the engine. "She won't want to see me. For sure."

Paula and Robyn got out and made their way to the front entrance. Neither spoke but Robyn found herself taking in deep breaths to help calm herself.

Although there were a ton of cars parked outside, she was still shocked by the crowd of people in line ahead of them. Women, children, senior citizens, along with teen girls holding onto toddlers and infants made their way slowly through the two metal detectors. According to Paula, visits were only conducted on weekends. The first letter in an inmate's last name determined which day and at what time.

When she and Paula reached the machine, they, like the others, removed their jackets and placed them and their purses on the belt. After being waved through and retrieving their belongings, they waited in another line that led to the desks where everyone had to sign in with the matrons wearing brown uniforms. Once that was accomplished, they were given a number and told to take a seat; they'd be called when Ardella arrived. Robyn wondered if her grandmother would treat them like Calvin and refuse to see them. In a way she hoped so, so this would all be over and they could fly home.

Their number was called fifteen minutes later. She and Paula followed a different matron through a set of doors and down a dimly lit hallway. At another door, with a wire-covered window, the matron knocked, and it was opened. Inside stood a stern-faced female guard. Ardella, dressed in purple prison garb, was seated at a table. It and two empty plastic chairs were the only furniture. It had been a year since Robyn had seen her, and in that time, her hair, tied back, had gone grayer and looked thinner. Robyn's heart pounded as she and Paula sat. To her surprise, her grandmother smiled, and said, "Thanks for coming to see me. How are you?"

Paula seemed caught off guard by the pleasantness but replied, "Doing okay. It's good seeing you."

Ardella turned to Robyn, "And how are you, Robyn?"

"Good. You?"

She replied with a shrug. "As good as can be expected, I suppose. Enjoying your new life?"

"Yes."

And then as if someone flipped a switch, Ardella leaned close and sneered, "Good! Enjoy it because I don't want to see you ever again!"

Robyn jumped with fright.

Eyes feral, Ardella turned to Paula. "You, either. Don't visit, don't call, don't write. If I die here, leave me to the state. I don't want you anywhere near me even when I'm dead. You got that?" She told the guard standing in the corner, "Take me back!"

The tight-lipped guard led her from the room.

The matron who'd escorted them had remained. She appeared sympathetic but said nothing as they stood and followed her back to the waiting area.

Outside, on the walk back to the car, tears stung Robyn's eyes. A grim Paula draped an arm over her trembling shoulders and gave her a comforting hug. "It's okay," she whispered. "We'll leave her be, just like she wants."

Anna Lee took one look at their faces and said softly, "It didn't go well, did it?"

Paula shook her head.

In the backseat, Robyn stared sightlessly through her tears as Anna Lee started the engine and drove them away.

THAT EVENING, ROBYN and Paula caught their flight back to Kansas. It was late when they finally got home. Robyn was getting into bed when Paula stuck her head in the room. "Sleep well, babe."

"You too."

"And, Roby, just because Della doesn't love us, it doesn't mean we aren't worthy of love. We are. As an old Baptist preacher once told me, 'God don't make junk.'"

Robyn nodded.

"Good night," Paula said with a soft smile.

"Good night, Paula."

AT CHURCH THE next morning, as the congregation sang the opening hymn, Paula, wearing an emerald green vestment, processed in behind the cross-carrying Devon, and his two flanking torchbearers, Wyatt and Lucas. Seeing her, Bernadine wondered about the trip to Oklahoma. She knew Paula had been optimistic, so she hoped everything went okay.

The opening prayers segued into the day's readings from the Old and New Testaments. As Mal walked to the lectern to do the honors, seeing him didn't raise her blood pressure. Was it possible that having gotten her say she could now move on to maybe having him as a friend? His strong rich voice carried well, and he read with just the right amount of expression and reverence. Done, Mal came down the aisle to return to his seat. As he passed her pew, his gaze brushed hers but didn't linger. She didn't let it bother her. Instead, she focused on Paula walking to the pulpit to give the day's sermon.

The theme was tied to expectations, and how often we trust people to show us love and compassion only to have them do the opposite. As an example, Paula gave them a thumbnail sketch of her aunt's reaction to her visit and how pleasant it had begun before the ugly ending.

"It's hard to be compassionate or forgiving when someone yanks the rug out from under your feet and you fall flat on your face," she told the congregation.

Bernadine noted the similarities to her own situation with Mal.

Paula continued, "I wish God could send us a magic potion that boosted our desire to forgive, but in reality, that would be too easy. There are no shortcuts. I believe forgiveness is meant to be hard to grapple with because it forces us to confront who we are. In my case, I have to figure out how to love someone who any right-thinking person would turn their back on. My being irate and angry in response doesn't hurt her spirit, it hurts mine. There's the old saying that holding a grudge is like drinking poison and expecting the other person to die."

Bernadine saw nods of agreement.

Paula acknowledged them with an "Exactly. So, because we are human, we fail a lot at this business of forgiveness, but it doesn't mean we give up on the concept. Eighteenth-century English poet Alexander Pope said: To err is human, to forgive divine. So, while I work on changing my heart, pray for me. And if you're working on your own heart, I'll pray for you. Do we have a deal?"

More nods.

"Thanks," she said looking out at the congregation. "Amen."

The amen was echoed and the service continued.

When church was over, everyone gathered in the fellowship hall to chat and snack. Bernadine placed cut carrots and celery, a small dab of ranch dressing, and a few small crackers on her plate. Spotting Rocky, Jack, and Kyrie Abbott seated together, she headed their way. En route, she was stopped by Bing Shepard. Since being permanently lamed in the arson fire, he'd mastered maneuvering with his cane, but she couldn't help think how unfair it was that he was forced to rely upon it in the first place. Were it not for Odessa Stillwell, he'd not need aid getting around.

Bing asked Bernadine, "Have you heard anything about Leo's supposed land sale?"

"No, and I'm willing to bet we won't, but Tina and I will keep turning over rocks."

"Okay. And if you haven't heard, the lawsuit the farmers down south brought against Mega Seed has been allowed to proceed. Mega Seed's lawyers tried to get it thrown out, but the judge said there was sufficient evidence for it to go forward. Good news."

"It is," Bernadine agreed. "I'll look up the ruling in the office tomorrow morning. And again, I'll let you know if we find anything that shows Leo is telling the truth."

"Thanks." He moved on and she did the same.

As Bernadine sat, Rocky said, "We may have issues with one of our chef candidates."

Bernadine paused with a raised celery stick. "Meaning?"

"Audra Perry is bringing her parents with her for the interview."

"Oh, that's okay. I'll have Tamar or Gen show them around while we meet with the daughter."

Rocky shook her head. "No. They're coming to sit in on the interview."

"What? Why? We're not hiring the whole family."

Bernadine asked, "How old is Ms. Perry?"

Rocky replied, "According to the date of birth on her application, she's twenty-five."

"Who has their parents sit in on a job interview at that age?"

Kyrie sipped his coffee. "Sounds like helicopter parents. There were a ton of them when I was in college. A few even tried to get the okay to live in the dorm."

"That's crazy," Bernadine replied.

"My feeling, too," Rocky agreed. "Ms. Perry sent me a text yesterday afternoon about them coming along, so I put in a call to one of her references, a small restaurant in Chicago where she worked two years ago. The woman on the phone said Audra Perry is an excellent chef, but they had to let her go because of her mom and dad's constant interference. She said Racine, that's the mom, and William, that's dad, constantly complained about who the daughter worked with, the shifts she was given, and that she wasn't being promoted fast enough. Apparently, when they decided to speak to the owner, that was that."

Jack cracked, "Great way to help your kid not be successful."

"Amen," Bernadine replied.

"Do you want to take her off the list and just interview Thornton Webb for now?" Rocky asked. "If you give me a few days, I can maybe find another candidate to replace her."

"No, let's see how much of a nightmare this really is. Maybe being fired made the parents learn their place. Is there any indication they're the reason she's leaving her current position in Kansas City?"

"No."

Bernadine wasn't in the mood for drama, she just wanted a great chef. "If things go south during the interview, we'll tell her thanks for coming and send them on their way. Is that okay with you?"

"That works. Henry Adams has enough show runners. We don't need someone's mama and daddy bucking to be in charge."

CHAPTER
10

Monday evening's Candidates Debate was being held in the school's kiva, and as people trickled in and took their seats, Bernadine said to Tina, "This is exciting. It's the first mayoral election we've had since I purchased Henry Adams."

"Nothing like democracy in action," Tina quipped.

Although Bernadine had agreed not to publicly endorse any of the contenders, she had her own private favorites. Sheila was her top choice because of what she'd shared of her vision at the Auxiliary meeting. Barrett came in second. Riley Curry and Thad July didn't stand a chance of getting her vote. Although, if the Paynes were suddenly abducted by aliens, Thad would have to do. He might be the mythical coyote but had way more sense than Cletus's dad.

As the seats began to fill up, she saw familiar faces: Tamar, Genevieve and TC, Reverend Paula and Robyn, and others. When Mal walked in with Trent, her attention lingered on him for a moment. As if sensing her scrutiny he turned and gave her a nod. She nodded in response and resumed scanning the crowd. Bing came in, followed by Clay and some of the farmers. As she'd promised Bing at church on Sunday, she'd checked out the news reports on the black farmers' suit against Mega Seed. The seed giant was accused of selling the farmers sterile seed. Even though a major agricultural college couldn't get the seed to germinate either, the company called the suit meritless. The court hadn't agreed. She planned to keep an eye on the case.

Construction boss Warren Kelly entered the kiva holding hands with his auburn-haired wife, Jayne, and they looked so much like two high schoolers on a date, Bernadine smiled their way. She was also pleased to see Gemma Dahl enter with Mike Freewater, but had nothing but a frown for Big Al Stillwell who chose a seat in the back.

Jack James was the evening's moderator and MC. Each candidate would be given ten minutes to explain their platform. Once everyone was done, they'd then take questions from Jack and the audience. He'd also asked the kids in his classroom to compose some of their own, and Bernadine was interested in what they'd come up with. If they planned to stay in town after graduation or move back to raise their families once their lives were established, they had a vested interest in how a future Henry Adams might look.

While the seats began filling up, up on the stage the candidates huddled with their managers. Riley in his signature black suit stood talking with Leo, who was wearing banker blue.

Tina said, "For being such a crappy individual, Leo always dresses well."

Bernadine agreed that he was a crappy individual. She

didn't care about the rest. She hoped he was ready for Riley going off the rails and pontificating on subjects he knew nothing about, because it was bound to happen.

Sheila, dressed in a sharp black business suit and heels, conferred with Lily, while Barrett and his manager, Luis, stood together on the far end of the stage. So far, Thad was a no-show. Parts of Bernadine prayed he'd changed his mind, but she doubted such a plea would be answered. Sure enough, he entered the stage from the wings riding in his chair with Griffin by his side.

Minutes later, the candidates took their seats onstage, the lights over the audience were dimmed, the house lights on the stage brought up, and they were under way.

Jack welcomed everyone, and the speaking order was established the old-school way: they drew straws. Barrett drew the shortest. He'd go first and be followed by Thad, Riley, and then Sheila.

Barrett walked to the mic and began by proposing more people be allowed to move in, a new subdivision be added, and a variety of businesses be encouraged to move in as well.

"We need growth," he said. "A town that isn't growing isn't going to be around very long."

He got some applause for that.

"For our farmers, I want to investigate the pros and cons of establishing a co-op venture for storing your grain in a silo we'd own. Why are you paying a company thirty miles away when we could be stockpiling our own here?" That drew an enthusiastic response.

"Gary and I have talked about Clark's Grocery contracting for more local fruit and vegetables, especially during the summer months, and possibly sponsoring a farmers' market."

Bernadine was impressed with the ideas he was sharing, and from all the applause many others seemed impressed as well.

Barrett continued, "I also want us to continue to participate in the innovative security partnerships established by Trent and Bernadine. But I'd like us to think about installing a low-level metal detector system for large gatherings like Movie Night. I think we—"

"I object!" Riley yelled, jumping to his feet. "That's part of my platform. You can't be stealing my ideas!"

Bernadine and Tina shared a look.

Barrett replied, "I'm not stealing your ideas, Curry."

"Yes, you are. Probably been using some of that high-tech stuff you own to bug my house and my phone. I want the Election Commission to investigate this."

Jack said, "Mr. Curry, I'm sure you're not the only candidate concerned about security. How about you let the colonel finish, and you can give us your idea when it's your turn."

As Riley sat down, his eyes shot daggers at Barrett. Bernadine wished she could see Leo's face, but he was seated in shadow on the far side of the room.

While Riley continued to glare, Barrett used his last two minutes to talk more about the metal detector. Bernadine wondered if such a thing was necessary, then told herself Sam Miller, who'd been shot last summer, would undoubtedly say yes. Her pretending Henry Adams was somehow magically immune to the gun violence so prevalent everywhere would expose the citizens to an unnecessary danger. That this was even being discussed in her little town made her sad.

Barrett thanked the audience for their time and took his seat. Next up was Thad.

"I want to build a casino here. And do you know why?"

Someone in the audience shouted, "No, why?" Laughter followed.

"Because there's nothing fun to do around here anymore. In the old days we had rodeos and poker games, tractor pulls, even a few shoot-outs. Now, nothing. So, to liven up the place and to bring in a hay wagon full of cash, I say we build a casino. Revenue would pay for roads, build homes, and draw in all those businesses Colonel Payne talked about, and keep us from having to raise taxes. A casino would bring in superstar entertainers, too. When was the last time any of you saw Janet Jackson, Earth Wind and Fire, or Buddy Guy live? A casino would fix that."

As applause erupted, Bernadine couldn't decide whether to laugh or cry.

He continued, "I agree that we need growth and more people, so let's give folks a reason to come here. A casino would be just what the doctor ordered. That's all I have to say. Curry and Mrs. Payne can use the rest of my time if they want." He steered his chair back to his spot.

Riley stood and walked to the mic. Being shorter, he fiddled with it until it was at the height he needed. "First of all, I don't appreciate Payne stealing my idea and I will be lodging a formal complaint with the Election Commission."

Thad grumbled, "Oh, give it a rest, Riley. No one's trying to steal any of your dumb ideas."

Riley swirled. "Didn't you just hear him talking about a metal detector?" he asked, angry all over again. "I came up with that. You can ask Mr. Brown." He called out, "Didn't I come up with that first, Leo?"

No response.

Off the rails we go!

Riley asked, "And besides, what's dumber than a casino run by a dumb Okie like you, July?"

"Dumb Okie!" Thad yelled. "I got your dumb Okie, hog boy!"

Jack stepped in. "Gentlemen, let's keep this civil, shall we?"

Riley said, "He started it."

"Please continue, Mr. Curry," Jack said, tone weary.

Tina whispered, "Poor Jack."

Bernadine agreed.

Focused again on the audience, Riley said, "Even though Mr. Marine over there is trying to steal my thunder, town security is the foundation of my campaign. No one should go to a Movie Night and be shot up, but that's what happened, and I blame everyone in the current administration."

Bernadine thought his assessment very unfair.

"That assassin should never have been hired in the first place. I know it. You know it." A few people clapped. "There'll be no Russian mobsters on my watch. I want metal detectors at the rec, the church, the Power Plant, and everywhere else people gather. Then I want some real security people to come in and remove the lame equipment we have installed now and put in something that actually works. No more of this experimental partnership business. Cronyism isn't keeping us safe."

Bernadine thought back on all the work they'd put in to get companies to invest in Henry Adams, and she wanted to march to the stage and punch Riley in the nose. As if sensing that, Tina put a restraining hand on her arm, "Down, girl."

Bernadine sat back and fumed.

"Once I win the election, I plan to clean house. There will be no gang members in my administration, former or not."

That drew boos and Bernadine was glad to hear them.

Luis shouted, "Stop dragging a young man who moved here to turn his life around!"

Genevieve yelled out, "Hypocrite! Tell everybody how much money you stole from me, Riley!"

As the skewering of Riley gathered steam, Bernadine leaned over to Tina. "Leo's probably having a heart attack right about now."

"Couldn't happen to a nicer guy."

Jack walked to the mic and shouted over the yelling, "Okay, everybody, quiet down!"

They did but reluctantly. As the silence settled, Genevieve called out, "Anybody voting for him needs their head examined."

People cheered.

Jack asked Riley, "Are you finished, Mr. Curry?"

"No. I have one more point to make. No disrespect to Mrs. Payne, but I don't believe this town is ready for a female mayor."

Boos rained down.

As they gained volume, he shouted to be heard. "Men are under attack all over the nation, just for being men, and I don't want that happening here!" Done. He sat.

Jack turned to Sheila. "Mrs. Payne."

Sheila walked to the microphone and said, "I agree with the necessity of bringing in new residents, and the need for a secure Henry Adams, but instead of raising taxes for all these initiatives, I propose a way to pay for them that will only cost us pennies."

She waited until people were on the edges of their seats, before saying, "Wind power." She then proceeded to blow everyone away with facts and figures. "Last year, millions of dollars were earned by rural communities and farmers like ours by leasing their land to wind turbines. Some families have saved their farms from foreclosure by partnering with these companies. There are already established programs in place here in Kansas, so this isn't experimental."

A buzz went through the room. "As your mayor, I'd like to invite the companies here so we can get a good look at what they have to offer, and then connect them to any farmers who want to participate. According to some of the information I've read, the profits have made a difference in the bottom line for many communities and it can make a difference for Henry Adams as well."

She moved on to her idea of having the town placed on the National Register of Historic Places, explaining the added revenue that could bring in along with her proposed museum. "Last but not least, I agree with Mr. July. I also want us to have some fun. I'd like to build a drive-in we can enjoy during the summer months."

Cheers erupted. She smiled shyly and let the hooting and hollering subside before continuing to talk about the logistics tied to a drive-in. When she finished, she added, "I know there are some who don't think a woman has what it takes to be mayor, even though Mayor Olivia July guided this town during its golden years, but if you vote for me, we'll work together as a community to prove the naysayers wrong. Thank you."

And she went back to her seat.

Women in the room jumped to their feet and applauded madly, some men, too. Were the election held that evening,

Bernadine was certain Sheila Payne would win by a landslide.

The audience participation portion was next. People wanting to ask questions of the candidates were invited to form a line behind the microphone standing in the aisle. Bernadine was pleased see that Amari July was first.

He asked, "If I was eighteen and could vote, what part of your platform would benefit people my age the most?"

Beside her, Tina whispered, "Great question."

Bernadine agreed.

Jack turned to the candidates. "Let's use the same order. Colonel Payne, your response?"

"I'd mandate that all new businesses hire a percentage of people ages eighteen to twenty-five, and that summer internships be set aside for high school kids."

"Paid internships, right?" Amari asked. "Nobody should have to work for free."

Barrett showed a small smile and amended his reply, "Yes, paid internships for high school students."

Riley, even though he was out of turn, was next to answer. "The biggest benefit from mine is that you won't get shot." He turned to Payne and glared. "Security for one and all is how I see it."

Thad replied, "A casino offers you a chance at a big payoff that could make you rich for the rest of your life, and who doesn't want that, no matter the age?"

She thought both answers lacked substance and forethought.

Next was Sheila. She checked her notes for a moment, then replied to Amari's question. "Not everyone wants to or can

afford to attend college. As mayor I'd like to sit down with the
president of the community college and talk about increas-
ing the numbers and varieties of classes tied to a trade. Right
now, there's only carpentry and heating and cooling. Adding classes where students could become certified plumbers
or electricians, or landscapers, along with other programs targeting farming science would be a plus for our area."

Tina whispered, "Can we have the election tonight so I can
vote for her?"

The rest of the question session played out along the same
lines. The colonel gave measured replies. Sheila offered detailed responses. Thad stuck to big money payouts, and Riley
to security. Both men came off as one-trick ponies.

RILEY'S PERFORMANCE HAD given Leo a serious headache. By
the time the debate ended and people began leaving, all he
wanted was to head home and treat it with lots of cognac. He
had no desire to see Riley, but he caught Leo in the parking lot
before he could make it to his car.

"I think I picked up quite a few votes," Riley boasted.

Leo wondered how anyone could be so delusional? Curry
was his candidate though, so he lied, "You might be right. We
should look at expanding the platform a bit more, however.
People want security, but that's not the only thing affecting
them."

"It won't be those wind vanes Mrs. Payne was pushing.
I heard someone in the government say those things cause
cancer."

Leo's headache worsened. "Something else then. Maybe
something tied to education or an idea that would benefit
families."

"Oh, okay, but you really think I did good in there?"

Leo refused to enable more craziness by lying again. "Your campaign signs and posters should be in tomorrow. The big highway billboard you wanted will be up by midweek."

Riley crowed, "Hot damn! Can't wait to see what pose you chose. My serious one, I hope." He struck the one he'd done for the photo shoot.

As the bulk of the crowd began trickling out of the building, Leo ignored Riley's comment and instead asked, "How much money did you steal from your ex-wife?"

"I didn't steal it. I borrowed it and had every intention of repaying her."

"How much did you borrow?"

"Fifty thousand."

Leo sighed inwardly. "I'm going to head home. I think I may be coming down with something."

"Understood. I'll think about what you said about expanding my platform, but first I'm having a beer to celebrate my win tonight."

"Good for you. I'll come by the salon and drop off the signs and posters after they arrive. Put them wherever you think best."

"Isn't that your job?"

Leo wanted to shake him until his teeth rattled and his head popped off his neck. "Technically yes. But you know where people are more likely to see them. You're the expert here."

"You're right. I do know more about Henry Adams. Okay. Stop by as soon as my stuff comes. Real anxious to see them. You think the campaign can lease me a car?"

"No." Leo got in his and drove away.

At home, Leo plopped down into his favorite, caramel-colored leather chair and took a long draw of the cognac in his glass. Curry's performance had been a campaign manager's nightmare. From accusing Payne of stealing his concept to calling Thad July a dumb Okie. He'd followed that by answering every question the same way: security. By the end, Leo thought if he'd heard the word one more time, he'd lose his mind. Once again, he wished he'd investigated the man more thoroughly or better yet, run for mayor himself; at least he wouldn't feel like he was up to his neck in quicksand. And the investigative report he'd received on Curry had only reinforced the feeling. From embezzlement to bigamy to posing as Trent July in order to steal a car, the man's antics were jaw-dropping. After his hog killed Morton Prell, Curry broke the hog out of the county pen and the two went on the lam. Eventually apprehended by law enforcement and returned to Kansas, the court determined the hog had killed Prell in self-defense and all charges were dropped. Curry then took the hog to Hollywood to be trained for the movies by a man named Scarsdale. When Curry couldn't pay the bills, he and the hog fled back to Henry Adams, only to have Scarsdale show up with a court order giving him possession of the hog.

Leo's phone sounded. Looking down at the caller ID he saw Al Stillwell's name. Not in the mood for whatever the man wanted, he let it go to voice mail. A minute later, his front door began rattling from the pounding someone was giving it. He wanted to ignore that as well, but hoping it might be the sheriff telling him Curry had driven off a cliff, Leo got up and went to the door. Through the fancy glass pane, he saw Stillwell looming on the other side.

"Open the door, Brown!"

Wondering if the night could get any worse, he opened it and let the man in. "What do you want?"

"I was at the debate. Quite the candidate you got there."

Leo gritted out, "What do you want, Stillwell?"

"The lease agreement. Is it done?"

"I told you ten days. Anything else?"

"Yeah, three things. One. Make sure the agreement is legal. Two. Next time I call, pick up the phone. And three. Tell Riley not to antagonize Thad July. July payback is legendary around here."

"I'll keep that in mind," Leo said dismissively.

Stillwell showed an ugly smug smile. "You and Curry deserve each other. Don't say I didn't warn you about the Julys."

He exited and stepped back out into the night. Leo flung the door closed.

"YOU WERE AMAZING up there, Sheila."

Surprised, she glanced over at Barrett as he drove them home. Preston had gone home with Trent and Lily. He and Amari had a report to write on the debate. "Thanks. I thought you did well, too."

"There's well, and there's totally prepared. You were the latter. You blew us off the stage."

"I appreciate you saying that."

"It's the truth, and I owe you an apology for saying you didn't have what it takes to do the job. I was wrong. When you talked about the trade classes, I wanted to raise the white flag and vote for you myself."

In response to his praise, emotion welled up and tears stung her eyes. "Thank you," she whispered.

"In fact, I'm pulling out of the race."

"What? Why?"

"Because my wife should be mayor and I want to help her get elected."

Her hand flew to her mouth. Shaking, she stared speechless.

"I'm serious, Sheila. Henry Adams needs you."

Her brain finally reengaged enough to ask, "Who are you, and what have you done with my husband?"

Barrett laughed. "Watching and listening to you on the stage made me realize just how wrong I've been. Will you do me a favor?"

"I'll try."

They'd reached their house, so he pulled up into the driveway and cut the engine. In the silent darkness, he turned her way and asked, "When we go inside, will you sit with me and tell me all the things I don't know about you?"

"Like what?"

"Like you being a trig ninja for one."

"Who told you?"

"Our son."

"I need to remind him that snitches get stitches."

They laughed.

When it was quiet again, Sheila viewed him wondrously. "Are you really interested?"

"I am. Very much so."

"Then, yes. You get your coffee, I'll get out of these clothes, make my tea, and we'll talk."

"Good and I don't want you dimming your light ever again. Don't worry about me. You go ahead and shine."

"Thanks for that and for your faith in me."

"It's what husbands do, or so the Dads and brilliant teen-agers like our son keep telling me."

She leaned over and kissed his cheek. "You're a good man, Colonel Payne."

"But I can be better, and that's my goal."

Inside, Barrett turned on the Keurig and waited for Sheila to return for their talk. Watching her on the stage exuding so much confidence and intelligence had been humbling. That he'd spent the past few weeks throwing barriers in her path in order to salve his ego made him look foolish in hindsight and regret the pain he'd caused her. And when she related her vision about the trade classes, he knew then and there, he'd be dropping out of the race to support her instead. In a million years, he wouldn't have thought of something so basic and yet so life changing. Her detailed platform spoke to young, old, farmers, and townies. She needed to be mayor. Bernadine Brown, Lily Fontaine July, and his soon-to-be-elected wife were the triumvirate Henry Adams needed to shape its future. The evening made something else clear. For him to be truly worthy of the remarkable woman he'd married, he needed to find the courage to make an appointment with Paula Grant. He owed it to Sheila and Preston. More important, he owed it to himself to deal with the shadows of his past and his oft-times rigid way of viewing life, so he could shape his own future.

CHAPTER
11

Tuesday morning, Bernadine, Rocky, and Tina gathered in her office to get ready for the chef interviews with Audra Perry and Thornton Webb. Ms. Perry and her parents had driven from Kansas City yesterday and overnighted in one of Franklin's motels. Webb had flown in.

At nine, Lily appeared in the doorway. "The Perrys are here, ladies."

"Bring them in," Bernadine replied.

The three entered and upon seeing the mom's tightly set caramel-colored face, Bernadine wondered what she was upset about. "I'm Bernadine Brown," she said, walking over to greet them. "Welcome to Henry Adams."

The mother spoke for the family. "Thank you. I'm Racine. My husband, William, and this is our daughter, Audra."

"Pleased to meet you. Let me take your coats."

The parents were dressed like bankers. Mom was in an expensive navy suit with matching heels and a pricey handbag. Dad was dressed in charcoal gray. Audra wore a pair of black jeans and a lightweight red cashmere sweater, gold hoops in her ears, and a thin gold chain around her neck. Mom's gold on her wrists and in her ears was tasteful but bolder and weightier. Bernadine wondered what Racine and William did for a living.

"Let me introduce my partners, Tina Craig and Rochelle Dancer James."

Tina and Rocky offered a hello. The family nodded in reply.

Tina asked, "Did you have a pleasant evening?"

William said, "We're used to more upscale accommodations, but we survived."

Rocky shot Bernadine a level look.

Bernadine said, "Our little town is still growing. We hope to have more upscale lodging sometime in the future."

Racine muttered, "It can't be soon enough."

Audra gave her a glare. "Please pardon their rudeness. They complain no matter where they stay."

Okeydokey. Bernadine noted the glares the parents flashed in response. This was going to be fun.

Audra said, "So, ladies, please tell me about the position."

Rocky spoke for the partners and outlined what they were looking for, and the status of the soon-to-be-built restaurant, something she'd explained to Audra during their phone interview last week.

William said, "The place isn't built yet? You didn't tell us that, Audra."

"There was no need to. Just like there's no need for you and Mom to be here."

Racine countered with, "We're here to look out for your best interests. We don't want you taken advantage of. How long will the construction last?"

"We plan to open in the spring," Rocky said.

Racine asked, "And you have the financing approved?"

Tina said, "We don't need financing. We're paying cash."

Racine looked so shocked, Bernadine had trouble hiding her smile.

William studied the three of them with renewed interest. "Cash?"

Bernadine said, "Yes. Audra, tell us—"

Racine butted in, "Does this place even have Wi-Fi? We're accustomed to emailing our daughter on a regular basis."

"Yes. Staying in touch won't be an issue."

Rocky, who'd apparently had enough, stood. "Mr. and Mrs. Perry, we're going to ask you to leave the room now, so we can conduct the interview. It's been a pleasure meeting you. There's coffee and food in the conference room. If you'll follow me, please."

They shared a look of astonishment.

Mom said, "We prefer to stay."

"Okay, then we're sorry you came all this way for nothing."

Audra said, "Mom, will you and Dad just go, please, so we can get this done?"

William's eyes roamed the faces in the room as if seeking support. It was obvious they'd never encountered this situation before.

Tina said, "If you don't want her to be interviewed, that's up to you. If you do, please follow Rochelle to the conference room."

Mom's jaw tightened. She picked up her handbag and got to her feet. "Come on, Will."

"But . . ." He exhaled his frustration, stood, and followed Rocky and his wife to the door.

Once they were gone, Audra said, "You ladies are the bomb. I love my parents, but if I get the job, can one of you adopt me?"

The interview went well. Since Rocky had the most experience in food service, she took the lead and asked about Audra's training and goals. "I graduated from Princeton with a degree in finance because that's what my parents wanted. Got my MBA from Wharton, then worked with a big firm in Boston. Hated it, and the smug people I worked with. Eighteen months in, I woke up one day and said, screw this. I'm tired of being miserable. Quit the job, cashed in some of the stock I inherited from my grandparents, and went to culinary school. My parents had a stroke."

Bernadine saw Rocky and Tina smile.

"I've always loved to cook and it's all I want to do. I'm an only child. Mom's a lawyer. Daddy has his own investment firm. They've had my life planned since the day I was born— the right schools, the right job. Marry the right guy, have the right kids. I feel like a hamster on a wheel and I'm exhausted. I know I don't have enough experience to head up your restaurant, but I'm willing to do whatever it takes to train under whoever you hire so that I can. I'll wash dishes, sweep floors, whatever you want. I got into the cooking game late, I just want to catch up."

Rocky said, "You're right about not having the experience to run the Three Spinsters, but I love your passion. Tell you what. I have an opening now in our diner. The head chef is an amazing young man. If you want to work under him until we get the restaurant up and running, you're welcome."

Her face lit up. "Really? When I can start?"

"Up to you."

"Tomorrow? Today. Five minutes ago?"

They laughed.

"Any of the above," Rocky said.

"OMG! Okay. I'd like to start right away. Is there a place where I can stay? I can pay rent."

Bernadine said, "Go talk to your parents, and once you're done, come back and we'll turn the logistics over to Lily July. She'll help you move your life to Henry Adams."

Audra began to cry and gave each of them a tight hug—totally inappropriate during a job interview, but they looked past that.

She took the tissue Bernadine handed her and dried her eyes. "Both my parents are only children too, so I don't have aunts, but now I feel as if I have three. Three Spinsters. Three Aunts."

They smiled.

"Thank you so much for this opportunity. I won't let you down. I promise."

She left them to go tell her parents.

The encounter took place behind the conference room's closed door, which meant Bernadine, Tina, and Rocky weren't privy to the conversation. They did hear quite a bit of shouting, however.

A short while later, Audra returned. Sadness filled her eyes. "I'm going to go back home first. My parents reminded me that I should probably give my current job my notice. And they're not real happy with my decision. I need to sort this out. Can you hold the job for me?"

Rocky said, "Yes, but not indefinitely."

Bernadine agreed.

"I know they're going to try and talk me out of this, but

I'm not going to let them. I want the job. I'll be in touch to work out things with Ms. July asap."

"Okay. We'll look forward to that."

She offered a weak smile and departed.

Her parents left the Power Plant without so much as a word. The Three Aunts decided that was okay.

THORNTON WEBB ARRIVED for his interview a few hours later. Bernadine admitted to being shocked by how big a man he was. Prizefighter big. Defensive end big, with a shaved head and a warm brown face as pretty as Muhammed Ali in his prime. She looked over at Tina, who raised an appreciative eyebrow. Rocky showed no reaction.

"Welcome to Henry Adams, Mr. Webb," Bernadine said. She made the introductions. He nodded at each before taking a seat. She offered coffee. He declined.

"I hope travel wasn't too exhausting. We lack a lot of the big-city amenities."

"I noticed but not holding that against you. This is rural Kansas."

She wasn't sure how to take that. He hadn't smiled so far and there was a touch of skepticism in his eyes, which made her wonder again why he'd applied for the job.

Rocky said, "It's rural but we like it here, so if that's a problem, we can cut this short right now."

He viewed her silently for a moment. "Wasn't trying to offend. Just making a statement."

Bernadine said, "The obvious question for all of us is, why would someone with your expertise and reputation want to move here?"

He shrugged. "I'm looking for a change. You reach a point

in your life where you need a challenge and moving here might be it."

Tina said, "We're looking for someone who'll give us four or five years. Is that you?"

"Possibly. Takes a while to establish a place's reputation. You ladies will be starting with none. I'm arrogant enough and a good enough chef to do that, but it won't happen overnight. Depending on how this interview goes, I'd be willing to put in the necessary time. Who knows, I may even stick around longer. I've never lived in a place without sirens or crowds. My question to you is, how do you plan on your chef getting access to the various foods needed for a quality place."

"Such as?" Bernadine asked.

"Fresh meat and seafood mainly."

"Would a jet work?"

His brow furrowed. "A jet?"

"Tina and I have private jets. Flying you out, or products in, shouldn't be an issue."

He appeared stunned. "Really?"

"On speed dial," Tina tossed back.

And for the first time since entering the office, Chef Thornton Webb showed a ghost of a smile. "Can I get a tour of the town? See where the restaurant will be? Get a feel for the place?"

Bernadine looked to Tina and Rocky. Each appeared pleased. "Sure."

Because the construction site was within walking distance of the Power Plant, they walked. The air was chilly, the sun shining. Webb asked, "How cold does it get here?"

Rocky said, "Capital letters cold from as early as mid-October until sometimes the end of April."

He smiled. "Strike one."

Amused, Bernadine protested, "Hey. Not fair. A little cold never hurt anyone."

"You're talking to a California man, Ms. Brown."

"Terence—he drove you here from the airport—moved here from Oakland last year. He survived his first winter just fine."

Tina threw in, "Take it from a girl from the Midwest. You'll get used to it. You might even learn to love it."

Webb appeared doubtful.

At the site, everything was going full bore: earthmovers, semis, workers with survey instruments. He glanced around at all the chaos, but kept his thoughts unspoken. He was introduced to Trent and to construction chief Warren Kelly and both men welcomed him to the community.

"I haven't accepted the job just yet."

Trent said, "By the time these women are done with you, you will. Believe me."

Warren laughed. "Listen to him, Mr. Webb, and they are a joy to work with and for."

Webb nodded.

Trent and Warren returned to duty and the tour moved on.

Webb asked, "Do you have a name picked out for the restaurant?"

Bernadine told him what it would be and why.

He stopped. "This town has been here that long?"

"Since 1879. We're trying to get Henry Adams listed on the National Register of Historic Places. Not many all Black townships have survived this long."

As they walked down Main Street, they gave him a brief

history of the town, the man it was named after, and the Exodus of 1879.

"Never heard of the Exodus."

"Consider it your homework," Rocky said.

Bernadine explained how she purchased Henry Adams on eBay, and the sorry state the town had been in back then.

He asked with surprise, "So you paid for all these improvements?"

She nodded. "When much is given, much is expected."

As they approached the church, Paula stepped out and walked toward her truck parked in the driveway. Seeing them, she waved. Rocky called her over.

"Want you to meet Chef Thornton Webb. He's interviewing for the restaurant. This is our priest, Reverend Paula Grant."

Paula shook his hand. "Welcome to Henry Adams. This is a great place to live and to work. The people are wonderful."

"A lady priest. Episcopalian?"

"Yes. Are you familiar with us?"

"I am. My restaurant in Oakland partners with the local diocese's soup kitchen."

"Always a joy to meet someone helping do God's work. I have to run. Nice meeting you, Chef Webb. Hope you'll consider moving here."

"Thanks."

As Paula left them, and their little tour group moved, Bernadine saw him visually track Paula's truck as it moved down Main. Rocky appeared to notice as well and sent Bernadine a quick but significant look.

Inside the rec center he was introduced to Tamar. "Pleased to meet you, Chef Webb."

"Same here."

"Do you know your family history?" she asked.

He studied her silently for a few moments, then admitted, "Other than that my grandparents on my mom's side moved to the Bay from somewhere in Oklahoma, no."

"It'll be something you can work on after you take the job."

He smiled. "Everyone seems to think it's a foregone conclusion that I'll be taking the job."

Tamar said, "Because you will. You need what we can give you. I can see it in your eyes."

He went still.

Tamar said, "Nice meeting you. Thanks for bringing him to meet me, ladies. Now, let me get back to work."

Dismissed, they exited.

He asked, "She always that mysterious?"

Rocky cracked, "Always. You can put that in all caps, too."

The last place to see was the Dog and as he entered, Chef Webb smiled. The lunch rush was just getting started so the place was only partly filled. The waitstaff was delivering orders. The very young Stevie Wonder was on the box begging his girl to sign a "Contract on Love."

"I like the atmosphere. Can I see the kitchen?" he asked Rocky.

"Of course."

She introduced him to head chef Randy Emerson and the other members of the staff. Bernadine saw Webb glance at Randy's tattoo sleeves featuring cuts of meat and smiled.

"Where are you from Randy?" he asked

"Texas."

"I like the sleeves. Nice work."

"Thanks, Chef."

"So, Chef. What's on the lunch menu today?"

Randy, sounding a bit nervous, gave him a rundown.

While they spoke, Bernadine said to Rocky, "Tina and I are going to back to my office. Let me know when he's done here, and we'll see about TC getting him to the airport for his flight home."

"Will do."

TWO HOURS LATER, Webb was on his way back to the airport. Bernadine sat in her office working on some things and reflecting on the day. She wondered if she'd imagined Webb's interest in Paula, then decided to leave it alone. Tina had been dropped off at Bernadine's to handle some phone calls and relax. They'd hook up again for dinner.

Lily came in. "So is Mr. Handsome Chef going to take the job?"

"He said he'd let us know in a few days. He seemed impressed with our little corner of the world, so we'll see. I do think adding Audra might be a good thing for her, though.

"Her parents were real unhappy when they left. I hope she can work things out."

Bernadine agreed. "What did I miss this morning while doing interviews and playing tour guide?"

"The survey company was out at Marie's, and guess what?"

Bernadine paused. "What?"

"Her house is sitting on a very large deposit of natural gas."

"Really?"

"They're still checking their data on the deposit, but yes. Their office did some calling around and had someone search through the old county deeds and records and found that her mother, Agnes, had a survey done back in the sixties. She knew about the deposit then, but never moved forward on the extraction."

"Why not?"

"I called Tamar and she said Agnes was afraid the gas companies would try and take her land if she gave them access to it, so she sat on the information, and basically it was lost through time. She never said anything to Marie about it, either."

"I wonder if that was why, when Marie and Leo were dating, Agnes kept telling Marie that Leo wanted the land, not Marie."

"Quite possibly."

"Wow." Agnes's last words to her daughter, Marie, had been to hold on to the Jefferson land. Bernadine was convinced Leo knew about the natural gas deposit back then. He and the Salem Oil company probably came across the information while doing research for the pipeline they'd wanted to install. "So, what does Marie plan to do?"

"She said she's going to do some reading up on it, then talk to you and Tina about what she might do next. The survey company says her land is sitting on a small gold mine."

"Is this the kind of gas that needs fracking to extract?"

"She was worried about that but was told it's conventional gas, and pumping is used instead. Fracking is used for what's called unconventional natural gas."

"And the difference?"

"From what the geologists told Marie, conventional is closer to the surface. She said if fracking had to be used, she'd just let it sit."

Bernadine was pleased to hear that. When Leo was trying

to get approval for his pipeline a few years ago, Trent held a special Movie Night and showed the 2010 documentary *Gasland* that chronicled the extensive damage the fracking process caused not only to the environment but to people's lives. A safe extraction of Marie's gas deposit would be good for the surrounding area, and if it proved to be as lucrative as estimated, she'd be set financially. Now that she was getting help for her gambling addiction, there was little chance of her squandering the newly found fortune at the tables in Vegas, or so Bernadine hoped.

"Any news on Leo and the land buy he told the farmers about?"

"No. Tina and I are pretty sure he's lying. We've had our people talk to developers and investment companies from Beijing to San Francisco to Boston and back, and no one's heard a thing. Of course, Leo lying isn't a surprise. I just wish he wasn't trying to bamboozle our neighbors. Again."

"I agree. Maybe the Fickle Finger of Fate will strike."

"The Fickle Finger of Fate?"

"Yes. From the old *Laugh-In* show. Amari found it on the internet and we're having a ball watching it."

"Ah. Just a bit before my time."

"Mine too, but it is funny. President Nixon was on one of the episodes."

"Goodness. Anything else I missed today?"

"No. Not that I can think of. Oh, yes! I got a text from Sheila this morning. Barrett is dropping out of the race."

"What?"

"Apparently, he was so impressed by her performance last night that he's withdrawing. Wants to help her get elected."

"Oh, my goodness." Bernadine found it amazing that the man who'd been so upset by his wife's running was now getting over himself so she could win the race. She wondered what made him change his mind, other than being one of the men Sheila mopped the floor with. "I have to give him kudos for making that decision and supporting her."

"I agree. She was over the moon."

Bernadine was so happy for Sheila. Barrett's attitude had been weighing her down like an anchor.

Lily continued. "Her campaign signs came in today. I'm going to help her put them up tomorrow. Preston and Amari have volunteered, too."

She paused before saying, "I think she can win, Bernadine. I don't see Thad or Riley coming anywhere close to her in votes, but stranger things have happened."

"True." One had only to look at the political mess in Washington to know the truth in that.

"But the gender prejudice Riley is pushing worries me. Trent said some of the construction guys agree with him and won't be voting for Sheila."

Bernadine didn't like hearing this. "Does Trent have any idea how widespread the feeling is?"

"He just mentioned it in passing. I'll ask or you can when you see him."

"Okay."

"We're putting her signs together at my house after dinner. If you want to help, come by around seven."

"Will do."

She returned to her office. Bernadine went back to her laptop, but the reality that some men were stuck in the horse-

and-buggy days in their view of women left her unsettled. She hoped it was just a few. Surely, Riley wouldn't win the election. Would he?

At a bit past five, Bernadine decided to head home. The day had been long and all she wanted was to put on her sweats and veg out until bedtime. She wasn't sure if she was up to helping with the campaign signs. She'd wait and see how she felt later.

At home, she was surprised to find Tina on the phone with her suitcase beside her. Tina held up a finger forestalling questions while she continued her conversation. "Okay. Be there as soon as I can."

The call ended and the worry on Tina's face concerned Bernadine. "What's happened?"

"Mimi fell and broke her hip."

Mimi was Tina's eighty-year-old mom. "Oh no!"

"That was my brother, Kevin, on the phone. She's at the hospital and stable, but docs are pretty sure she'll need surgery. Kevin said they're waiting on the X-rays to come back."

"Did she trip and fall?"

"Fell skating. We keep telling her to stay off the skates. Does she listen? Of course not."

Bernadine knew this was serious, but Mimi, a former roller derby star, was a force of nature and Mimi was going to do Mimi. "Well, tell her I send my love. Don't you yell at my girl too much. That she's still active at her age is a blessing."

"Not when you fall and crack your behind, it isn't."

Bernadine smiled. "Is Mike on his way?" He was her copter pilot.

"Yes. We'll fly to Tulsa, leave the chopper, and switch over to the plane. It's in a hangar there. I should be in Milwaukee before midnight."

Bernadine gave her a hug. "Take care and travel safe."

"Will do. Wasn't sure where you were in your day, so TC's on his way to take me to the field by the firehouse so Mike can pick me up."

"Okay. Keep me posted."

"Will do. Oh, Mal stopped by."

Bernadine stiffened. "Why?"

"He left you something."

On the couch was a box wrapped in shiny purple paper.

Tina said, "I think he planned to leave it on the porch but I saw him drive up and opened the door."

Bernadine's curiosity was piqued. "Did he say what it was?" There was a lovely burgundy bow on top.

"No. Only that it was for you. Then he left."

A car horn sounded. "That's TC. I'll text you when I get to Milwaukee."

Bernadine's attention swung from the box to Tina. "Okay. Hope Mimi will be okay."

"If she stays off those damn skates."

Tina and her brother had been trying to get Mimi to give up skating for years but to no avail.

TC came to the door, carried Tina's suitcase out to the black town car, and the two departed.

In the silence left behind, Bernadine crossed over to the box and picked it up. After unwrapping it, she opened the white box inside. Seeing what it held, a fond smile curved her lips as she lifted the contents free. It was a kite, and even though it was folded inside clear packaging, she saw that it was a beautifully detailed dragon. Just like his. She'd asked him for a similar one when their relationship first began, but he'd encouraged her to wait because she didn't have the necessary skills. Since those days they'd flown kites together many times, and with each outing she grew better and better. And now . . . It was teal colored with burgundy-accented wings. The fierce face was also burgundy, and the teal underbelly was accented with a line of gold triangles. It was gorgeous and she wanted to rush right out and watch it fly. The sun was already setting though, so she'd have to wait, but even that disappointment couldn't stop her from feeling like a kid at Christmas. *You get big points for this, Malachi July. Big points.* She marveled at his gift for a few minutes more before setting it aside to fish her phone out of her tote. He deserved a thank-you, but should she call him or play her cards close to the vest and just text? A voice in her head said, *Call the man!* So, she did.

"Hey," she said when he picked up. There was all kinds of noise in the background. It sounded like drums, voices, and laughter.

"Hey."

Wherever he was it was loud. "Just called to say thanks for the kite."

"Hold on. I can barely hear you. Let me go outside."

Curious about his location, she waited.

"Okay. Sorry. I'm at Tamar's helping Thad with his signs. Half the family is here."

"Ah. I called to say thanks for the kite. It's beautiful."

"You're welcome. I'm glad you like it."

Nervous as a girl talking to a boy for the first time, she wasn't sure what to say next. Forcing her voice to stay calm, she said, "I'll let you get back to the signs. Thanks again."

"You're welcome, again."

"Bye."

The call ended and she wondered why she was so nervous. They'd talked on the phone a thousand times, but it was the first time in a while that she hadn't wanted Mal's head on a platter while doing so and that had to mean something. She just wasn't sure what. Her stomach growled, reminding her that she hadn't eaten, so giving the kite one last admiring look, she took to the stairs to change clothes and start dinner.

CHAPTER
12

The salon was closed on Mondays and Tuesday, so when Riley reported to work Wednesday morning, he was still high on his debate performance. He planned to ask his customers how they thought he did and couldn't wait to hear their praises. He nodded a greeting to Kelly seated at her desk on the far side of the room and hung up his jacket.

"So you attacked my husband's character at the debate Monday night?"

He froze, turned, and looked into Kelly's wintry eyes. He hadn't heard her walk up. Unprepared for the confrontation, he swallowed and quickly tried to think of a reply, but she wasn't done. "My Bobby is the sweetest man you'd ever want to meet. He's a great dad and has dreams of giving his family a beautiful future." She had a black comb in her hand and pointed it at him. "Keep his name out of your mouth. You hear me?"

"He's a former gang member."

"And you're a former thief. The pot doesn't get to call the kettle black."

Riley flinched.

She walked back to her side of the shop. Shaken, he released the breath he'd been holding just as Leo Brown came in the door.

"What's wrong? You look like you've just seen a ghost."

"Nothing. What can I do for you?"

Kelly yelled, "Tell your candidate if he drags my husband again, I'll be dragging his fake, rose-wearing behind to Topeka and back!"

Brown stiffened.

"Don't pay her any attention," Riley said quietly, hoping she couldn't hear him.

Brown studied Riley for a moment, but instead of asking more questions, he said, "I have your signs in my trunk. Wanted to make sure you were here before I brought them in."

Riley's mood instantly brightened and he followed Brown out to his newly leased black import. In the trunk were six campaign signs. Riley was confused. "Where are the rest?"

"That's it. It's not like you've got a big city to cover."

"But I need more than six."

"I got you the billboard. Our money went toward that."

"Oh." But he realized Brown was right. It wasn't as if Henry Adams rivaled Los Angeles in size, and as far as he knew, none of the other candidates had a big fancy billboard overlooking the highway. "I want you to arrange a meeting with the Election Commission so we can file a complaint about Payne stealing my metal detector idea."

"Not necessary. He withdrew his candidacy."

"Scared of being fined, I'll bet."

"I'm sure you're right. I need to get going. Put the signs

wherever you think they'll do the most good and I'll be in touch."

As Brown drove off, a buoyant Riley gently placed the signs in the backseat of his car.

For the rest of the workday, Riley floated on a cloud. Even though his five customers offered him no more than a shrug when asked how he'd done at the debate, he had campaign signs. They sported the slogan "Be Secure with Curry," and his face was set in the serious pose he'd requested. Kelly hadn't directed another word his way for the rest of the day, but it didn't matter. Once he won the election, he'd be quitting, and wished her luck finding someone as equally skilled with a pair of clippers.

As he drove home to change clothes, Riley made a mental list of the places he planned to put his signs. He ate a quick dinner of tuna and crackers, donned jeans and a sweatshirt with a picture of Babe the pig on the front, and drove back to Main Street. He stopped at the Power Plant first. Mrs. Payne and July already had their signs by the curb. It was the best spot, so Riley stuck his sign in the ground right in front of July's since no one was going to vote for a dumb Okie anyway. He used the same tactic in front of the rec, the Lofts housing the salon and coffee shop, and the Dog. Because his signs hid July's so well, it made it appear as if Riley and Mrs. Payne were the only candidates running.

There were no other campaign signs on the lawn in front of the church. Pleased at the idea of getting there first, he stuck his in the grass and was admiring it when the lady reverend came outside.

"You'll have to remove the sign, Mr. Curry."

"Because?"

"Separation of church and state. God doesn't vote or endorse candidates."

"I think it will be okay."

"I don't. Pull it out, please, or I will."

She was speaking to him in a nice enough tone but there was a determination in her eyes that he decided not to mess with. He pulled up the sign.

"Thank you, Mr. Curry."

He grumbled, "You're welcome." And got back in his car and headed to the highway to check out his billboard.

He pulled off onto the shoulder and got out. The billboard loomed high above the cars and big rigs whizzing by. Seeing his face and campaign slogan way up there made him so proud, tears stung his eyes. Never in his life had he imagined being such a celebrity. He thought about all the people driving past who'd remark not only on his slogan but on his striking, statesmanlike appearance, too. Brown had done a heck of a job. Wiping his eyes, mayoral candidate Riley Curry got back into his car and drove home.

An hour later, his phone rang. He didn't recognize the number but knew the area code covered the Los Angeles area, so he picked up. It was a man named Chauncey Mayo and he'd gotten Riley's number from Cletus's trainer, Ben Scarsdale.

When the call ended twenty minutes later, Riley was breathless with excitement. Cletus's film company wanted to honor the hog's Animal Oscar nomination with a ticker-tape parade down Henry Adams's Main Street. There'd be bands, the other animal nominees, and various top celebrities. Since Riley was the soon-to-be-elected new mayor, he'd given Mayo and his people the green light. Mayo would be flying in the next day to nail down the details. Riley toyed with the idea of letting Bernadine Brown know about Mayo's arrival but decided surprising her would be better.

ON THURSDAY AFTERNOON, Lily came into Bernadine's office and said, "Riley Curry is here with a man named Chauncey Mayo. They'd like to speak with you."

Bernadine wondered what craziness to expect now. Barrett called earlier on behalf of the Election Commission. Thad had filed a complaint about the placement of Riley's campaign signs. Not wanting to know what that meant, she'd politely cut him off in the middle of the explanation and told him to handle it in whatever way he and commission members saw fit. She was trying to make the day a short one so she could fly her kite. She was certain whatever Riley wanted would derail those plans. "Did he say what about?"

Lily shook her head.

She sighed. "Okay. Send them in."

Lily returned with Riley and a tall, blond man with a beard who appeared to be in his early thirties. He was decked out in skinny hipster jeans and a gray sleeveless bubble vest over a checked shirt. As soon as he entered, he walked over and shook her hand. "Chauncey Mayo. Call me Chaunce," he invited with a white-toothed smile. "Pleased to meet you, Ms. Burns."

First misstep. "Brown," she said correcting him. "Bernadine Brown."

"Oops. Sorry. My bad."

She eyed Riley, who looked everywhere but at her. "Have a seat," she offered. "And tell me why you're here."

"Thanks. I'm from Watershed Productions in Hollywood. You heard of us, right?"

"I have."

"We're the company behind the movie *Cletus Goes to Hollywood*."

She felt a headache rising. "And?"

"Mr. Curry wasn't sure if we needed a permit for the parade. He said you run the administrative offices and you'd know, so, do we?"

"Do we what?"

"Need a permit for the parade?"

"What parade?"

"Cletus's Homecoming Parade."

Bernadine sat back in her chair and drew in a deep breath. When she was certain she could speak calmly, she said, "Cletus's Homecoming Parade." Her eyes pinned Riley to his chair and he squirmed. "I'm afraid Mr. Curry hasn't shared any information about a parade."

Chaunce wasn't fazed. He launched into a spirited tale of bands and floats and confetti that left Bernadine so outdone, she had to take in another deep breath. She met the eyes of the smiling Chaunce. "There isn't going to be a parade, Mr. Mayo."

He paused and stared at her for a moment. "What do you mean? Mr. Curry has already given us the go-ahead. We just need to make sure we don't need a sign-off from the county or whatever entity that handles these things."

"I'm the entity."

"But he's the mayor. You work for him, correct? He says jump. You ask how high."

Riley cleared his throat loudly and rolled his shoulders in a way that let Bernadine know he knew he was in trouble up to his dyed black hair. "Mr. Curry is not the mayor, Mr. Mayo."

Riley spoke up. "But I will be after the election."

Her glare made him jump, then go silent as a piece of fire-wood. "Riley, how about you let Chaunce and I speak privately. Have a seat in the conference room. We won't be long."

He opened his mouth to protest but he appeared to see the fire in her eyes and the steam rolling from her ears, so he nodded and exited.

Chaunce had confusion all over his face.

"Now. Mr. Mayo. Riley Curry is running for mayor. The election will be soon, and he has as much of a chance of winning as you do."

He cocked his head.

"Even if I did give you clearance to have this parade, your company would have to spend a fortune flying in extras for the crowd scenes, because I guarantee no one within fifteen miles will attend."

His jaw dropped. "Why not?"

"To put it politely, Cletus is not well liked here. For many reasons."

"But—"

"He's such a pariah, there's a court order restricting his movements within the town limits. He killed a man—it was in self-defense, but the man is still dead. He wrecked Riley's house to the point it's been condemned, and the contractors that razed it were forced to wear haz-mat suits to do the job. Do you need to hear more?"

Chaunce's eyes were as wide as the Mississippi and he coughed a few times as if choking on his reaction. Finally finding his tongue, he asked, "So what is your role here?"

"I own Henry Adams. As in my name is on the bill of sale. Riley Curry is known for fudging the truth, so I'm sorry you flew all this way for nothing. There will be no parade."

"My boss is not going to be happy."

"I can't help that."

"Suppose we offer a donation to your favorite charity?"

She was done discussing the subject, and so had no response.

"You can't stop a Hollywood studio."

"I can buy your studio tomorrow and have you and your boss out of a job by Friday. Just because I'm female and in a small town doesn't mean I'm impressed by Hollywood."

"We'll sue," he threatened.

"Fine, and when my lawyers are done, I *will* own the studio. Have a nice flight home, Mr. Mayo."

He sat there a moment sizing her up.

She waited.

He finally got to his feet and said icily, "A pleasure meeting you. Not. Tell Mr. Curry I'll be in touch."

"I'm not his secretary."

Full-on angry, he stormed out.

Bernadine opened the intercom to Lily's office. "Lil, Riley should be in the conference room; can you send him back in here, please."

A moment later he walked in. Sheepishly. "Yes?"

"There will be no parade. Goodbye."

"But—"

"Good. Bye."

Riley hung his head and departed.

Lily came in and took one look at Bernadine's face and asked, "What did Riley do this time?"

When Bernadine told her, Lily's jaw dropped. Bernadine then said, "So, between I'm the mayor Riley Curry, and Mr. Chauncey, call me Chaunce, Mayonnaise, I've had it. I'm going home and fly my kite."

"Your kite?"

She closed her laptop and picked up her purse. "Yes, my kite."

"Like the ones you used to fly with Mal?"

She put on her jacket. "Yes. I need the stress relief."

"When did you buy a kite?"

"I didn't. It was a gift."

"From Mal?"

Bernadine took her keys out of her purse.

Smiling, Lily crossed her arms and eyed her speculatively. "Did I miss something?"

"I'll see you tomorrow."

"So you aren't going to tell me."

"Bye, Lily."

As she headed down the hall to the exit, a laughing Lily called out behind her. "I'm going to find out. You know there are no secrets in Henry Adams."

Bernadine kept walking.

She drove to Tamar's because that's where she'd always flown kites in the past. There was such peace and serenity down by the banks of the creek. When she reached the gate and saw all the vehicles and tents in the yard, she remembered the Oklahoma clan was in town to help with Thad's campaign. Their presence meant there'd be no peace or serenity, and Mal was probably somewhere around, too. Disappointed, she drove on, wondering where to go next. She ruled out the subdivision. Bernadine loved her neighbor friends, but she and the kite would draw curiosity, maybe unwanted company, and definitely unwanted questions, so she kept driving and thinking. The sight of tiny raindrops slowly dotting her windshield made her groan aloud. As it increased to full, flat-out rain, she turned on the wipers and blew out a breath. *No kite flying for me.* Doubly disappointed, she drove home.

AT THE END of the school day, Robyn grabbed her backpack, said goodbye to everyone, and ran the short distance through the rain to the church. Paula's door was closed, which meant she had a session going on inside. Uncertain how long Paula might be, Robyn fished her e-reader out of her backpack and, after taking off her damp hoodie, settled in. She was reading *A Blade So Black* by L.L. McKinney. It was about a girl like herself who was using her awesome powers to battle evil and save her friends and the world. Before moving to Henry Adams and becoming friends with Leah, Robyn didn't know books like *Blade* even existed, but now that she did, she was devouring titles of what were called Young Adult Fantasy, as if she needed them to breathe.

Robyn was so engrossed in the story, she had no idea how much time had passed when Paula's door opened. Out stepped her cousin and Brain's dad, Colonel Payne. Seeing her he looked uncomfortable, so she gave him a simple nod and went back to her story. Although his appearance was a surprise, she hid it so he wouldn't think she was judging him for being there. Paula walked him upstairs to the door and returned a short moment later.

"How was your day?" she asked.

"Pretty good. I have a lot of homework, but what else is new." She closed her e-book and followed Paula inside.

As Paula gathered her belongings so she could drive them home, she said, "I got a text from Calvin. He found a nice family to rent Tyree's house—a couple with three little kids."

Robyn hoped they'd have a better time living there than she'd had.

"Also, Della's house burned down."

"What happened?"

"Young people were using it as a secret late-night party spot and apparently had candles to provide light. Fire department thinks either one was left burning or got knocked over but the place burned to the ground."

Robyn was outdone. "I guess you and Cal won't have to worry about what to do with it anymore."

"No, but someone needing a home could've used it. Now, it's going to be torn down."

"Was anybody hurt?"

"Not that I know of."

That was good news, but her grandmother's house held nothing but bad memories so, unlike Paula, Robyn was glad it was gone.

They drove home through the rain, and after dinner, Paula stayed at the table to work on Sunday's sermon. It was Robyn's day to do the kitchen cleanup, so she stashed the leftovers in the fridge and fed the dirty dishes to the dishwasher.

Paula looked up and asked, "Do you want to tour some colleges over the holiday break?"

Robyn shrugged. "I suppose."

"You sound so excited."

That made Robyn smile. "I'm just not sure what I want to do after I'm done with school. Did you know when you graduated?"

"I thought I wanted to be a lawyer because one of the women in our apartment building was one, but after Mom died and I went to live with Tyree, all I wanted was to leave Blackbird."

"Totally feel you on that." Robyn rinsed one of the glasses and put it on the dishwasher rack. "All the kids in my class seem to have their lives figured out. Leah says she was born to be a physicist. Amari wanted to race cars, but now wants to study anthropology. Zoey's going to be a musician. Wyatt's down with cartography. I feel like something's wrong with me because I don't."

"There's nothing wrong with you. Most of them have had enough time to settle into life. They have supportive parents and a great teacher. They've traveled and had lots of beneficial experiences. You've lacked that during your early years, but it isn't your fault."

Paula's response mirrored her own thinking that her friends had been exposed to way more than she had. "So how do I figure out what I want to do?"

"Pick something you're passionate about, or curious about. Sometimes our purpose picks us. You're only eighteen, Roby, you have plenty of time to decide on the future, and if you don't want to go to college, you can pick an alternative. You can do the Peace Corps or help President Carter build homes with Habitat for Humanity. You have some money socked away, so you have options."

"I never thought about doing something like the Peace Corps or any other group that helps people."

"Working on behalf of the less fortunate can be immensely rewarding, not only for them but for you as well."

Robyn thought that over. "So, if I do want to look at colleges, which ones should I pick?"

"I'd put Spelman on the list, of course, but do some research and see what schools you might want to visit. I think a mix of big ones and small ones might be the way to start. Do you want to go to KU? Out of state? Do you want warm weather? Snow? Factor all those things in when you make your list."

"Sounds like homework."

Paula smiled and nodded. "Homework for your future."

"One last question. Do you think I'll ever have a boyfriend?"

"Do you want one?"

"I don't know."

"Then how about you concentrate on getting Robyn ready for life first, and if and when the time comes for a boy, you'll be better prepared to decide who to pick."

"What do you mean?"

"You want someone who appreciates you for you. Who's kind to you, supports you, and won't try and control your life, or keep you from having friends."

"There are guys who do that?"

"Yes, women too, and unfortunately people who fall prey to them in the name of love."

"Oh. I don't want that."

"And you shouldn't."

"Not trying to be nosy but why haven't you married somebody?"

Paula shrugged. "Haven't found the right person yet. Having to share me with God scared off a lot of men."

Robyn thought she understood that. "Thanks for letting me interrupt you."

"Anytime."

Robyn finished her chores, did her homework, then booted up her laptop to begin researching colleges, the Peace Corps, and Habitat for Humanity.

CHAPTER
13

Now that the candidates had their signs in place, campaigning began in earnest. Riley spent his days at the salon trying to convince everyone who entered that he was the only man for the job. He was pleased hearing that some of the men agreed and wouldn't be voting for a woman. He spent the rest of the time bragging about his billboard.

Thad and the Julys campaigned by holding court at the Dog and driving all over town blowing kazoos and drumming in the bed of an old hay wagon with his smiling face plastered on the side along with his slogan: "Take a Gamble on July." Sheila spent her evenings meeting with the various constituencies in the area: farmers, families, construction workers, men and women in the trades. She even met with the staff at Clark's Grocery. Barrett went with her as her driver, and watching her interact, ask questions, and listen intently made him incredibly proud. His blooming pride was one of the things he'd discussed in his session with Paula a few days ago. It was their first meeting and he'd been as nervous as a new recruit at boot camp. Preston had been correct, however. Paula was easy to talk to, and never made him feel as if something was wrong with him for being there. In discussing his uneasiness, she assured him it was natural, and that she'd not pressure him to reveal more about himself than he wanted to lay on the table. He was still uncomfortable though, so much so that he hadn't mentioned anything to Sheila about it. Paula emphasized that it was his choice to share the visits with Sheila or not. His conversations with her were confidential and always would be.

Now, Barrett and Sheila were on their way home after leaving a meeting with a few of the community college professors and students registered to vote in Henry Adams. Driving, he glanced over. "Tired?"

"I am. Who knew talking to people night after night would be so exhausting. I just want a hot shower and my pjs."

"What's on the schedule for tomorrow?"

"I meet with the Franklin City Council in the afternoon to get their ideas about any projects they might like to partner with Henry Adams on. Bernadine said Franklin wants to send their kids to Jefferson Academy but are balking at paying what she considers a fair price for teacher salaries, supplies, and the rest."

"They want to play but not pay?"

"Basically, but that's not going to happen. I believe they're thinking they can sweet-talk me or bully me into supporting their position."

"They'll learn you're tougher than you look."

"Hopefully, I won't have to prove it to them."

"There's something I didn't ask you when we talked the other night."

"What was it?"

"What did you want to be when you were growing up?"

"A lady astronaut. My father thought it was the funniest thing he'd ever heard."

"How old were you?"

"Eight? Maybe nine?"

"What did your mom say?"

"Nothing, but she knew I had a thing for numbers and math, so on the one hand, she wanted me to keep my love for those hidden—in order to get a husband. But on the other hand, she encouraged me to take the advanced math and science classes when I hit high school. I never understood the opposing goals. It was like: Be smart, but be a lady first? Still don't get her reasoning. I was appreciative, though. Why do you ask?"

"Just watching you at these meetings and wondering if you ever thought as a little girl you'd one day be running for mayor."

"Oh. Never. What did you want to be when you were little?"

"A Marine, of course."

She laughed softly. "Of course."

"I wanted to be just like my grandfather and my father—but not the abusive parts." He went silent for a moment as the old memories rose up to haunt him, then confessed quietly, "I'm seeing Paula about all that."

She didn't act surprised by the admission. "Paula's good people. She's helped me a lot."

He pulled into their driveway and cut the engine. He sat with her for a moment before looking over and saying, "Trying to figure out if it makes me less of a man."

She shook her head. "No, Barrett, it doesn't. At least not in my eyes. I think it takes a lot of strength and courage to ask someone to help you shine a light on the dark places inside."

"You think so?"

"I know so. Not sure if I'm supposed to say this, but I'm proud of you. Sometimes those dark spaces keep us from being whole."

"I'm trying to decide if I want to go again or not."

"Up to you, but don't make the decision right away. Let yourself think it over for a little while first."

He nodded. "Thanks for the encouragement. Have I told you lately how much I love you?"

"No, but you can tell me now."

He gave a soft chuckle and ran a worshipping finger down her cheek. "You are so much more than I deserve. I love you, Sheila Payne." Leaning over, he kissed her softly.

When the kiss ended and he drew back, she whispered, "I love you too, Colonel Barrett Payne."

Leaving the car, they went inside.

OVER AT HIS mansion, Leo turned away from Big Al Stillwell's silent but menacing presence to watch Riley strutting around the solarium shooting the breeze with the farmers who'd shown up for the evening's meet and greet. Leo had provided food and drink, and the flat screen was tuned to the big KU at Duke basketball game. He counted twenty-five men, five more than had shown up for the last meeting. Leo assumed word had gotten around about the money he'd given away, and the new faces were probably anticipating a repeat. They were correct. Due to Riley's disastrous performance at the debate, and his overall obnoxious personality, Curry needed every vote

Leo could buy. Although Leo didn't worry about Thad July being a serious contender, the Paynes certainly were. Not only had Sheila Payne been impressive enough at the debate to be elected president of the United States, her husband was no longer in the race, which meant his supporters would probably throw their votes her way, but Leo didn't have the time to worry over that now. He had to get Riley through this, first, but he was encouraged by the small but positive response he'd been receiving to playing up the gender divide between his candidate and Mrs. Payne. In his comings and goings a few men had let him know they'd be voting for Riley because he was male. One man at the Franklin drugstore asked if it was okay to pass out the buttons he made that said: "Curry—the only MAN for the job." Leo of course said yes.

But now he focused on the evening's event. He muted the TV, had everyone take seats, and opened the meeting. "For those who don't know me, I'm Leo Brown, Mr. Curry's campaign manager. Welcome to my home and thank you for coming. Riley's platform is a sound one, and if you're still on the fence as to who you'll be voting for, I hope tonight helps cement your decision to give him your support. Who has the first question?"

"Can you give us an update on the land buy, Riley?"

Riley puffed out his chest. "I've been busy crisscrossing the county getting the word out on my vision, so I'm going to turn that question over to Leo. He's coordinating that for me."

Lying through his teeth, Leo talked about the new corporations that were signing on, and that some of the interested parties would be sending preliminary survey crews to check out properties. "These multinational corporations are extremely busy this time of year, and their development teams are either overseas or up to their necks evaluating other sites. We should expect some serious news and visits come spring."

Leo was pleased to see eagerness shine in the eyes of some in the room. "So please bear with us if you don't hear anything from them right away. Their interest is solid. Just remember Riley needs your votes to help smooth the way for the process going forward."

Riley then asked the men, "Has everyone seen my billboard? Leo, how about we take a break and caravan to the highway and take a look at it?"

Leo forced himself to respond in an even tone, "Maybe later. Right now, you might want to pass out that gift Mega Seed sent over for your supporters." For the five hundredth time, he wished he hadn't gotten involved with Curry.

Riley responded importantly, "Well, get the bags."

Leo growled inwardly at being spoken to like a servant but with help from some of the others in the room, he did as he was told. He'd strangle the annoying little man later. He set the large bags of seed at Riley's feet and prayed he remembered everything they'd rehearsed over the last few days.

Riley opened by talking about Mega Seed underwriting his campaign and being tapped as one of their spokesmen. He quoted the stats on crop yields and boasted that he'd convinced Mega Seed to give the seed away for free to his supporters in exchange for endorsements about its performance. He went on to say how well it had performed in the lab. He had the speaking points down and Leo relaxed.

One farmer asked, "This isn't the Mega Seed product that's in court, is it?"

Riley looked to Leo who, having been caught off guard by the question, recovered enough to say, "No, and because that complaint has no merit, the case is about to be thrown out."

The farmer shook his head. "No. Courts ruled last week that the lawsuit can go forward. It was on the news."

Leo froze and lied, "Regardless, this is not that seed. I'm sure once the suit goes before a competent judge with the ability to discern all the science tied to the case, he'll rule in favor of the company."

The farmer didn't look convinced. On the far side of the room, Leo saw Big Al's smirk.

Another man asked Riley, "Are you in favor of the USDA program that's been paying compensation to members of the National Black Farmers Coalition because of the government's past discriminatory practices?"

"I am. In fact, I pride myself on knowing all there is to know about the payments and how to sign up for them."

Leo heard Stillwell laugh darkly.

"Really?" someone asked. Leo swore he heard sarcasm in the tone.

"I do," Riley declared. "I'm an expert on issues that affect the local farming community."

The same man said, "Then you're either a liar, full of shit, or both, because that program shut down years ago. It was a trick question, Curry. Wanted to see how much you really know about our issues."

Riley's eyes went wide. He stuttered, "I-I was testing you to see if you knew the program had been shut down."

Muttering rumbled through the room. The gathering was on the fast track to hell.

Leo quickly stepped in. "How about we pass out the seed and the monetary bonus Mega Seed is offering as a way of saying thanks for using it in your fields come spring."

Some faces lit up, others didn't. Riley passed out the seed and the cash while Leo sighed at how quickly this had soured. He'd been so busy talking to printers about the campaign signs, arranging for the installation of the billboard, and making sure Curry knew what he was supposed to say this evening, he'd paid no attention to the seed case. It had been winding its way through the courts for the past two years. The assurances sent to the field offices by the company lawyers had employees like Leo believing the case would be summarily dismissed. But according to what he'd learned just now, they'd been wrong, and because they were, it might put a wrench in the outcome of the plan he and the conspiring companies had come up with. In order to succeed, they needed the seed planted by as many of the targeted farmers as possible. Failure meant heads would roll, and Leo's would be first on the block.

At the end of the evening, the seed and money were disbursed, KU beat Duke, and the farmers including Stillwell made their exit. All twenty-five except Stillwell took the seed, but he was pretty sure it was only to get the two hundred dollars that went with it. There was no guarantee they'd actually plant the seed and it was a worry Leo wasn't sure how to fix.

Once he and Riley were alone, Riley said, "I thought we did good tonight. I remembered all my talking points. I didn't like the trick question, though. That was rude."

Leo needed a drink. "I agree. It was rude. Mega Seed will be pleased that so many people took their product."

"We should offer more money next time. Make sure people keep coming back."

That was the last thing Leo's handlers would want to hear. "I'll run that by them. You go home and get some rest."

"Will do. Think I'll drive over and say good night to my billboard first."

Leo nodded. It was the only response he had for such craziness.

With Riley gone, Leo poured a healthy helping of cognac into a glass only to have his phone alert go off. He picked it up and in response to what he viewed, his hand shook. He opened the FaceTime app and saw the aged, ghoul-like face of Mega Seed president Virgil Quelp. "Evening, sir."

"How'd the meeting go, Leo? They take the bait?"

"Some did."

"How many is some?"

"Twenty-five farmers showed up. Twenty-four left with the seed." Leo knew better than to share his concerns about how many would actually plant it, though.

"That's not a bad number. Keep it up. Salem Oil needs that pipeline and we need that land."

"Understood."

"How's the mayoral campaign?"

"Going well. He's a strong candidate. In a tough fight, though. Running against a very savvy woman."

"Hate these damn feminists. Women have no business in the political arena. Can you bribe her to drop out?"

"I don't think so."

"Try."

"Yes, sir." He sighed inwardly and changed the subject. "I hear the court sent the seed case forward."

"Damn lawyers. We're now putting a clause in the farmers' contracts that any seed sent out for testing will result in a big fine. That should quash any further suits. I'm still certain we'll win. Those uppity farmers underestimate our resolve, and how much we're willing to spend to get this decided in our favor."

Leo thought Mega Seed foolishly underestimated the intelligence and outrage of the black farmers behind the lawsuit, but he kept that to himself.

Quelp said, "Okay, Leo. Keep me posted on the happenings there, and make sure you get that seed distributed the way we need it to be. Salem Oil fired you once. I can make it twice. Good night."

The screen went black and Leo tossed back bitterly, "And good night to you too, you treacherous old bastard."

On Saturday morning, Bernadine awakened to rays of sunlight spilling into her room. Leaving the bed, she walked to the patio door and moved aside the snow white gossamer curtains so she could see out. The sky was the clear frosty blue that seemed to go with autumn, and the grasses on the plains swayed in the wind. Seeing that made her think about her kite. It looked to be a perfect day to send Mimi the dragon up to test her wings; however, the Julys were still at Tamar's. With each day's sunrise bringing winter ever closer, she didn't know how much longer she had before the weather brought snow and she had to store the kite until spring. Sighing, she put the kite out of her mind and began what she envisioned to be a nice, slow, easy day. She'd left all her work at the office, so she could dive into a couple of new books and check out the movies on Netflix she'd been anxious to see.

Dressed in her sweats, she went to the kitchen and took Crystal's latest smoothie creation out of the fridge. The few she'd made before had been fruit based and fairly tasty. This one was dark green, and according to Crys all veggie. In it was kale—which Bernadine detested—spinach which she loved, carrots, and a few other ingredients she couldn't remember. She poured the thick mixture into a glass and had to admit it didn't look very appealing. Raising the glass, she gave it a quick sniff and took a swallow. Yelling at the awful taste, she forced herself to take another swallow, then poured the rest down the garbage disposal and made herself some bacon, eggs, grits, and toast.

She'd just sat down to eat when her phone pinged. It was a text from Mal. *I'm going out to fly my kite. You want to come along?*

Beset with all kinds of thoughts and emotions, she hesitated then responded, *Where? Tamar's?*

No. Too many people.

She looked out at the beautiful day. The offer was so tempting. But it was Mal. A voice inside countered: *So what!* Smiling, she sent back her reply. *I'm in. Where should I meet you?*

Clay and Bing's. 10 ok?

It was now 8:30. *Yes.*

See you there. Wear your boots. Probably muddy.

Spending the morning with Mal was definitely not something she'd planned on doing. But? She told herself this was only about her kite. Period. Setting the phone aside, she started on her breakfast.

Bernadine arrived at Clay and Bing's farm at ten sharp. Mal's souped-up red Ford truck was parked out front. Seeing it gave her a slight case of the nerves, which made no sense so she drew in a deep calming breath. The large wooden pens that held the hogs and cattle were empty. She assumed the livestock was either chilling in the barn or a butcher's freezer.

Leaving Baby, she carried her kite to the front door and rang the bell.

She was met by Clay. "Morning. Come on in. Hand me the kite. I'll put it here on the chair." Thanking him, she followed him through the front room with its comfortable-looking sofa and chairs, then past the nice-size dining room with its large polished table and four pushed-in chairs, and into the kitchen. It was as homey as the rest of the place. Mal was at the table sipping coffee. His dark eyes met hers. He gave her a slight nod. Heart thumping, she returned the gesture similarly and forced her attention to Bing, seated on his left. A large manila envelope stuffed with papers was in the center of the table near his coffee mug. His cane rested on the back of the chair. "Morning, Bernadine."

"Morning, Bing."

He gestured her to a chair. Clay took the empty one to her right.

"How's everyone?" she asked, hoping small talk would help calm her nervousness.

They chatted for a moment about the upcoming Halloween party and how much fun it would be and then the election.

Bing said to Mal, "No offense, Malachi, but everyone I've talked to is voting for Sheila Payne."

"No offense taken. So am I."

They laughed.

Mal continued, "Thad is just in this for the fun. If he did win, he'd be back in Oklahoma by nightfall. He's still real mad at Riley for calling him a dumb Okie, and for messing with his signs. Riley might want to keep an eye out, because I guarantee, Thad's going to pay him back before the last vote's counted one way or another."

Bernadine knew from the town's legends that the Julys were serious about retribution and often took revenge in comical ways.

"Speaking of Riley," Clay said. "He and Leo passed out seed from Mega Seed the other night, along with more cash. I also saw a farmer at the feed store yesterday wearing a button that said: Vote for Curry. The only man for the job. And the word *man* is in capital letters."

Bernadine responded, "I've heard that a few men who won't vote for a woman have gotten on his bandwagon. In a way I know he can't possibly win, but can he?"

Bing shook his head. "I think not. Anybody voting for him has a couple of screws loose."

Bernadine blew out a breath. "I can't wait for the election to be over, so he can lose and go back to just being a local annoyance, and Leo can leave town."

Bing asked her, "Did you read up on the lawsuit against his company?"

"I did. Glad the case is going forward, but I don't get why Mega Seed would sell those farmers dead seed."

"For their land."

Bing must have seen the confusion on her face, so he explained, "If you sell farmers seeds that fail to germinate, nothing grows. If nothing grows, you have nothing to sell. Nothing to sell means you can't pay bills, what's owed on equipment, storage, or your taxes. Land is the only collateral for the most part so, the land goes into foreclosure. Guess who buys the land from the bank?"

She went still.

Bing said, "There were almost two million black farmers in the 1920s. Now, there's fewer than fifty thousand. What bad weather didn't wipe out, the government's Agriculture Department did by refusing loans, and making black farmers jump through hoops for aid and resources white farmers received with no problem."

Clay added, "The way farming works now, you can only plant Big Agriculture's seeds. Plant your own and companies like Mega Seed will see you in court. Tractor manufacturers have built their new machines so farmers can't service them when they break down. Only the manufacturer can do repairs."

"That doesn't sound fair."

"No, it doesn't, which is why some farmers in California took Big Tractor to court."

"Do they have a good case?"

Clay shrugged. "We'll see."

Bernadine thought this over for a moment and asked, "So is the seed Riley's giving away sterile, too?"

Bing said, "No, according to what he told the farmers the other night, but I sent some samples to a friend in the KU agriculture department. He's going to see if it germinates and let me know."

Bernadine had trouble understanding Mega Seed's motives. "But why here? Are they trying to steal our farmland, too?"

Bing picked up the manila folder, removed a large piece of paper, and unfolded it. On it was a map of Graham County. He said, "We pinpointed the farms owned by the first set of farmers Leo invited the night he talked about the corporations wanting to buy land."

Bernadine eyed the blue dots. They marched in a fairly straight line between the county's northern and southern borders. She studied it, and realized she'd seen something similar before, but couldn't remember where. After wrestling with the question, the light came on and her jaw dropped. "The pipeline," she said.

Eyes wide, she looked from Clay to Bing, and to Mal, who raised his coffee cup to her in tribute. "I told them it wouldn't take you but a minute or two to figure it out."

Bernadine viewed the map again. "They're trying to take the land so they can put in that damned pipeline." *Leo, you dirty dog!*

"We don't know that for sure," Bing said. "We do know Leo was fired from Salem Oil and now works for Mega Seed. If you were going to run a play like this, wouldn't you send in someone who already has an in with the people you're trying to bamboozle?"

Bernadine anger rose. "Hold on, I need to make a quick call."

They waited while she pulled her phone from her purse and hit speed dial. "Tina, hey, girl. Question. Salem Oil and Mega Seed. Are they owned by the same multinational?"

It only took Tina a second to reply, yes.

Telling Tina she'd explain later, Bernadine ended the call and relayed the answer to the men. She viewed the map again and wanted to punch Leo's lights out. "Have you shared this map with anyone else?"

"Only Mike Freewater. We're going to wait until the seed report comes back. And if it's sterile like we think it is, we'll call the newspapers and let the publicity bust Leo's and the corporations' chops."

She thought that a good plan. "Thanks for showing me

this. I'll keep it under my hat for now, too. Great work, gentle-men."

They nodded.

Bing added, "And maybe the courts will be more inclined to do something now that white farmers are being targeted, too."

Bernadine said, "Hopefully, inclined enough to send every-body from both companies straight to jail. How long do you think it'll be before your friend knows if the seed's viable?"

"Two, maybe three weeks. No longer than that."

Although she'd said she'd keep the info under her hat, she knew her legal people would want a heads-up regardless of the outcome of the seed testing. "I'll be having my legal people reach out to the Black Farmers Coalition to see if we can offer any assistance with their suit, because this stinks." And it did. How dare they conspire to bulldoze the livelihood of farmers for their own greedy gain. "Do they lack a conscience?"

They talked for a few more minutes, and when they were done, Mal asked, "You ready to go kite flying?"

"Yes. Otherwise I may march over to Leo's and set fire to what little hair he has left."

Mal chuckled. "Then come on. Where's your kite?"

Outside, as they walked away from the back of the house, Bernadine was glad she'd worn her Wellies. The ground was soft from the rain of a few days ago and the mud would've ruined a good pair of shoes. It was still a beautiful sunny day. The air was a bit chilly but it was October and she knew they were lucky it wasn't straight-up cold. Wearing a lightweight parka and with her gloves in a pocket, she carried her kite and walked silently beside Mal. She had no idea where they were going, but she was content being outside and knowing she'd soon be sending Mimi up for her first dance.

They'd been walking for about twenty minutes when he looked over and asked, "You okay?"

"I am."

"Still mad at Leo?"

"I think I'll always be mad at Leo."

"Still mad at me?"

She glanced up, and after weighing her feelings, replied truthfully, "No."

He studied her for a moment, then nodded.

They walked on in silence.

She realized she really wasn't mad at him anymore. Whether it was due to the passage of time or having gained closure from blasting him that day in the parking lot of Dog, she didn't know. What was certain was that being with him no longer made her feel like there was a gallon of battery acid in her stomach.

They came to a halt a few yards away from a stand of trees. Behind them Clay's farmhouse seemed miles away across the open field of grasses.

"There's a table in the trees where we can sit."

She followed and saw the weathered picnic table and a firepit encircled by large stones positioned a few yards away from a wide stretch of water. "Is this the same creek that runs behind Tamar's place?"

"It is, but it's deeper and wider at this point. Great for the whitetail deer and turkeys. Gives them a place to drink. We hunt out here sometimes."

She looked up at the trees, most of which had already shed

their leaves, and at the steep bank on the far side of the water. Mal shucked free of his camo-designed backpack and set his kite down.

It was so quiet she could hear the water. The breeze was still high, the sun still bright, and all the tension brought on by Leo and his mess was forgotten. "Thanks for bringing me out here."

"You're welcome. Didn't know if you'd agree, but it was such a nice day, figured I'd take a chance and ask."

"I'm glad you did. I've been wanting to take Mimi out."

"Mimi?"

"It's what I named the kite—after Tina's mom."

"Ah."

Time seemed to stand still in that moment. Memories of them being together this way in the past washed over her. The intensity in his eyes made her believe he was thinking along the same lines, and not sure what might become of it, she broke the contact. "Let me get my line tied on and send this lady up."

Bernadine sat, and after tying a lark's head knot, attached her Dacron line to the kite. She was reminded that he'd taught her the knot. It had taken her a few times to learn how to make it, even while she'd fumed at her failed attempts, he'd been his ever-patient self, encouraging her, until she mastered it.

They were now ready. Separating herself from him by a few yards so their kite lines wouldn't cross, she let Mimi catch the wind and fed her the line as she climbed. The kite soared quickly and smoothly. The gold diamonds on her belly caught the sunlight and glowed like Zoey's coins. Her happiness showed itself in her wide smile. Looking Mal's way, she saw him smiling back. A second later, his black dragon took flight. The big kite sported accents of red and silver, and like Mimi, caught the sunlight as it climbed and soared against the bright blue sky overhead.

Once Bernadine was certain Mimi could probably see to Milwaukee from her spot in the sky, she stopped giving her line and let her dance. The kite swayed and frolicked in the steady breeze, and her owner swore this was the best gift she'd ever received. Mal had two lines on his kite, so he could make it rise and fall like she imagined a real dragon might move. It was fascinating. Made her a little envious too, but also determined to one day be equally as skilled.

"Watch this!" he called. Expertly handling the twin lines, he made his kite undulate more precisely.

"Show-off!" she yelled.

"That's my name! Don't wear it out."

She laughed.

After an hour, Bernadine's arms began to tire and the constant looking up had her neck and shoulders complaining. Time for a break. She fished the staplelike stake out of her pocket, fed it through the holes of the oblong disc holding her line, and pushed the staple firmly into the rain-softened ground. Mal did the same, and for a moment they stood and watched their kites dance unassisted in the wind.

"I have a thermos of coffee if you want to take the chill off."

"I do."

Leaving the staked kites, they walked back to the table. Mal fished the thermos and two go-cups out of his backpack. The coffee poured out steaming hot. After helping herself to the small packets of sweetener and creamer, she sat and sipped. Content, she watched the kites. This outing was the most fun she had with Mal since their split.

"Penny for your thoughts."

"Just thinking it's been a while since I had this much fun." She chose not to tell him everything on her mind.

"Ditto."

"Thanks again for the kite and invitation."

"You're welcome, again."

And because her hand was the one that turned the world, Bing's map came to mind, bringing with it thoughts of Leo. "I hope we can find a way to send Leo to jail."

He gave her a look.

Confused, she asked, "What?"

"You're supposed to be relaxing and enjoying yourself. Not working and turning the world. Remember?"

She started to protest but thought better of it because she had come out here for fun. "You're right. Thanks for the reminder."

"Here to serve."

She grinned ruefully. He'd always provided the balance her often too full life and mind needed.

"Hungry?"

"A little."

"Good. Let's have lunch."

While she watched, Mal reached into the backpack and withdrew two foil-wrapped packages and two canned sodas. "Be right back."

He walked into the trees, and a moment later returned carrying a large black tote wrapped by a heavy chain that fed into a padlock. As if sensing her unasked questions, he explained as he set the tote on the ground. "Like I said, we sometimes hunt out this way. We stash supplies inside so we don't have to drag stuff back and forth." He pulled a ring of keys from his pocket and fit a small silver one into the lock. "It's chained up to keep out varmints and thieves."

He pulled the chain free and removed the tote's top. Out came a small bag of charcoal, a rectangular box of kitchen matches, paper plates, plastic utensils, wet wipes, paper towels, and napkins, which he placed on the table.

"What are we having for lunch?"

"An outdoor gourmet delight."

She laughed. "What?"

He didn't elaborate so she watched as he poured charcoal into the pit, added some newspaper from the tote and started a fire.

"We need to find a couple of sticks."

She gave Mal a side-eye but followed him over to the trees. He picked out two thin but sturdy branches, and using a wicked-looking hunting knife he withdrew from a sheath around his waist, he cut them down, peeled away some of the outer bark, and whittled the ends to a sharp point.

"Is this gourmet delight hot dogs?"

"You are one smart cookie, Cookie."

Amused by all that he was, she trailed him back to the table.

The branches were the perfect length to roast the hot dogs at a distance that kept her parka from going up in flames. The dogs had come from Clay's freezer, and although they'd thawed a bit, it took a while before they actually started to cook. She'd never done this before, and because she was Bernadine Brown, and Bernadine Brown didn't like lengthy processes, she complained, "Next time can we just bring carryout?"

He looked over and asked quietly, "Is there going to be a next time?"

Her heart stopped and she stammered, "I-I don't know. Maybe? Yes?"

Mal smiled. "I like it when you're tongue-tied."

She stuck out her no longer tied tongue, said, "Buns please, sir. I think this one is finally done."

On the table were buns and condiments, and once she had her gourmet delight prepared to her satisfaction, she took a bite and groaned with pleasure.

He laughed. "That good?"

"Oh yes." They were heavenly. She'd had grilled hot dogs before but not ones cooked over an open flame and for some reason the flavor seemed enhanced. "This is wonderful."

"Still want carryout, if maybe, yes, we do this again?"

She rolled her eyes.

"I like teasing you, too."

Today was the first time she was allowing herself to enjoy the way being with him had made her feel in the past. Without discussing their breakup, they'd slipped back into the easy companionship they'd once shared, which was admittedly better than her desire to run him over with her truck every time they were in the same room. "What are we doing here, Mal?"

He didn't pretend to not understand the question. "I don't know. I've been asking myself the same thing since we got here."

Bernadine thought about what she wanted to say next and chose her words carefully. "I don't know the answer either, but if we don't put a name to it, and go slow, would you be open to seeing where it leads?"

His face remained unreadable for a second or two, then he nodded. "I would." Holding her gaze in the silence that followed, he asked, "Are you sure?"

"I am."

He held up his can of cola in a silent acknowledgment of their agreement. "To the unknown."

She raised her own. "To the unknown."

Later, after repacking the tote and bringing their kites down, they trekked back to Clay and Bing's. She put Mimi in her truck while he put his kite in his Ford. Noticing Bing watching them from the doorway, she smiled inwardly, resigning herself to the fact that by the time she got home everyone in town would know she and Mal spent the day together. *Nothing like small-town living.*

She got in her truck and Mal walked over. "Thanks again," she said.

"You're welcome. I enjoyed myself."

"I did, too."

"Take care."

She started the engine and drove away.

At home, she took a hot shower, slipped into some comfy clothes, and made some tea. Drinking it, she reflected on the day. She had no qualms about the agreement she'd made with Mal. It felt right. Raising her cup in the quiet of her kitchen, she echoed the words, "To the unknown."

CHAPTER
14

Sunday night, Leo sent Big Al a text letting him know the lease agreement was ready to be signed, but got no response. An hour later, there was heavy knocking on the door. He answered it and found a stern-faced Stillwell on the other side. Stepping back to let him enter, Leo groused, "Why can't you ring the bell like normal people?"

"Because you might say you didn't hear it."

He sighed at the man's reasoning and led him into his office for the first time. He watched the farmer take in the expensive furniture, the tastefully displayed awards he'd received from Salem Oil, and the mahogany bookcases filled with books. Whether the farmer in his oil-stained overalls and denim jacket was impressed, he didn't let on. "Have a seat."

He sat and Leo slid the four-page document to him across the gleaming desk.

Stillwell picked it up. "Why so many pages?"

"Because it's a business agreement."

"I'll have it back to you in a couple of days."

"No. I need you to sign it now."

"Why?"

"Because my lawyer is relocating his office and anything that comes in after tomorrow gets put on the back burner for at least three months while the firm makes the transition. Also, the State of Kansas needs that filed in sixty days to make it legal, so it needs to be signed and sent tonight."

"I need someone to read me the fine print, so I'll know what's in it. I'm a farmer not a law professor."

"Do you want the lease or not? You not being able to read is not my problem."

Stillwell's furious face almost made Leo regret shaming the man the way he had. Almost. In truth, Stillwell's lack of comprehension was a gift that would keep on giving.

"How do I know you aren't cheating me?"

"I've nothing to gain from doing that. The last thing I want is you angry with me. You're a pretty scary dude, my friend." Leo gave him an innocent smile. "The agreement begins January first next year. That'll give me time to pack up and sell this place. If you want to buy the house, the arrangements are spelled out in the agreement, too."

"I don't. I'll probably tear it down."

Leo was appalled.

"What am I going to do with it?" Stillwell asked. "It's sitting on farmable land, and I'm definitely not going to live in it."

"I understand," Leo lied. All the more reason to get Stillwell to sign off now. The house was worth more than farming would bring in if the man planted soybean and corn for the next hundred years. The ignorance and shortsightedness of rubes like Stillwell never ceased to amaze, but Leo had no qualms taking advantage of them.

"Give me a pen and show me where to sign. And make me copies."

Leo paused, wondering if Stillwell could be talked out of the copies but decided it didn't matter. Once he signed the agreement it was over. He'd need a lawyer to contest it and Leo doubted Stillwell had the money to hire one with enough clout to get it thrown out.

Leo passed him a pen, told him where to sign, then made the requested copies, which Stillwell folded and put in the pocket of his dirty jacket.

Stillwell stood. "If you cheat me, I'll kill you, Brown."

Leo chuckled. "Don't be so dramatic."

"Do I look like I'm playing?"

Leo stiffened.

"My mother's in prison for the rest of her life. My daughter won't talk to me. Cheat me, and I'll gladly do the time because I'll have nothing left to live for."

The bridled violence in his glare made the hair stand on the back of Leo's neck. He forced himself not to shake. "I'm not going to cheat you."

"See that you don't."

And he walked out.

Leo's heart was still pounding when he heard the front door slam announcing Stillwell's exit.

Later, preparing to turn in, Leo had all but convinced himself Stillwell had been bluffing. No one in their right mind would make such a boldfaced threat. *Would they?*

He killed the lights and settled into his king-size bed. It took a long time for sleep to come.

As HALLOWEEN APPROACHED, pumpkins appeared on the porches in the subdivision and in the windows of the rec, the Dog, and the coffee shop. Costumes for the big party were given their last few touches and farmers were trucking in pumpkins for the carving contest. In keeping with his campaign of "Take a Gamble on July," Thad held a rally in the ballroom of one of Franklin's seedier hotels, complete with blackjack tables, poker games, and young women dressed like Vegas showgirls serving drinks. Many men came. Because there were also two slot machines on the premises, and slot machines not operated by a licensed casino were illegal, the motel management called the sheriff. Will Dalton and his deputies arrived and arrested everyone, including Thad, Diego, most of the other Julys, and two of the girls serving drinks for being underage.

Bernadine, seated at her desk Monday morning, viewed the anger in Tamar's eyes as she related the story. Bernadine knew better than to laugh but it was hard to keep a straight face. "Was Griffin there, too?"

"Of course not. He's the only one with sense. He tried to tell my brother the party was probably illegal, but when has Thaddeus ever listened? He told the hotel he was throwing a birthday party."

"Coyotes going to coyote."

That crack earned Bernadine a hot look from the town matriarch, so she apologized. "Sorry." She wondered if Mal had been hauled off to jail too but figured Tamar would've said that.

"So are they still locked up?"

"No. Griffin posted bail for Thad and the rest of his knuckleheads this morning. They go before Judge Amy in a couple of days. Will says they'll probably get off with just a fine."

"And a stern lecture from Judge Amy."

Tamar nodded.

"Is Thad going to stay in the race?"

"Who knows."

Bernadine's phone sounded. It was a text from Lily. She read it and said to Tamar, "Sheila and Riley are being interviewed at the Dog about the election by the local news." She picked up the remote and clicked on the flat screen.

On the screen, Sheila appeared poised as always and was focused on the young male reporter asking her about her campaign. She kept her responses informative but brief. Riley, on the other hand, kept looking into the camera while pontificating. His target—Thad's gambling party. "I knew July's campaign was a joke from the start. The authorities should lock him up and throw away the key. Is he really that dumb to think he could get away with something like that? When I win the mayor's race—"

The reporter cut him off. "I'm sorry, Mr. Curry. We've run out of time. Back to you guys at the studio."

Bernadine turned off the flat screen.

Tamar said, "He's really bucking to wind up on a flagpole, isn't he?"

"Riley's going to Riley."

LATER THAT AFTERNOON, Al Stillwell showed up in Bernadine's doorway and she froze. "Can I help you?"

"Need to talk to you about something."

Wary, she said, "Sure. Come on in."

He handed her some papers. "Leo Brown said he's going to lease my land back to me. This is supposedly the contract."

Bernadine took the document. "Why bring it to me?"

"Because you have lawyers and I don't, and I need to know if this is legit. I quit school when I was twelve to help my folks farm, so I don't read well."

Bernadine knew it must have cost him to admit that to her.

"I want your people to look it over. He told me I had to sign it right away because his lawyer was moving his office, or some crap."

"When did he give this to you?"

"Late last night."

"And you signed it then?"

"Yeah, in his fancy office. He told me it wouldn't go through the state if I didn't."

Now what, Leo? "Why bring this to me?"

"Like I said, you've got lawyers, I don't. And you owe me."

Bernadine met the challenge in his hostile eyes and thought back on the deadly havoc his mother had caused. He was big, had a violent temper, and in many ways scared her to death, but she didn't owe him a thing. "You believe I owe you. I don't. We'll agree to disagree. I'll have my people go over this. It may take a day or two, but honestly, if you've already signed it, you're going to need a lawyer if something's not right."

"I got a plan."

"Okay. Give me your contact information and I'll let you know what they think."

He wrote down his number and left without another word, which prompted her to sarcastically say, "You're welcome."

Sitting there, she leafed through the four pages and wondered again what Leo might be up to. Truthfully, the lease might not be anything more than what Leo claimed, and Stillwell was simply being paranoid, but if the wording did defraud him, then what? Leo had always been smart. As a man of color who'd climbed to the top rungs of the corporate ladder he had to be. He was also arrogant to a fault though, and when you consider yourself the smartest person in the room, you can be brought down by someone you consider intellectually beneath you because you're too busy smelling the rarefied air of your own inflated ego to see the attack coming. Not giving Stillwell an opportunity to have the lease looked at before signing was a definite red flag. Something wasn't right. Once again, she hoped Leo knew Big Al Stillwell wasn't someone to play with.

After sending the lease to her legal people, and calling Tina to catch her up on goings-on and to ask after Mimi, Bernadine decided to have lunch at the Dog. Usually she and Lily lunched together but Lily was wearing her campaign manager hat today. A local lady farmer invited Sheila to lunch at her home and to meet some of the woman's friends. Bernadine was pretty sure Sheila knew every man, woman, and child in the county, by now. For someone who'd seemed afraid of her own shadow when she first arrived in Henry Adams, her personal growth was an astonishing something to behold. Bernadine couldn't wait for her to win the election.

Bernadine decided to walk to the Dog. She needed the exercise and the fresh air. She was just about to leave when her sister, Diane, entered her office. "Hey," she said, caught by surprise. "What are you doing here? You didn't tell me you were coming."

Diane was fashionably dressed as always in a stunning pale-gold tunic over black leggings and a pair of black short-heeled booties. Her permed hair was on point as was her makeup and jewelry. The single life looked good on her.

"I'm off for the next couple of days. Just thought I'd make the drive over to see if we could do lunch and catch up. I'm doing me time."

"Self-care is vital. Glad to see you. I was on my way to the Dog. Do you want to eat there?"

"Sure. That works."

They'd had issues in the past because Diane was spoiled and had a sense of entitlement their parents had encouraged—which shredded Bernadine's self-esteem. Diane was thin. Bernadine was not. Diane was popular. Bernadine wasn't. When Diane's dentist husband, Harmon, divorced her after thirty-plus years of marriage, her world came crashing down, and she'd shown up at Bernadine's door a complete wreck. The visit, lasting weeks, hadn't gone well, but forced Diane to face reality and finally grow up. Now she had a new life in Topeka. They were on better terms as siblings, but a part of Bernadine kept her sister at arm's length because she still tended to be a spoiled entitled-acting witch.

Diane asked, "Do you want to drive or shall I?"

"I'd planned to walk, wanted to get some fresh air."

"I don't want to show up all hot and sweaty."

"It isn't a long walk."

"I know, but still."

Bernadine sighed inwardly. "Then I'll drive."

Having gotten her way, Diane smiled.

As always, the Dog was busy. It was lunchtime after all. The two sisters stood in line behind the people ahead of them while Sister Sledge's "We Are Family" blared from the candy apple red jukebox. Diane asked quietly, "Can't you pull rank or something, so we don't have to wait."

"No." Bernadine had no intentions of pissing off the people ahead of them by jumping the line.

The wait wasn't long. The hostess escorted them to a booth and promised to send a waitperson right over. Bernadine waved and nodded greetings to some of the people she knew, like Bing and Clay and Genevieve and Roni. Bernadine figured she probably knew every man, woman, and child in the county, too.

Mal walked up. "Ladies, good afternoon. How are you? What can I get you to drink?"

Before Bernadine could respond, Diane said, "You're just the person I wanted to see."

Mal glanced at Bernadine before asking, "And why is that?"

"For some reason, my calls to you are being blocked. Probably some glitch in your phone. Can you check it?"

"No need to. I told you the first time you called I wasn't interested in going out, but you kept calling."

Bernadine picked her jaw up off the table and stared at her sister.

Diane replied, "I thought you were just being coy or didn't want to have to listen to my sister complaining about us."

"There is no us. No means no, Diane. So can I bring you ladies something to drink?"

Pleased that Diane had been put in her place, Bernadine replied, "Some hot tea, please."

"Constant Comment with lemon?" he asked.

She nodded. It was her favorite.

"Diane?"

"Just bring me water. Thanks."

"Be right back."

Sulking, Diane picked up the menu. "I can't believe he blocked my calls."

Bernadine knew the menu like she knew her name, but she scanned it anyway and didn't say a word.

Diane added, "I mean, I have men coming out of my ears."

"Then maybe concentrate on them."

"Are you two back together?"

"That has nothing to do with this conversation."

"You are, aren't you?"

Bernadine didn't respond. Her private life was none of her sister's business.

"I suppose that explains it," Diane said, sounding miffed. "But the real question is, why he'd choose you over me? I'm still the beauty of the family."

Bernadine was accustomed to the insults. She'd been on the receiving end of them her entire life. Now that she was a far more confident adult, the digs were less painful, but still stung. She took the high road. "How are the kids?" She hadn't touched base with her niece, Monique, and her nephews, Harmon Jr. and Marlon, in weeks.

Diane continued to sulk. "They're fine. Marlon and Anthony are trying to adopt." Marlon and his partner, Anthony, lived in Hawaii.

Diane turned to Bernadine. "I just remembered I have an appointment scheduled this afternoon. I need you to drive me back to my car so I can go."

Liar liar pants on fire. "No. I'm here to have lunch. If you want to leave because of what happened with Mal, fine. Go. But you'll have to walk. Where you parked isn't that far."

"Mal has nothing to do with me leaving."

"Whatever you say, but I'm eating first. Walk or stay."

Diane picked up her handbag and scooted to the end of the bench. "You can be such a bitch."

"Bye, Diane."

She left the booth and moved swiftly to the exit.

Bernadine sighed and gazed out of the window to wait for her tea.

Mal returned carrying a tray holding a teapot, a cup, and her sister's glass of water. "Where's Diane?"

"Gone. She suddenly remembered an appointment back in Topeka."

He set the teapot and cup within reach. "Didn't like me calling her out?"

"No."

"She hurt your feelings before she left though, didn't she?"

"How'd you guess?"

"It's in your eyes, and seeing how I'm the one who hurt you the most recently, I should know what it looks like, don't you think?"

She was so moved by his admission she didn't know what to say.

He took the decision out of her hands by asking gently, "Ready to order?"

Still stunned, she was.

After taking down her request, he turned to go.

"Mal."

He stopped and looked back.

"Thank you."

"You're welcome."

Bernadine was partway through her turkey burger and

sweet potato fries when Riley entered the dining room, accompanied by Chauncey aka Chaunce Mayo, and a slick-haired, highly tanned, middle-aged man in a black pinstriped suit. She assumed the George Hamilton look-alike was the boss he'd told her about, or some other studio high muckety-muck. After the conversation with Mayo in her office, she couldn't believe he'd returned, but waited to see what this was about. Riley buttonholed Mal. They spoke and Riley gestured to the men as if making introductions. Mal nodded politely in response, but gave Riley a skeptical side-eye before walking over to the sound system. He cut the music, which of course got everyone's attention. He picked up the mic. "Can I have your attention for a minute? Riley has an announcement."

Bing shouted, "We're not voting for you!"

Laughter followed. Riley's jaw tightened. His accomplices looked caught off guard and warily scanned the faces of the small sea of people turned their way.

"This isn't about the election."

"Good! Because we're not voting for you!"

He waited for the second round of laughter to subside. "These men are from Hollywood."

Silence.

Riley cleared his throat. "As I said, they're from Hollywood, and they want to put Henry Adams on the map by throwing a parade down our Main Street for Cletus to celebrate his Oscar nomination!"

Bernadine was outdone by them thinking they could use this method to circumvent her nixing the parade. She didn't have to worry, however. The boos and catcalls were instantaneous.

Genevieve called out, "Is that killer hog going to be on a spit?"

The Hollywood duo now appeared shocked. Riley tried to soldier on, explaining how much fun the parade would be, but by then, the pushback was so loud, Bernadine couldn't hear a word he was saying. *I tried to warn them.*

A red-faced Mayo tugged Riley's sleeve and said something. Riley handed Mal the mic, and he and his crew quick-stepped it to the exit to the cheers and thunderous applause of the diners.

Bernadine returned to her lunch. *Lesson learned.*

AT THE TOWN meeting that evening, the department heads gave their reports, a sheet was passed around to get the names of seniors needing absentee ballots for the election, and after, Trent asked Sheila to come up to the podium. Her first words were "This has nothing to do with the election."

The responding cheers brought out her smile. "I'm here in my capacity as the VP of social affairs to talk about Halloween."

More cheers.

"Halloween is this Saturday and we'll be having our first Henry Adams costume party night and a pumpkin-carving contest. Tamar came up with the theme, which is superheroes and kids' movies. Those who have not made prior arrangements for your costumes with our Mistress of Needles, Gemma Dahl, too late. She's not taking any more orders."

"No, I'm not," she called out. "Done. Finished. Tired."

"For the pumpkin-carving contest, there will be one prize for those over eighteen and one for under. Grand prize for

both will be a fifty-dollar gift card courtesy of Clark's Grocery." Murmurs of approval moved through the room.

She added, "That gift card might be a great down payment
on your Thanksgiving dinner so be sure you enter. Thanks,
Gary."

"You're welcome," he called out from his seat.

"After you get your pumpkin carved, if you aren't going
to use the guts, please put them in a Ziploc bag and bring
them here. Rocky and her staff are going to roast the seeds for
snacks that will be available for free while supplies last, and
the rest will be pureed and put into soups, muffins, donuts,
and other tasty things that will be put on the menu. As most
of you know, the pumpkins are on the grounds behind the
rec. You can pick up yours anytime if you're entering the contest, but it needs to be back to rec by noon if you're entering
the judging. Any questions?"

There weren't any, so she returned to her seat.

Trent thanked her and asked, "Any other new business or
concerns before I end the meeting?"

No one spoke up, so he brought down the gavel.

As Sheila walked with her men to Barrett's truck, she
asked, "Have either of you ever carved a pumpkin?"

Barrett cracked, "That's not a skill called for by the Marine
Corps."

Preston grinned. "Not many carved in the inner city of
Milwaukee, either."

"Then we should enter. Barrett, please stop by the rec on
the way home and we'll get one apiece."

Preston looked pleased.

Barrett didn't.

"It'll be fun," she promised.

He looked doubtful and asked, "Have you ever carved one?"

"No, but I'm not deterred by that. I still think it'll be fun."

"Okay, Ms. Soon-to-Be Mayor."

The Payne family joined the rest of the town's citizens in the field behind the rec to pick out a pumpkin. They were of varying sizes and spread out on the ground as if still waiting to be harvested. As the Paynes came alongside Gemma and her kids, Sheila asked Jasmine if she'd ever carved before.

"Yes, ma'am. Lucas and I got pumpkins every year."

Barrett asked, "Any advice?"

Lucas said, "Find one that's sort of firm on the outside, so the carving goes easier and lasts longer. And the bigger they are, the more guts they have."

Preston tossed back, "Pumpkin carving, time shares in Maui and Disneyworld. Is there anything you two kazillionaires haven't done?"

Lucas laughed. "Quit hating." Lucas and his sister, Jasmine, were very wealthy as a result of their late parents' estate.

Jaz added, "Yeah. You just work on figuring out a way for us to time travel, Mr. Wizard."

The Paynes laughed and continued their search. They finally found what they hoped were three good candidates. After helping themselves to the carving tools and design printouts offered, they drove home.

While Sheila went upstairs to prepare for another day on the campaign trail tomorrow, and Preston went to FaceTime his friends, Barrett poured himself a small shot of bourbon, took a seat on the living room sofa, and reflected on his day. He'd had his second session with Paula earlier. With her gentle guidance he'd unpacked some of the baggage he'd been carrying around since his teen years. Most of it had to do with his father's abuse of his mother and himself. Talking about it had been painful but also cathartic as Paula helped him unravel the knots tied around his emotions. With her he was able to see that following his father and grandfather into the service and becoming a warrior made him believe his hurt and pain could be ignored because acknowledging such things were for the soft, not the strong. He hadn't allowed himself to grieve when his mother died or feel anything after his father's fading health forced him into an assisted-living facility, a facility Barrett wasn't allowed to visit because his father refused to see him. Paula pointed out the likelihood of that stemming from his father being ashamed and embarrassed by his decline and inability to take care of himself. Being infirm was for the weak, not the strong. And for Barrett it all made sense. Finally. The entire time growing up, he'd been at the mercy of a man who used the power of his fists to prove his manhood and superiority. After a catastrophic stroke, his father needed help with everything from using the toilet to eating. There was no superiority in that. He'd lived for three years after the stroke but they never once spoke, visited, or shared a smile. Barrett wondered if his father really wanted to die estranged and alone. There was no way of knowing but Barrett was certain it was not something he wished for himself. He thought about Preston. His son had made him not only a good father but also a better person. Might he have been able to do the same for his own father, given the opportunity? He'd like to think the answer would've been yes, but unfortunately, he'd never know that either and that was painful, as well.

Barrett realized he hadn't touched the drink, but that

didn't matter. He got up and went upstairs. He knocked on Preston's open door.

Preston was at his desk. He glanced away from his laptop. "Hey, Pops."

"Hey, son. Can I bother you for a minute?"

"Sure. What's up?"

"Just came up to say thanks for making me a good dad and a better person."

Preston scanned his face. "Are you okay? You're not getting ready to die on me and Mom, are you?"

He smiled. "No, son. Just have had a couple of talks with Paula."

"Helped you figure out some stuff?"

"Yes. Most of it dealing with my father, so I wanted to let you know what a great son I think you are."

"Thanks. I appreciate that. And thanks for adopting me. No telling where I'd be if Ms. Bernadine hadn't brought me here. Dead maybe."

Barrett had never met a more honestly frank young man. "It would've been my loss, so I'm glad you're here, too. I'll let you get back to what you were doing."

"Okay. And Pops, thanks for letting me know how you feel. That means a lot."

"You're welcome."

Barrett entered his bedroom to find Sheila on the love seat, surrounded by papers and wearing her reading glasses. He smiled at that. His lovely wife was a bit vain and rarely wore them outside the house. She was so focused on the laptop beside her, a few seconds passed before she noticed his presence. She finally glanced up. "Hey."

"Hey. What are you doing?"

"Pulling together the information on the state's wind energy initiative. I'm meeting with some farmers tomorrow who're interested in signing up."

"That's such a great idea."

"I agree. What're you up to?"

"Just left Preston. Wanted to thank him for making me a better dad and a better person."

She eyed him speculatively for a moment before asking, "Did you have another session with Paula?"

"I did and she's helping me be a better dad, husband, person—all of that."

"I'm glad it's working out."

"So am I. I want to apologize again for all the years I made you feel small and unseen. You deserved so much more."

"We're moving forward and that's what counts. No more apologies needed. Okay?"

"Okay." He'd told Paula about his affair and the depth of his remorse. Sheila's willingness to forgive was the most cherished gift he'd ever received. "You go back to what you were doing. Let me know when you're done."

"Will do."

He left her alone and went downstairs. Being able to move forward was a gift as well.

CHAPTER
15

Friday morning, Bernadine was already at her desk with her coffee and laptop when Lily arrived for work. "Morning, Lil."

"Hey, Bernadine. How are you?"

"Okay. Just got the report back on the contract Leo had Big Al sign."

Lily walked fully into the office. "Is it legit?"

"If you call cheating him via convoluted legalese legit."

Lily sighed. "Al's going to Hulk smash him."

"I know. I sent Al a text a little while ago. He'll be by later this morning." Bernadine remembered something she'd been meaning to ask Lily. "What happened with your secret spy friend? Have you heard anything more from her?"

"No. She quit a few days ago. Leo tried to hit on her."

"Good lord."

"I know. He asked her if she wanted a raise, and told her what she had to do to get it. She quit on the spot."

"Leo is such a dog."

"Yes, he is. She said when she told her husband about the come-on, she had to keep him from riding down on Leo and kicking his behind."

"Well, I believe he's digging his own grave with this seed business, so we don't really need any further inside information at this point." Putting her ex out of her mind, Bernadine shifted gears. "Are you ready for the Halloween party?"

"I am. My costume is ready to go."

"So is mine." The costumes were supposed to be secret, so she and everyone else in town were anxiously awaiting the big reveals.

"And you and Mal?" Lily asked. "What's up with that?"

Bernadine paused, thinking over her reply. "Let's just say we're trying to figure things out."

"I have a thousand questions, but I'll keep them to myself."

Bernadine's smile curved her lips. "Thanks, Lily."

"You're welcome. Okay, I'm off to turn my parts of the world. See you later."

After Lily departed, Bernadine admittedly had a thousand questions of her own about the road she and Mal were on. That they were no longer on one headed for hell was a good thing. She was still moved by his words at the Dog about being able to see the hurt in her eyes, and she wasn't sure why. Maybe because his insight had been so unexpected or because his words finally convinced her that he did understand how damaging his betrayal had been. Whatever the reason, another one of the barriers she'd erected between them fell at that moment, joining a few others that silently crumbled the day they flew the kites.

Her reverie was interrupted by a knock. It was Marie Jefferson. "Morning, Marie."

"Hey. Do you have a few minutes?"

"Sure, come on in. Sit. Can I get you some coffee?"

"No thanks."

"What can I do for you?"

"I've decided to go ahead and have the gas extracted next spring, but I need a lawyer or two, or three. Can you help me with that?"

"I can. Having good legal advice is always the way to go. Do you want me to see if I can find you an industry expert you can hire as an adviser who can answer your questions about the process or the science or anything else you may have concerns about? The person can also be your advocate if anything sticky comes up."

"Hadn't thought about having an advocate. That's a great idea. May need a financial adviser, too."

"I'll see about hooking you up with both."

"Thanks."

"What do you want to do about the land transfer? The taxes are paid. I'm assuming you no longer want to sell."

"No, I don't. At least not right now, but I would like it put into some kind of trust after I die."

"We'll get the lawyers to look into that, too."

She nodded thanks and added softly, "Last month I was looking the poorhouse in the face. Now?"

"As Reverend Paula would say: God always shows up on time."

"Amen," Marie replied. "Thanks for everything."

"You're welcome."

Marie stood. "Let me get over to the rec before Tamar sends the bloodhounds after me. I volunteered to help her and her crew with the decorations for the Halloween party."

"Okay. I'll let you know when I get your team hooked up."

"Great. See you later."

"Bye, Marie."

Bernadine was pleased that everything had worked out for Marie. Over the years, they'd had a few differences, but she was a vital member of the community and Henry Adams needed what she brought to the table, educationally and historically.

In anticipation of Al Stillwell's arrival, Bernadine printed out the contract and the notes her legal people had attached. She was certain Stillwell wouldn't be pleased by what the note contained. That he'd be needing a top-notch lawyer to get him out of the already signed contract was a given. She hoped he had sense enough to direct his anger at Leo and not her way.

Big Al showed up a bit before lunchtime. She'd heard he was living in Oklahoma and working for one of the oil companies there, which may or may not account for the stained and dirty clothing he always wore.

"So, what did your people say?" he asked.

She handed him the document and the notes. "That the contract entitles you to lease ten acres."

"What!" he shouted. "He was supposed to lease me the entire two hundred."

"You signed for ten. You'll be needing a good lawyer to challenge it, though. According to the notes they sent along, there's a clause buried in the wording that says any challenge you bring will forfeit the agreement in its entirety."

"That bastard!"

Bernadine agreed.

"This can't be legal."

"My people didn't speak to that. But you need to obtain representation as quickly as possible."

"I can't afford a fancy lawyer."

Bernadine remained silent. She'd had the contract evaluated and wouldn't be offering further assistance. The last thing she needed was drama tied to Leo Brown leaking into her life. Stillwell was on his own.

He stood. The tense set of his jaw and the fire in his eyes spoke to his mood. "I have to work tonight so I need to get back." He turned and left.

In the silence after his exit, Bernadine offered another sarcastic, "You're welcome."

Lily's voice came over the intercom. "I'm ordering lunch from the Dog. Do you want something?"

Bernadine had planned to walk to the diner for lunch but looking out the window at the driving rain changed her mind. She gave Lily her order and went back to work.

A short while later, a knock broke her concentration and she looked up to see Mal in her doorway. In his hand was a white plastic bag.

"Brought your lunch."

"Thanks." She rose to take it. She hadn't seen him since the day of her sister's visit.

"Diane make it home okay?"

She nodded. "She sent a text when she arrived. As much as she likes to one-up me, I'm surprised she didn't tell me she was trying to talk to you."

"Maybe my lack of enthusiasm had something to do with it."

"Maybe." She took the plunge and asked, "If Tamar doesn't work us to the bone this evening, do you want to go for coffee after we're done at the rec?" Tamar had volunteered everyone to help set up for the Halloween party.

"Sure. At the Dog?"

She thought about all the gossip that would cause. "How about my place instead? A lot less staring."

His eyes showed he understood. "Sure. I'd like that. You can catch me up on your week."

"And you can do the same for me."

They viewed each other silently for a few moments. Bernadine sensed barriers dropping right and left.

"I'll see you later," he said.

"Okay."

And he was gone. She didn't know if what she'd proposed was a date, but they'd agreed to not give their new path a name, so she'd stick to calling it, just coffee.

THE WORKDAY WAS winding down, so as Riley swept up the area around his chair, he was looking forward to the weekend. He had no plans to attend the town's Halloween party Saturday night. Still stung by the vocal drubbing he and the movie producers received at the Dog, he wanted nothing to do with anyone in town. Once he won the election he planned to hand out a bunch of payback to people like his ex-wife and that old pest Bing Shepard. In the meantime, he'd be treating himself to some popcorn and camping out in front of his television to watch the first annual Animal Oscar Ball being shown live later on the Animal Planet channel. Cletus, the other nominees, their trainers, and a host of celebrities and industry people would be attending the black tie affair. Yesterday evening, he'd watched the Cletus Goes Home homecoming parade. Mayo and his staff shot the event on a Hollywood lot made up to look like a typical small town. There were floats, a high school band, and a small crowd of paid extras posing as Henry Adams citizens. Riley was saddened by the fact that he hadn't been invited but took great satisfaction in booing loudly at the television when the camera showed trainer Ben Scarsdale, arm in a sling, waving from Cletus's corn-and-hay-filled float. Cletus was dressed up in denim overalls and a straw hat. Although Riley continued to miss him terribly, he hoped his hog was enjoying his fame and time in the spotlight.

With his work area now clean, Riley removed his smock, placed it in the hamper, and walked over to get his check from Kelly. She'd been standoffish all week, which he attributed to him calling out her gangbanger husband, but he couldn't help it if the truth hurt.

She handed him the check and picked up her coat and purse. They were closing early for the Halloween weekend goings-on. Riley looked up from the dollar amount shown on his paycheck in confusion. "This isn't right. It's eighty dollars short."

"Correct. It's to make up for the five dollars here and there you've been stealing and putting in your pocket."

His heart stopped.

"Not sure why you thought I wouldn't notice. Because I know you aren't making a lot here, I've been letting it go. I figured you needed it for stuff like gas, but when you come for my Bobby like you did at that debate, I come for you."

He silently prayed she hadn't called the sheriff.

"And look up there."

He followed her red-nailed finger to a small black button above the doorframe. "That's a camera I had Mr. Payne install just for you. Have a good weekend."

Riley's hands shook as he put the check in his wallet. Taking his jacket down from the coat-tree, he left the shop without a word.

To make himself feel better, Riley paid a visit to his billboard. Parking his car on the side of the busy highway, he got out. He never tired of seeing his handsome confident face, and as he admired himself, the heart-stopping panic Kelly caused slowly dissipated. He reasoned that if he was paid more, he wouldn't have had to supplement his measly salary. Viewing his face for a few moments more, he got back in his rattling old car and drove home.

By the time he had dinner and popped his corn, Kelly was no longer on his mind. Remote in hand, he settled in on his couch and clicked on the TV and Animal Planet.

It was a red carpet event. There were actors in tuxedos and pretty actresses in glittering designer gowns. The lady commentator spoke with the producer of Cletus's movie, Alvin Malone, and his young blond wife, Helga, clad in a shimmering pink gown. Malone was the very tanned man who'd accompanied Chaunce Mayo to the Dog earlier in the week. Having met him, Riley felt like a Hollywood insider. Their interview done, the Malones went on their way and were followed by other top-notch industry people. And then, much to the delight of the people behind the barriers that lined the carpet, the nominees arrived. Cletus strutted into view wearing a black tux with tails and dark glasses. Riley cheered. His hog was dressed similarly to the way he'd been attired for his wedding to Eustacia Pennymaker's pet sow, Chocolate.

Riley wondered if Eustacia was watching. He wanted to call her and find out but remembered she told him to never contact her again after he reached out to her a few weeks ago to ask if she'd contribute to his campaign. Her loss, he figured. The commentator was now talking with Riley's nemesis, Ben Scarsdale. His arm still in a sling. When asked about it, the trainer attributed the injury to the fall he'd taken on the daytime television show a few weeks back. Riley took a perverse pleasure in having seen it happen. Then the mic was lowered to Cletus. She asked him how he felt about his nomination and all the hoopla tied to the event. Cletus replied with a happy squeal. Riley was so proud tears stung his eyes.

Cletus and Scarsdale went on their way and were followed by the other nominees: Brutus the goat, Charley the chimp wearing a tux and white sneakers, a pit bull named Maxine, and Feathers, a red-tailed hawk. Riley had seen all their movies and enjoyed them but expected Cletus to walk away with the award for Best Actor and Best Picture. Hands down.

The lady commentator and her camera crew moved into the ballroom where the gala was being held. There were huge pictures of the animal actors on the walls. A quartet on the stage played classical music and the guests mixed and mingled, while white-coated waitpeople floated through the crowd carrying trays holding drinks and frou-frou bites to eat. The animals being feted strolled through the room. Cletus walked beside Scarsdale, while the chimp and goat walked with their female handlers. The pit bull was on a pink ribbon-like leash. Feathers rode on the shoulders of his tuxedo-wearing trainer. The lady commentator stopped the Malones as they spoke with Scarsdale.

"Mrs. Malone, can I get you to pose with Cletus?"

Mrs. Malone gave the reporter a fake smile and declined but her husband encouraged her. Obviously not happy, she bent low, put her hand on Cletus's neck and the hog bit her on her thigh. She screamed and jumped. Furious, she smacked Cletus hard on the head with the program in her hand. Cletus protested with an angry squeal and charged her, knocking her to the floor. Her outraged husband kicked Cletus in the side, reached down to help his wife, only to have Cletus sink his sharp teeth into the man's hand. Malone howled and tried to free his fingers, but Cletus wouldn't let go. The one-armed Scarsdale attempted to grab Cletus, only to be bitten, too. Squealing, Cletus went on a rampage, knocking over tables, using his bulk against guests and waiters. Women screamed, trying to get out of his path. A few men tried to corral him, but wound up being chomped on as well. Pandemonium ensued as Brutus the goat joined the melee, biting and ramming. Charley the chimp broke away from his trainer and began throwing whatever he could get his hands on: the plastic champagne glasses, dropped purses, the frou-frou appetizers, and the small plates from the trays abandoned by the terrorized waitstaff. Feathers took to the air and began dive-bombing the guests now running in panic to the exits. A wide-eyed Riley jumped to his feet. His popcorn fell to the floor. The scene was a madhouse. Women in stilettos fell off their shoes in the stampede to the doors. Men stopped to help them up, only to be bowled over by other guests intent upon fleeing for their lives. Someone pulled the fire alarm and while it clanged, the camera showed people holding programs over their heads to protect themselves from the attacking hawk. The only animal that didn't go berserk was Maxine the pit bull. She sat calmly on the stage with her trainer and the gaping classical quartet.

The lady commentator did her best to report on the chaos, but as she wrestled with Charley the chimp for possession of her microphone, she was butted from behind by Brutus and the feed died.

Speechless, Riley eyed the black screen and fell back onto the couch.

The spectacle, which had streamed live, immediately lit up social media platforms worldwide. Television programs were interrupted by stern-faced anchors while chyrons touting Breaking News scrolled across the screen. Cable news networks promised live reports as soon as their crews were in place. Inside the rec, the people of Henry Adams getting the gym ready for the Halloween party watched the ball via the flat screen. When the screen went black, they were so stunned by the pandemonium, no one made a sound at first, and then, they laughed until they almost fell down.

Afterward, at home, Bernadine made coffee, while jazz played softly and Mal hung out at the counter. "So how many lawsuits do you think Cletus's studio will be dealing with by this time tomorrow?" she asked.

"Probably one for every person there. That hog's been involved with some crazy stuff over the years, but that mess tonight had to be the craziest."

She chuckled. "It really was." When the coffee maker was done, she grabbed one filled cup, Mal took the other, and they sat at her dining table.

"I did feel sorry for all the people he chomped on. No telling what kind of germs that hog has in his mouth."

"I'm sure Scarsdale had him vaccinated, because there are diseases that can jump from animals to humans. They're rare though, but one not so rare is rabies."

"Yikes."

"After what we saw tonight, I don't think they'll be awarding Cletus anything but a one-way ticket to a sausage-making factory."

She laughed. "As long as they don't send him back here, I'm okay with whatever happens to him."

"Me, too." He took a short sip, before asking quietly, "So how are you doing turning the world?"

She answered truthfully, "I'm good. Trying not to work myself into a heart attack. I've stopped bringing work home on weekends."

He raised his cup. "Congrats. That's a good thing."

"Makes me a bit anxious, still, but I'm getting better at just sitting. What about you?"

"Still hoping folks will forgive a foolish old man. Seeing Paula once a week to try and work out how I got myself in this mess."

Bernadine stilled. She'd had no idea he'd been seeing Paula.

"Talking to her was easier than I thought it would be, maybe because I've had to put myself on the line at AA all these years. Men tend to bullshit themselves about their insecurities and whatever else they have going on inside, and sometimes all that denial leads to doing stupid stuff like my embezzling. More men need to sit down with someone like Paula. She's been a big help."

She didn't know what to say.

"I'm not telling you this to get pity strokes. Just letting you know what's going on with me."

"Okay." Bernadine was impressed, though. Very much so. A few months ago, Mal had acted as if a slap on the wrist was all he deserved for his crime. When no one agreed, he tried wallowing in victimhood, which made his relationships go from bad to worse. Getting his nose broken from a sucker punch and having an angry Luis call him out apparently forced him to take an honest look at himself in the mirror. She assumed he hadn't liked what he'd seen if he was talking to Paula, and she had to give him props for that.

So they sat, drank coffee, and talked about everything and nothing: Tina's rehabbing mom, the nefarious Leo and his equally nefarious pipeline plan, the latest on the Three Spinsters, the election, and Halloween.

Bernadine asked, "Did you all ever have Devil's Night in Henry Adams?"

"No. Never heard of it until I saw the pictures of Detroit burning itself down."

"It didn't start out that way. When I was growing up, Devil's Night was a night for pranks. Trash cans turned over, soaping people's windows—that kind of stuff. Of course, my parents never let their daughters participate."

"So how did it turn into houses being set on fire."

"Arson. Tied to suburban folks wanting to get rid of their abandoned Detroit property. You pay someone to torch your place, get a fat check from your insurance company, and you walk away."

"Wow. Never knew that, but no Devil's Night here. We did trick or treat when we were growing up, but once people began moving away, and there were fewer places to go, my friends would come to Tamar's or to Marie's and we'd do stuff like bobbing for apples, play hide-and-seek in the dark, cook hot dogs outside—if it wasn't raining or snowing."

Bernadine thought back and replied wistfully, "Our streets would be filled with kids. No one could afford real store-bought costumes, so you'd dress up with whatever you could find at home. I went as my daddy one year. Wore one of his old coats and a hat. Momma used a piece of charcoal to draw me a mustache and a beard."

They shared a smile.

"So do you have your costume for tomorrow?" she asked.

"I do. You?"

"Yes."

"And it is?"

"You'll have to wait until tomorrow. It's supposed to be a surprise, remember?"

"Okay, be that way, then."

She was enjoying his company and he seemed to be enjoying hers.

When time came for him to leave, she walked him to the door.

"Thanks for the coffee," he said quietly.

"You're welcome."

"Would it be okay if we had dinner Sunday?"

"Your place or here?"

"Here, if you'd be more comfortable."

"I would. How about we have Crystal cook if she's not busy?"

"That works for me."

"Okay. I'll see you at the party tomorrow and we'll talk about time and all that."

His eyes and voice softened. "This was fun."

"I had a good time, too."

"You take care."

"You, too."

And he was gone.

She closed the door and stood there for a moment. Another step forward in whatever they were doing, and she was okay with that.

As MEGA SEED president Virgil Quelp angrily berated Leo on the phone, Leo ran a hand over his perspiring face. "No, sir. I didn't know someone here had sent the seeds out to be tested. Yes, sir, totally my fault. Totally."

The verbal flogging continued. Quelp called him incompetent and inept and promised Leo he'd never work anywhere ever again if he didn't get the mess with the seed fixed. "Yes, sir. I understand the importance of what the company is trying to achieve and how crucial this mission is."

In truth, Leo wanted to tell him to go to hell but knew he'd be fired in a heartbeat and he needed his job. "Of course, sir. I'll take care of it right away. I'll have it done by end of business on Monday. Yes, sir. I won't let you down."

The call finally ended, and Leo threw the phone across the room. He didn't know what caught him more off guard—the fact that someone had sent seed samples to the college for testing or that Quelp knew about it and Leo hadn't. Either way he was caught between a rock and a hard place and didn't have a clue as to how to make it all go away. He got up and poured a hefty amount of cognac into a glass. As he tossed it back, he thought about how the well-heeled burn of the aged liquor would be one of the things he'd be giving up if he couldn't find a way out of this mess. Quelp and the men in charge of Salem Oil were influential enough to ensure he'd have trouble finding work as an elementary-school cafeteria worker if they put the word out on him. In reality, Leo realized his plan had been doomed from the start, mainly because he'd considered himself so much smarter than the people he'd been sent in to scam. That and the fact that he'd hitched his wagon to the annoying little madman Riley Curry. Thinking of Curry, Leo remembered the Hollywood ball the hog was supposed to be attending and he checked his watch. The event was undoubtedly over, so he opened his laptop to see if he could catch a replay. He found it, and as he sipped his cognac and watched the horror unfold, his jaw dropped. A knock at his door interrupted his viewing. Wondering who it could be at this hour, he looked through the peephole and sighed. Pulling the door open, he started to chew out the person on the other side, only to have a fist explode in his face. He was out cold before he hit the floor.

THE NEXT MORNING, it appeared as if Devil's Night had come to Henry Adams. While folks were sleeping, someone climbed up to Riley's billboard and added hog's ears and a snout to his face. The transformation was so well done, it was obviously the work of a person with artistic skill. The sight drew morning television news reporters to the spot and caused a big backup on the highway from gawking drivers. Riley's campaign posters in town were given the same piggy makeover. Views of his pranked face drew amused head shakes and laughter from those watching the reports over breakfast at the Dog. However, Riley, upon seeing it on his TV, was hopping mad. He called Leo, got no response, so he called Sheriff Will Dalton who came out to take the report. Riley insisted the Julys were the culprits and wanted every last one of them arrested. Will asked for proof. Riley had none. Will took down the report and went out to Tamar's. No Julys confessed, so he cautioned Thad and his kin as he always did when they were in town and drove back to his office.

At noon everyone gathered in the chilly wind outside the Dog to check out the pumpkins entered in the contest. Some were great like the one Crystal did of a dragon, and the nice traditional jack-o'-lantern carved by Reverend Paula and Robyn. Leah's E = mc2, was placed next to Preston's very lopsided rendition of Saturn. Wyatt did a map of the state of Kansas, and Zoey's had a music staff and notes. The July entry was an amazingly detailed smiling coyote seated next to a pig on a spit. Sheila took one look at it and declared, "We have a winner!" In agreement, applause, hoots, and hollers filled the air.

That evening, the gym at the rec was filled with costumed residents who'd come to celebrate Halloween. Henry Adams had never thrown a celebration quite like it. There was music, dancing, laughter, games, and with the theme of Comics, Disney, and Superheroes, Bernadine thought it was a big hit. The gym had been thematically transformed by pumpkins, ghosts, skeletons, and ugly witches standing over cauldrons bubbling smoke from dry ice. One corner of the room resembled a graveyard with fake stones and a tree filled with spooky-eyed black cats, while fake spiderwebs hung from the ceiling. Many in the Ladies Auxiliary dressed up as Disney villainesses. She'd come as Ursula from the *Little Mermaid*, and with her blue body suit, white wig, and matching blue eye shadow she thought she was pretty fly. Also looking good was Roni Garland as Hela from *Ragnarok*. Wearing all black and sporting a black antler headpiece, she was ready to take on Thor and anyone else who got in her way. Gen sashayed in as Cruella, complete with white fake fur coat, two-toned hair, and a long cigarette holder. Any dalmatians in the area were in danger.

Lily, as Maleficent, came over to where Bernadine stood and shouted over the voices and music, "This is wild!"

"I know!" she said, laughing. "So much fun!"

Marie, wearing green face paint and the black dress and hat of the Wicked Witch of the West, snarled at them and shook her broom as she passed by. Luis, decked out as T'Challa, gave them the Wakanda Forever salute. Beside him, his son, Alfonso, who looked like Harry Potter all the time, came as Harry Potter, armed with a wand. His daughter was dressed as the Easter Bunny.

Mal strolled by in a black leather coat and the black eye patch of Nick Fury. He gave Bernadine a sexy wink and she melted like a teenager. An amused Lily shook her head. "You two are a mess."

Bernadine simply smiled in response and took in some of the other costumes. Gemma, who'd done most of the sewing, was dressed as Cinderella and wearing a lovely yellow ball gown. Beside her was her handsome Prince Charming, Mike Freewater decked out in a Marine dress uniform. Tamar, with her silver hair streaming down her back and wearing her silver bangles and an African print caftan, looked as she did all the time, but she told everyone she was N'Dare, the Kenyan mother of superheroine Storm. Sheila drifted over to say hello. She'd come as Nubia, Wonder Woman's twin sister. Beside her, Barrett was dressed in a pair of jeans, a tee, and a gray hoodie.

Confused by his attire, Bernadine asked, "You decided not to dress up?"

"I'm Luke Cage."

Sheila rolled her eyes. "In other words, he decided not to dress up."

"Hey!" he said in mock defense.

Bernadine and Lily laughed.

Across the room was the apple-bobbing station. Wyatt, dressed like Iron Man, knelt beside the tub and removed his helmet. His fake Tony Stark mustache and goatee made those nearby almost fall over laughing.

On the far side of the room, a blindfolded Devon, dressed as James Brown, complete with cape and perm, was trying to hit the suspended piñata. "I thought the theme was Comics, Movies, and Disney," Bernadine said to Lily.

"I know, but Devon is going to do Devon. Just like Zoey will always do Zoey." Miss Miami had come as one of her superheroes—Beethoven. Somebody else doing their own thing was Preston. He'd come as Albert Einstein. He and Zoey appeared to have gotten their wild-looking gray wigs from the same store. Trent was Inspector Gadget. As he walked by, he playfully flashed Lily with his trench coat and she choked on her punch laughing.

"That's your husband," Bernadine cracked.

Crystal was Cat Woman, the Eartha Kitt version. Amari added to the original Batman theme by being the Frank Gorshin Riddler in a green bowler and green suit covered with purple question marks. Thad rolled in as the pope. He was dressed in a white robe and had a miter atop his braids. Tamar was not amused.

Reverend Paula arrived as the female version of Bass Reeves, Indian Territory's most famous Black deputy US marshal. She explained that some historians believed Reeves to have been the true life model for the Lone Ranger. In her Stetson, jeans, vest, and star, she looked ready to arrest any outlaws on the premises. Seeing her made Bernadine remember the interest Thornton Webb had in her during his visit, and she wondered if he did take the job, how that interest might play out, if at all. Robyn, in a red leather hoodie, a black tee, and jeans, carried a black sword. She explained to Bernadine and Lily that she was Alice, a teen monster fighter from one of her favorite books: *A Blade So Black*. Jack James strolled by as Sherlock Holmes, complete with a houndstooth coat, hat, and the signature pipe. Beside him Rocky, wearing a big Afro wig and a short rabbit fur jacket, strutted as Cleopatra Jones. Teacher Kyrie Abbott wowed the crowd as Marvel's Sam Wilson aka the Falcon. And yes, the costume had wings.

The Best Costume award for the young people went to Jasmine dressed as Shuri, from *Black Panther*. Tiffany had come as Shuri as well and was so put out by Jaz wearing the same thing, she angrily demanded her dad take her home. Gary refused. Her pouting and bad attitude did win her something though—a spot in the kitchen on trash detail for the rest of the party, courtesy of Tamar.

Gen as Cruella and Kyrie as the Falcon tied for Best Adult costume and received rounds of applause and the gift certificates from Clark's Grocery.

Throughout the evening, Bernadine's attention kept straying Mal's way, and each time, his patched eye was waiting.

The first time it happened she was embarrassed to be caught, but then gave in and let herself look her fill while he did the same. Later, when Smokey's voice began to croon "Ooo Baby Baby," he walked over. "Will you dance with me?"

She nodded. As they found a spot in the middle of the floor, every eye in the place turned their way. Noticing the smiles and hearing the small smattering of applause, she said, "You'd think they'd have something better to do."

Holding her close, he moved them slowly to the beat. "Small-town folks. What're you going to do."

What she did was ignore them and savor how nice slow dancing with him felt. Hearing Smokey singing about his mistakes made it seem as if the lyrics were speaking directly to her and Mal. Dancing with him was so nice in fact, they stayed on the floor through two more songs until BTS began to play and the young ones took over.

"What time do you want to have dinner?" he asked escorting her back to her spot.

"Six?"

"Sounds good. I'm heading home. Need my beauty sleep." He looked down and said with a sincerity she felt in her bones, "Thanks for the dance."

"You're welcome. See you tomorrow."

As she watched him leave, Lily, who'd been dancing with Trent, walked up and said, "You two really need to tie the knot and be done, you know that, right?"

"Get behind me, Satan, and hush."

"I'm just saying."

Bernadine rolled her eyes and watched the young people on the floor, but Lily's words stayed with her for the rest of the evening.

CHAPTER
16

S unday morning, Riley was tired of Leo Brown not answering his calls or texts, so he got in his car and drove to
the mansion. He wanted to know if Sheriff Dalton had spoken
to him about the report he'd filed, and if Leo knew a lawyer who'd take on the lawsuit he wanted to bring against the
Julys for suffering and mental anguish. Newspeople from as
far away as New York City called all day Saturday asking for
Riley's reactions to Cletus's rampage at the ball and the defac-
ing of his billboard. Snapping "No comment," he'd hung up
each time. That evening, after he was sure the interest from
gawkers had died down, he'd driven out to the billboard to
get a firsthand look. It was even worse than he'd imagined.
Gone was his classic pose. Gone was his look of strength. In
their place was the head of a hog that resembled an eerie cross
between Cletus and himself. He had a snout, hair-tipped ears,
little piggy eyes, and a grinning mouth filled with misshapen
teeth. It was so hideous, he wanted to cry. He'd bet every dime
he'd borrowed from Genevieve's bank accounts that the Julys

were responsible—even if he didn't have proof. He'd gazed up at the sick joke for a few more minutes, cursing the Julys the entire time, then drove home.

Now, as he pulled into the driveway of Brown's mansion, Riley hoped his campaign manager had a plan for what to do about it all. The election was next week. The billboard needed to be taken down or painted over, and his vandalized campaign signs needed to be replaced. He'd tried to tell Brown six weren't going to be enough. Had he listened they might've had some to use as replacements.

Up on the porch, he rang the doorbell. When no one responded, he pushed the small ivory button again. Nothing. Pulling the screen door open, he knocked on the inside door, then knocked again, harder this time. Because that brought no results, he went around to the back of the house, hoping to look in through the solarium, but the drapes were closed. Next, he tried to pull up the garage doors to see if his car was inside. They didn't budge, so he figured they were the fancy kind that opened with a remote. Frustrated, he took out his phone and called him, but it went to voice mail. Again. Had the man left town? If he had, surely he'd have sense enough or been decent enough to let his candidate know.

Having run out of ideas, Riley got back in his car and drove home.

AFTER CHURCH, BERNADINE came home to find an old, beat-up, pale blue pickup truck parked in front of her house. Wondering if the owner might be someone visiting one of her neighbors, she pulled Baby into her garage. Stepping out and seeing Big Al standing menacingly near the open garage door scared her half to death. Calming her racing heart, she asked, "Yes?"

"Wondering if you've seen Leo Brown?"

"I haven't."

"I've been trying to catch him since leaving your office, but he's not at home or answering his phone."

"I can't help you, sorry."

He turned and walked away. Still shaken, she watched as he got back in the old truck and it rattled away. She didn't know where Leo might be, but had she cheated Stillwell out of his land, she'd be trying to book passage to someplace far, far away, like Mars.

Her second guest of the day arrived a short while later. Riley. He was looking for her ex-husband, too. "I haven't seen him, Riley."

"Do you know who I can call that might know?"

"I don't, sorry."

He looked perturbed. "Okay, thanks." And he drove off in a car that sounded a lot like Big Al's battered old truck.

Finding this all very curious, Bernadine again wondered where Leo might be, but she didn't care enough about him to do more than that, so she went on with her day.

Crystal arrived at five to drop off dinner. She was covered with snow. "Man, it's really crazy out there."

The weather people were predicting a serious snowfall over the next twenty-four hours. Winter had arrived.

It took Crystal a couple of trips to her car to bring in what she'd prepared. There were wings and green beans, red-skinned potato salad, and a tin of unbaked blueberry muffins dusted with cinnamon and sugar. "Put the muffins in the oven in about half an hour, so they'll be hot," she suggested as she took off her coat.

"Will do."

"Hope this dinner turns out better than the last time."

"I'm sure it will."

Crystal studied her in the way only Crystal could before saying, "I'm glad you two are unpacking your issues. You're as good for him as he is for you."

"You think so?"

"I know so. You two getting back together means I don't have to worry about you when I leave Henry Adams."

It was Bernadine's turn to do the studying. "You're leaving?"

"Maybe. I'm applying to some schools in Cali and one in Savannah. My grades are up, and two places have asked for samples of my portfolio."

"That's exciting, Crys."

"I know, but none of it would be happening if it weren't for my awesome mom. Thank you so much for having my back."

Tears stung Bernadine's eyes as she hugged her child. "You just needed some loving. The rest you accomplished with hard work and that God-given talent of yours."

Crystal held on tight. "I want you to grab some happiness too, Mom."

"I'm fine."

"I know, but think how much happiness you could add if you and the OG were living under the same roof."

Bernadine pulled back. "Have you been talking to Lily?"

"About what?"

"Mal and me."

"No. Why?"

"Nothing. Just asking." Bernadine gave her one last squeeze then kissed her cheek. "Keep me posted on the schools."

"You know I will."

They parted and Crys put on her coat. "Okay. Have a good time with your boo."

Bernadine chuckled. "I'll do my best."

"And think about what I said about that whole one-roof thing."

"Yes, ma'am. Be careful driving home."

"I will."

Bernadine stood in the door and watched her back out of the driveway. The snow was falling in thick wind-whipped sheets. Once the car disappeared, Bernadine closed the door and turned on the Weather Channel to get the latest on what was shaping up to be one whopper of a first snowfall.

The cinnamon scent of the baking muffins was wafting deliciously through the air when she opened the door to let Mal inside. Snow covered him like one of the historic mountain men. "Man. It's bad out there. Police are telling people to stay off the roads. Lots of accidents on the highways. Main Street is like an ice rink. Had to crawl here." He stomped the snow off his boots on her doormat.

"Glad you made it."

She took his coat and hat and hung them on the knob of the closet door. Both were too wet to go inside. He'd brought a six-pack of Pepsi with him, so while he took off his boots, Bernadine put the cold cola in the fridge. She was checking the muffins when he joined her. "Smells good in here."

"Crys's muffins. Blueberry with cinnamon sugar on top."

"She might want to consider opening a restaurant."

"I know." She told him about Crystal's art school pursuit. "I'm hoping one of the places accepts her."

"Same here."

Mal's phone sounded. He took it from his suitcoat pocket

and read the text. "It's from Trent. He's calling off the snow removal team for the night. Weather's too bad. We'll start plowing in the morning." He put the phone away. "I don't know, Bernadine, I may have to eat and run."

She stirred the green beans. "If you get stuck, you can always make it over to Trent's and spend the night there, or use my guest room. Either way, you'll be covered."

She glanced his way. Their eyes held. Her heart skipped a couple of beats. To pull herself together she placed the lid back on the pot of green beans. "I think the muffins might be ready."

They were, so aided by a couple of potholders, she eased the pan out of the oven and onto the counter. "Time to eat."

"Let me wash my hands." Mal left her to go to the powder room and Bernadine drew in a few calming breaths. Although she hadn't offered him a spot in her bedroom, giving him permission to spend the night sort of fell out of her mouth on its own. That they might wind up sharing a bed for the first time since their split was a possibility, but knowing him the way she did, he'd leave that decision in her hands. Malachi July made love like it was his calling on earth, but never without the assurance of her consent.

As always, Crystal's meal was a hit. Every dish was flavorful and perfectly seasoned. While they ate, the weather ran in the background. They weren't surprised to hear the storm had been upgraded to a blizzard. Fifteen inches were now expected over the next twenty-four hours. Highways were closed and the local school districts in their portion of the state announced a snow day for Monday. Outside the wind howled like an enraged beast. The lights flickered off, then came back on. A few moments later, they went out again. The house filled with early-evening darkness and silence. They waited for the power to return but when it didn't, Mal asked, "Do you have wood?"

"Yes. Out in the garage."

While he went to get the wood, she thought about Crystal alone in her loft and sent her a text. She texted back that she was at the rec with Tamar, Rocky, and the waitstaff. The rec had an emergency generator so everyone unable to leave Main Street had gathered there. Feeling better, Bernadine sent love and put her phone away.

Mal made three trips to bring in enough wood to hopefully last until morning. He piled the first load into her living room fireplace and set it aflame.

People on the plains weren't new to winter power outages, so all over Henry Adams and the adjacent areas, those without fancy generators gathered their candles, lanterns, flashlights, and bottled water, then dug out extra blankets, insulated sleeping bags, heavy quilts, playing cards, and board games, to hunker down and ride out the storm.

Bernadine turned off all the electronics to keep them from being damaged when the power returned, then she and Mal pulled the cushions off the sofa and sat in front of the fire. "You ready to get whipped in Scrabble?" he asked.

"No, but I'll whip you if you want."

"Then let's go, missy."

They set up the board. Aided by the wavering flames of the fire and her big battery-powered lantern, and with Stevie Wonder as their background music on her battery-operated DVD player, they began. Scrabble had always been one of Bernadine's favorite board games. Growing up, she'd ruled as house champion, beating her parents and sisters regularly.

However, Mal was the ruler in Henry Adams and she'd been humbled by her huge loss to him the first time they'd played a few years back. Her reading material consisted of nonfiction business books, newspapers like the *Wall Street Journal,* and the occasional autobiography, like the one tied to the former First Lady she had yet to finish. Mal read political magazines, sci-fi and fantasy, mysteries, true crime, and everything in between. As a result, he had an amazing vocabulary. The only other person in town with an equal command of words was Genevieve. It was always a treat to watch the two of them go head-to-head over a game of Scrabble. Unfortunately for Bernadine, she was not Genevieve. For her, beating Mal would be like winning the lotto.

As the play began, she held her own. The tiles were kind and she picked up a variety of good letters. As things progressed though, Mal's score increased, and her letters became more and more useless. She was not happy.

"Are you pouting, little girl?" he teased softly.

She stuck out her tongue. "Just play, July."

"You sure?"

She glared.

"Okay, since you insist." He set down the word: *quixotic.* "Bam! Who loves you, baby?" The game was over. He'd won again.

She hung her head in defeat. Raising her eyes and seeing amusement shining in his, she said, "I hate you right now."

He laughed softly. "I love the smell of jealousy by firelight."

She was so done with him.

"Another game?"

She looked at him as if he'd asked the dumbest question ever. "No."

Laughing, Mal fell back against the sofa pillows they'd placed around them to create their nest in front of the fire. "I'm sorry, but you always look so outdone when you get whipped."

Unable to hide her smile, Bernadine fussed, "Hush!"

He sidled close. "I think you need a hug."

She let him pull her into his side and she laid her head on his chest. He placed a kiss on her forehead. "Should I let you win next time?"

"No. I want to beat your behind fair and square."

"Not going to happen in this lifetime, but you can dream."

She looked up at him and realized how much fun they'd always had together. She'd missed this part of their relationship very much.

"Penny for your thoughts."

"Just thinking how much I've missed this part of us."

"So have I." He traced a slow fingertip down her cheek. "Shall we keep it going?"

"Yes."

He gave her a squeeze. "Sounds like a plan."

During the game, the temperature in the house had fallen dramatically. "Let's put more wood on the fire," he said to her. "And I'm going to get my coat."

"Bring mine too, please." She didn't want to know what the thermostat presently read, but it was cold enough to need not only coats but hats and gloves, too.

He returned with their coats. They put them on and she said, "Grab a flashlight. I want to go upstairs."

He followed her up and they pulled all the pillows and bedding off the beds, took them downstairs, then went back up to gather every spare blanket, quilt, and bedspread in the closets. Once that was accomplished, they covered themselves and settled in.

He asked, "Warm enough?"

"I think so," she said lying cuddled against him.

"We should've done some popcorn."

She laughed softly. "Maybe next time. I'm way too warm now to brave the tundra again."

"Me too, to be honest." He looked down at her. "Will you be offended if I go to sleep on you."

"Not at all."

"Thanks for offering me a port in the storm."

"Thanks for accepting."

He placed a gentle kiss on her brow. "Good night, baby girl."

"Night, Mal."

And they slept.

BERNADINE AWAKENED TO the smell of bacon and a very stiff body. Struggling to sit up, she groaned, and Mal appeared standing above her. "Morning," he said.

"Morning. Please tell me the power's back."

"It is."

"Thank God. If I have to sleep on the floor again, I'm going to need hospitalization. I'm stiff everywhere." She rubbed her bleary eyes.

"If you want breakfast, there's bacon, eggs, and toast. I need to get going. Our esteemed mayor is raring to fire up the snowblowers."

She sat up fully. "Bathroom first, then coffee, then food. Is it still snowing?"

"Just a little. Weather says the storm is heading to Illinois."

"I hope the Windy City is ready. Are you leaving now?"

He nodded.

She was saddened by that. "Okay. I'll see you later. Thanks in advance for breakfast."

"You're welcome."

She wanted to tell him to come back once he finished plowing and shoveling, but she kept it to herself. They were supposed to be taking it slow. She got to her feet. Her coat was as wrinkled as the bedding. She took it off and stepped out of the nest. "Don't overdo it out there."

"Don't worry. I'll text you when I'm done."

"Please do."

He seemed as reluctant to leave as she was to see him go. So she told him, "Go on before the mayor shows up and yells at us both."

He nodded. "Stay in until the roads get better."

"I'll be right here."

"Good."

He left and she missed him as soon as the door closed behind him.

TRENT AND THE grounds crew spent the entire day and into the evening, snow blowing, plowing, shoveling, and salting. The kids, led by Amari and Preston, cleared the walks and driveways in the subdivision with the family snowblowers, and once done had a huge snowball fight that brought a smile to Bernadine's face as she watched the fun-filled melee through her front windows.

That afternoon, Bernadine answered her doorbell and was surprised and concerned to see Deputy Davida Ransom on her porch. Letting her in, Bernadine asked, "Has something happened?"

"We got a call from Leo Brown's boss. They haven't heard from him in a while and asked our department to do a wellness check. No one is at his home. Do you have any idea where he might be?"

"I don't." Bernadine told her about being asked the same question by Al Stillwell and Riley.

"I just left Mr. Curry's place. Did Mr. Stillwell give you a reason why he was looking for Mr. Brown?"

"He had questions about a land lease he and Leo are executing."

Davida took notes. "Okay. I'll run down Mr. Stillwell and see if he was able to make contact. Do you have names of anyone who may know where he's gone?"

"No. He has a couple of ex-wives but I've no idea how to get in touch with them or where they live. He has a brother named Sylvester, but I haven't spoken with him in at least a decade. I don't know where he lives or if he's still alive."

"I should be able to find that out." She closed her notebook. "Thanks, Ms. Brown. If you hear anything, please call us."

"I will."

Deputy Ransom went back out into the snowy day and Bernadine closed the door. The search for Leo had taken an interesting turn.

Mal called that evening and she could hear the weariness in his voice. "I wanted to swing by and see you," he said, "but I'm a dead man walking."

"Not a problem. Have you eaten?"

"I have. Now going to take a shower and head to bed. I'll see you tomorrow."

"Okay. Get some rest."

"You too."

And the call ended. Happy that he'd checked in, Bernadine settled in for her evening. Scrolling through the newsfeed on her laptop, a story on Cletus caught her eye. As a result of the ball's mayhem, the movie studios and the trainers of the terrorizing animals were being sued by a slew of people. Producer Alvin Malone needed six stitches in his hand from being bitten by Cletus and was so angry about his wife being bitten too, he'd pulled the film *Cletus Goes to Hawaii* from distribution. He was quoted as stating the hog would never make another movie in Hollywood again. The article went on to reveal that trainer Ben Scarsdale had been hospitalized due to a heart attack, and that Cletus's nomination for the Animal Oscar had been rescinded. There was no indication as to the hog's present condition or location. Bernadine wondered if the world of Cletus could get any stranger or crazier.

ON ELECTION DAY, the residents of Henry Adams arrived at the Power Plant to vote for a new mayor. The members of the Election Commission were there to make sure there were no irregularities or tampering with the ballot box. Having no campaign manager to get him through the day or organize a victory party, Riley spent his time at home. He was promised a call about the results as soon as all the votes were counted. Even though Leo Brown had skipped town, Riley was confident he'd be the one moving into Trent's office at the Power Plant. He was concerned about Cletus, however. He'd seen the news reports about all the lawsuits, Malone pulling the film, and Scarsdale being in the hospital, but none of the reports said anything about how Cletus was doing or where he might be.

Later that afternoon a large truck pulled up into his snow-lined driveway. The driver, wearing a heavy coat and overalls, got out and came to the door.

"You Riley Curry?"

"Who's asking?"

The man rolled his eyes. "Do you own a hog?"

Confused, Riley answered, "Yes. The most famous hog in Hollywood used to be mine."

The man thrust a clipboard and a pen at him. "Sign by the X, and take this." He handed Riley a sealed envelope.

Still not understanding what any of this meant, Riley saw another man get out of the truck and open the back and put up a ramp. Down the ramp came Cletus and Riley yelled with joy. He quickly scrawled his name, then ran out into the snow. He didn't know who squealed louder. Him or his hog. Kneeling, Riley hugged him like he was made of gold, then led him past the truck and inside. He was so elated he never even noticed the truck drive away. The envelope held a note from Ben Scarsdale that read: *He's all yours! May you both rot in hell!*

Smiling, Riley hugged Cletus again. "Welcome home, big boy."

SHEILA SPENT THE day at home as well. If she won the election, there'd be a party at the rec on Saturday to celebrate, but like her opponents, she had to wait for the winner to be announced.

"You're going to win," Preston told her when he got home from school that afternoon.

Amari, who'd come with him, added, "Nobody's going to vote for Mr. Curry."

"Stranger things have happened, guys. We'll see."

"You'd get my vote if I were old enough," Amari assured her.

"Ditto," her son said.

"Thanks."

The boys went up to Preston's room to work on a group assignment from school, and she was left in the kitchen alone. She glanced up at the clock on the wall. Barrett was at the Power Plant. Due to his ties to Sheila, he wouldn't be allowed to help with the tally, but he'd be at the polls until they closed at seven. According to a text he'd sent to her a short while ago, a large number of people had shown up to cast their votes. She was pleased that so many were exercising their constitutional rights, but she wished 7:00 p.m. would hurry up and arrive so the ballot counting could begin.

WHILE THE TOWN waited to find out who Trent would be passing his gavel to, Sheriff Will Dalton and his people were still searching for Leo Brown. His brother, Sylvester, hadn't heard from him in over a month, and his ex-wives hadn't either, but wanted the name of his lawyer to ask about a will in case Leo was dead. The deputies found his car in the garage, and his phone on the floor in the living room. His car keys and wallet were on the mantel of the big stone fireplace. A small spot of blood was discovered on the floor by the door. It was sent to the lab for testing. A search of the abandoned Stillwell homestead and barns turned up nothing. They brought in a canine that led them to the driveway, but no farther.

AT 10:00 P.M., all three candidates were called and told that Sheila Payne was the newly elected mayor of Henry Adams. Sheila was so ecstatic tears filled her eyes.

Barrett, just as happy, hugged her tightly, "Congratulations, Your Honor."

"I won! I actually won!"

"Yes, you did. You did an amazing job campaigning, and you'll be just as amazing when you take office."

She cupped his jaw affectionately and said seriously, "Thank you so much for supporting me."

"You're welcome. After all these years, it was my turn to step up to the plate for you. You deserved it. Now, let's have some of the bubbly that Bernadine slipped me a few weeks ago just for this occasion."

"She gave you champagne for me?"

"A bottle of her best and two crystal flutes."

He retrieved the bottle and the crystal from their hiding place in the garage. Once back, he popped the cork, poured some for her, and then some for himself.

"To the future," he said.

They touched the flutes gently, sipped, and smiled.

RILEY WAS DISAPPOINTED by his loss even though he'd received more votes than anyone had expected. Thad July had gotten less and, according to the talk around town, had left his sister's place to return to Oklahoma. But now that he had Cletus back, Riley didn't much care about anything else. When Bernadine allowed him to move into Eustacia's old place, she'd specifically said no hogs on the premises, but he figured what she didn't know wouldn't hurt her, so he'd keep the return a secret while he looked for another place to stay.

BERNADINE AND MALACHI had dinner together every night in the days that followed the election. One evening, they watched a movie. The next night, she worked while he read. Thursday night, he convinced her to join him for a walk in the snow, so she bundled up, held his hand, and they set out under the stars. Each visit convinced her that Crystal was right. She and Mal needed to be under one roof, so she came up with a plan, but wanted to wait for the right moment.

FRIDAY MORNING, AT an oil-processing plant in California, an employee pulled a drum off the line because it didn't seem to be draining properly into the system's pipes. Not sure what the problem was, he pried off the lid, saw what appeared to be a body inside with the oil, and promptly lost his breakfast. His supervisor sent him home and called the police.

Saturday morning Will Dalton showed up at Bernadine's door. "Did you find Leo?" she asked as she let him inside.

"We're waiting on tests but I'm 90 percent sure we have." He explained the incident at the California plant.

"Good lord."

"The serial number on the drum was from a batch from the field where Stillwell works, so we picked him up. He confessed right away."

She was stunned. "So, him asking me about Leo's whereabout was a red herring?"

"I guess you could call it that."

"Wow."

"He said he told Leo if he cheated him, he'd kill him."

"And Leo cheated him." She was still blown away. "Now what happens?"

"He'll go before the judge and the court will take it from there."

"What about the remains?"

"We contacted his brother and the ex-wives. No one seems willing to step up."

Bernadine reminded herself that although he was a jerk, she had loved him at one time. "If you can give me the phone number of wherever the remains are being held, I'll make the arrangements. Has his daughter, Alfreda, been contacted?"

"Yes. She didn't want to be bothered, either."

That was sad, but Bernadine supposed she understood the young woman's thinking. Her grandmother Odessa had been responsible for the deaths of two of Alfreda's friends, and now, this. She wondered how Odessa would react to Al's arrest for Leo's murder?

Will said, "Sorry to be the bearer of bad news."

"It's okay, at least he's been located. Thanks for letting me know."

"You're welcome."

He left and Bernadine sighed. What a terrible way for Leo's life to end.

THAT EVENING, MAL arrived to escort Bernadine to Sheila's victory party.

"You look nice," he said to her.

"You're not looking too bad yourself, sir. I'm so happy for Sheila."

"We all are. Trent may be the happiest of all, though. He's been wanting to pass on that gavel since day one."

Trent would still be responsible for construction and grounds, so it wasn't as if Bernadine would be losing his expertise now that Sheila had his old job.

"I've had a great time with you this week, Mr. July."

"As have I, Ms. Brown."

"I don't want it to end, so can I ask you a question?"

"Sure. Shoot."

"Will you marry me?"

For a moment Mal appeared stunned. He studied Bernadine silently. He then eased her in against his heart and whispered, "Are you sure?"

"Very." She met his serious set gaze.

"Even though—"

She cut him off, saying gently, "Even though. We've come a long way and through a lot, and I love you very much."

He pulled her in tighter. "I love you, too. You're the best thing that's ever happened to me. God, woman. You're putting tears in my eyes."

There were happy tears in hers as well.

He asked, "How about we keep this just between us for now, so we don't steal Sheila's thunder tonight?"

"That's a great idea. You have a good heart, July."

He wiped his eyes. "Well, shall we go?"

"Yes, let me get my coat."

As they rode to the party in his truck, Bernadine knew there were going to be a lot of logistics to figure out to make their lives as a married couple a reality, but they'd do it together. And that was all that mattered.

What also mattered was the eviction notice she'd be sending to Riley and his hog first thing in the morning.

The End

About the author

About the book

Insights,
Interviews
& More . . .

Meet Beverly Jenkins

Sandra Vander Schaaf

BEVERLY JENKINS is the recipient of the Michigan Author Award from the Michigan Library Association, the Romance Writers of America Lifetime Achievement Award, as well as the Romantic Times Reviewers' Choice Award for Historical Romance. She has been nominated for the NAACP Image Award for Outstanding Literature and was featured in the documentary *Love Between the Covers* and on *CBS Sunday Morning.* Since the publication of *Night Song* in 1994, she has been leading the charge for inclusive romance and has been a constant darling of reviewers, fans, and her peers, garnering accolades for her work from the likes of the *Wall Street Journal, People* magazine, and NPR. ᔆᕽ

Author's Note

Dear Readers,

This has been our tenth trip to our favorite small town, and I hope you enjoyed it. As I traveled the country after the release of book nine: *Second Time Sweeter,* many of you had strong opinions about the Mal and Bernadine situation and how it might be resolved. In truth, since I had no clear-cut plan, I decided to let Bernadine lead the way. Bernadine and Mal getting married will make many readers smile. But will it really happen? Will somebody get cold feet? Will sister Diane stand up during the ceremony and denounce the whole thing? Will Bernadine try to book the Taj Mahal? Will Cletus be the ring bearer? Will Devon insist upon being the reception's entertainment while dressed as James Brown? Stay tuned.

Until Next Time,
B

Book Club Discussion Questions

1. Was the Bernadine and Mal split resolved to your satisfaction? If not, why not?

2. Were you surprised by Sheila's decision to run for mayor and all the things she'd kept hidden about herself?

3. What might have happened if Barrett had not dropped out of the race? Would it have affected the Payne marriage? If yes, how?

4. What part of the story touched you the most? What part made you laugh out loud?

5. Do you want to see Reverend Paula find love? If yes, why? If, no, why not?

6. Name the number one factor in Leo's personality that led to his death.

7. What's next for Riley and Cletus?

8. Will Mal and Bernadine really marry? Name some things that might make them call it off.

9. Who's your favorite Blessings series character?

10. Should the Blessing series continue, or do you think it's played out and should be ended?

11. Marie having a gambling problem caught me off guard. Did it surprise you, too?

12. If you were writing the next book, which character would it focus upon? ∽